Praise for the Hamptons Home & Garden Mysteries

"A delightful sneak peek into life in the Hamptons, with intricate plotting and a likeable, down-to-earth protagonist. A promising start to a promising series."
— *Suspense Magazine* on *Better Homes and Corpses*

"*Ghostal Living* is a marvelously entertaining tale of revenge, murder, quirky characters—and disappearing books! With a clever protagonist, wonderful details of life in the Hamptons, and plot twists on top of plot twists, Kathleen Bridge will have mystery readers clamoring for more."
— Kate Carlisle, *New York Times* bestselling author

"An excellent read."
— *RT Book Reviews* on *Hearse and Gardens*

"The descriptions of furniture and other antiques, as well as juicy tidbits on the Hamptons, make for entertaining reading for those who enjoy both antiques and lifestyles of the rich and famous."
— *Booklist* on *Better Homes and Corpses*

GW00658335

Books by Kathleen Bridge

Hamptons Home & Garden Mysteries

Better Homes and Corpses
Hearse and Gardens
Ghostal Living
Manor of Dying

By the Sea Mysteries

Death by the Sea
A Killing by the Sea
Murder by the Sea

Manor
of
Dying

Kathleen Bridge

BEYOND THE PAGE
PUBLISHING

Manor of Dying
Kathleen Bridge
Beyond the Page Books
are published by
Beyond the Page Publishing
www.beyondthepagepub.com

Copyright © 2019 by Kathleen Bridge
Cover design by Dar Albert, Wicked Smart Designs

ISBN: 978-1-950461-11-0

This book is dedicated to Ellen (Elle) F. Broder for all her support and inspiration over the years. With much love. This one's for you!

Acknowledgments

As always, to my wonderful agent Dawn Dowdle at Blue Ridge Literary Agency for her unending guidance and friendship. Without her I wouldn't be a published novelist. Thanks to Bill Harris and everyone at Beyond the Page Publishing for letting me continue the Hamptons Home and Garden Mysteries. I look forward to a long future together. To Chef Lon Otremba for his recipe contributions in both of my series. I'm forever grateful. And lastly, to my loving family, for putting up with and supporting all the hours I've had to spend away from them, doing what I love.

Chapter 1

As we approached the jagged rocks crowning the rough waters like menacing shark fins, I took a moment to reconsider what I'd signed up for. What had I been thinking when my friend Elle asked me to go to Shelter Island in the middle of winter to inventory a former mental asylum and the site of a grisly sixty-year-old murder?"

I know what.

Count me in!

My interior design business, Cottages by the Sea, had been on a short hiatus. It seemed no one relished trekking out to the easternmost tip of Long Island to choose sofa fabric during the coldest December on record. I couldn't blame them and kept busy decorating my own cottage. It had been slow going, but it was paramount that every nook and cranny should turn out the way I'd envisioned. And it had.

Now that I'd finally moved into my oceanfront nest on a cliff overlooking the Atlantic, I savored the peace and tranquility of having the small town of Montauk to myself. Winter afforded us locals, as I now considered myself, more breathing room. No tourists, no traffic, and best of all no one traipsing on my beach. Give me a crackling fire in my stone fireplace, a mystery novel in my hand as I looked out the window toward the Montauk Point Lighthouse, fat cat Jo sitting by my feet, occasionally biting them when I moved without warning, and I was cozily happy until spring's thaw.

The ferry lurched forward. I glanced over at Elle, noticing her white-knuckled grip on the pickup's steering wheel. "Relax. You can't change the trajectory of the ferry. It's only a short ride."

"I'll relax when we reach the island's shore and we drive off this thing. I'd hate to be on board during a hurricane or snowstorm."

Looking out the truck's windshield I saw a different picture of the bay than I had when I'd stayed at Sag Harbor's Bibliophile Bed & Breakfast last August. The Hamptons was another animal in the winter months. Most of the boats at the yacht club were hibernating in dry dock or had set their course for the warm waters of the

1

Caribbean. The shoreline disappeared behind us and all I saw ahead were choppy steel-gray waters. Pellets of sleet *rat-tat-tatted* against the windshield in Morse code—D A N G E R—blurring our approach to the south shore of the island. So much for the break in precipitation the weather forecasters had promised.

Elle gripped the wheel tighter. As a distraction, I asked, "How many times have you been to Nightingale Manor?"

"Once. The estate and grounds are really magnificent."

Secluded Nightingale Manor had been chosen as the location to film a premium-channel miniseries, *Mr. & Mrs. Winslow*. Set in the late 1930s, the series was being touted as following in the tradition of Dashiell Hammett's Thin Man movies, and like those it featured a wisecracking, madly-in-love husband-and-wife detecting team, private-eye Jack Winslow and newlywed Lara, Jack's former gal Friday at the East Side Detective Agency. After Jack inherits a fortune from his great-uncle, the couple move from the Lower East Side of Manhattan to a mansion on Long Island and find themselves solving murders committed by the area's high-society elite.

Elle and I were given the task of inventorying the items from Nightingale Manor to be used in the filming. We'd also be assisting the set designer in recreating the series' 1930s time period.

Using my sleeve to rub a hole in the frosted passenger's window, I said, "From what I've seen in old photos on the internet, the mansion looks dark and dreary, very much like a haunted mental asylum. What fun."

"Fun? Meg Barrett! Don't even think about it! Haven't you had enough death for a lifetime? We have a job to do. Don't need any distractions. Leave the decades-old murder in the past where it belongs." Elle had been growing out her dark brown hair from a short pixie style. We were opposites in looks and it was easy to see we weren't blood related. But we were sisters all the same. I'd felt a kinship from the first day I met her at *American Home and Garden* magazine. We shared the same passion for collecting and decorating. And getting in trouble.

I liked Elle's new, more mature look; it went along with her recent status of being engaged to Detective Arthur Shoner, top brass at the East Hampton Town PD. My father was a retired homicide detective on the Detroit PD. Now we both had ties to law enforcement. Something that came in handy when involved in murder investigations — as we'd both found out the hard way.

Elle continued, "I think you'll be surprised when you see what Nightingale Manor looks like in the twenty-first century compared to when it was a private sanitorium. The stone façade's been sandblasted, and I can only imagine the grounds in the springtime. There's even 180-degree water views from almost every window."

"Aha! If you knew what the mansion looked like when the murder took place, that means you've been doing your own snooping."

"I wasn't digging into the gory murder or perusing haunting photos of the crime scene, as I'm sure you've been doing. I just wanted to search the internet for any interior shots of Nightingale Manor from back in the day. Felicity, *Mr. & Mrs. Winslow*'s set designer, told me a good portion of the old furnishings have been stored away in unused parts of the mansion. Of which there are many. By the way, thanks for telling me about the old murder. I would've preferred to wear blinders."

"Did you meet Dr. Blake Nightingale?"

"Who?" she asked, turning on the truck's wipers to keep a sheet of ice from forming on the windshield.

"The current owner of Nightingale Manor. Southampton's premier cosmetic surgeon — his clientele, the Hamptons elite. He's the grandson of the doctor who started Nightingale Manor Sanitorium in the late 1920s."

"No. Besides Felicity, I only met the housekeeper, Willa."

"There's a recent scandal involving him that I found pretty interesting."

"Go on."

"He was the star of a hit reality television series, *Bungled*. The show centered on patients whose cosmetic surgeries had gone awry, sometimes maiming them and leaving them worse than they were before they went under the knife. Dr. Blake, as he was called on the show, apparently fixed bungled cosmetic surgeries while a camera crew looked on. 'Bungled to Beautiful' was the show's tagline. *Bungled* was a moneymaker until an unhappy client showed what her face looked like a month after filming. All the Botox and filler injections wore off, not to mention she'd gotten a nasty eyelid infection that made her look like Rocky in *Rocky II*. Dr. Blake had lied that she'd had successful corrective surgery. He'd done his own bungling and tried to cover it up with injectables."

"There's something so wrong with that on so many levels," Elle said.

"I agree. You ever see *Bungled*? I know you're a big reality TV fan."

"Not that kind of reality. Only home-and-garden, antiques and fixer-upper shows. Is *Bungled* still on the air? I want to know so I can block it. Women need to own their wrinkles and laugh lines, so they don't get bungled in the first place."

"Even though the patient who is suing had signed a non-disclosure agreement, the network yanked the show off midseason."

"I'm sure the doctor's scandal won't have any bearing on the filming of the miniseries. I'm so excited we were brought in to help with the set for the first episode. Jack and Lara Winslow come to Jack's great-uncle's estate for Christmas."

"Let me guess, the great-uncle gets murdered and Jack is the beneficiary of his fortune?"

"That would be my guess from what the set designer has told me," Elle said. "We're only hired to work on the pilot episode, but if we do good, I hope we'll be asked back for the other seven in the first season. The time period is in my wheelhouse."

"What time period before nineteen-eighty isn't?" I asked, smiling.

"Look who's calling the kettle black. And you know what a fan I am of the movies from the late thirties. Especially the Thin Man films. I picture myself as Myrna Loy and Arthur as William Powell."

"Of course you do. Maybe you can talk Detective Shoner into a small mustache?"

"You can call him Arthur. Especially now we're engaged."

"He'll always be Detective Shoner to me. I've tried to call him Arthur, it just won't stick. If it wasn't for me, you two wouldn't have met."

"If it wasn't for you *and* the murder of the Queen of the Hamptons, Caroline Spenser. But you're right. It seems all roads lead to murder in the Hamptons. Especially if you're involved." The ferry hit a huge wave head-on and our heads jerked backward.

"I should have checked what hotels on Shelter Island are open off-season. Making this commute in the winter . . ." Elle moaned.

Because my hat covered my ears I'd missed her last words. Even if I took it off, I wouldn't be able to hear what she was saying over the roar of wind and the ferry's engines unless she faced me, then I could read her lips. Something I'd been doing since my teens when I was first diagnosed with a hearing loss.

"Your commute is a breeze from Sag Harbor," I said. "I've got a forty-five-minute drive from Montauk, longer if the roads are bad."

Elle looked at me, worry in her dark brown eyes. "I can do this alone. I'll bring Maurice. He's dying to come."

Maurice was her longtime assistant, who'd been working at the shop from when Elle's great-aunt Mabel was alive. "Then who'll watch Mabel and Elle's Curiosities?" I asked.

Her shop was an eclectic vintage and antiques shop on the first level of an old Victorian whaling captain's house in Sag Harbor. It was also the first place I shopped for special items to put in my clients' cottages. Elle even allowed me full use of her carriage house to work on my refurbishing projects.

Before my mother's death from breast cancer when I was thirteen, my mother owned a thriving antiques shop in Michigan called Past Perfect. I can still remember my father letting me pick out things from the shop to bring back to our house in Detroit. After I moved to New York and attended NYU, I continued my obsession with home décor and got a job at a home and garden magazine, working my way up to editor in chief. The magazine was where I met the antiques-and-collectibles editor Elle Warner. One cheating ex-fiancé later, I fled Manhattan for Montauk and the peace and tranquility only the sea and salt life could offer. Much to my delight, after Elle's great-aunt left her everything in her will, Elle moved to the Hamptons full-time. Now we were both pursuing the things we loved. The only difference was that Great-aunt Mabel left Elle very wealthy. I, on the other hand, basically lived hand to mouth, or should I say client to client. Which was one of the reasons I jumped at the chance to help Elle at Nightingale Manor.

"The shop's only open Saturday and Sunday," Elle said. "Not many people out shopping for antiques or vintage in the winter. Seriously, I don't want to worry about you driving to Sag Harbor in bad weather."

"I'll be fine. Especially in my new Wagoneer. Eyes on the road! I mean water," I said to Elle.

"Funny, har, har. I'll be happy when I can drive off and hit the roads before they're covered in ice. We're only staying for two hours. Tops. We can't miss the last ferry back. Plus, I have someone picking up that armoire we worked on and I'm counting on you to pull me back in case I get sidetracked digging through all the treasures."

"Aye, aye, Captain Warner. So, you ready to hear about the murder?"

"Go ahead. Get it out of your system. It'll distract me from that incoming wave about to tip us over."

"Last night, when I came by to purchase a book of ferry tickets to save on our trips back and forth to the island, I got to talking to my new best friend, our ferry captain Chris Boyd. He was a wealth of Shelter Island and Nightingale Manor information." Little did Elle know that since she'd called me a couple weeks ago, I'd been researching everything I could about the future location for the filming of *Mr. & Mrs. Winslow*. I'd stumbled upon an old article in the *East Hampton Star* about the murder that took place in the early 1950s, and from there I was off to the races.

"Am I sure I want to hear this?" Elle said, grabbing my wrist as the ferry plowed through another white-capped wave and she went sliding across the vintage pickup's bench seat.

"Don't worry. Captain Chris said they've never shut down the ferry, no matter what the weather. He's been doing this run from Sag Harbor to Shelter Island for over fifty years and never missed a day."

"And that's a good thing?" Elle asked. "Sounds kind of reckless to me."

"Shall I continue?"

"Can I stop you?"

"Here goes. Nightingale Manor had been a getaway of sorts for the Hamptons rich and famous suffering from an assortment of maladies. When it first opened in the late 1920s as a private retreat, no one used the words *asylum* or *sanitorium*. It wasn't until the 1940s that they were forced to get accreditation in order to perform electroshock therapy and lobotomies. Then the name changed to Nightingale Manor Sanitorium. Before the forties, the public was under the impression that Nightingale Manor was a luxury resort for Manhattan's vacationing elite to hide when they needed a rest between projects. In reality, the small hospital sequestered patients in private suites where they could safely have their nervous breakdowns or dry out from their last alcoholic or drug binges under a doctor's care. That doctor was Tobias Nightingale."

"Cosmetic surgeon Dr. Blake Nightingale's father or grandfather, I'd guess?" Elle interjected.

"Grandfather."

"I wonder if the production crew and actors know about Nightingale's notorious past?"

"Doubt it. I had to do a lot of digging before I could find anything about it. Most likely the reason the current Dr. Blake didn't change the name of the estate. Remember, Nightingale Manor Sanitorium was an exclusive, private asylum. From my research, back in the day it was very easy for relatives to commit their family members without their say and there was little hope of them ever returning home. Thankfully, times have changed."

"And procedures have changed, too," Elle said. "No more lobotomies."

"True. Although shock therapy is still being used, sometimes with good results."

"Look, I see the dock. Hurry. Give me a quick recap of the murder so I can focus on other things, like meeting the actors playing Jack and Lara."

"At the beginning of the 1950s, two feuding actresses came to the asylum, Arden Hunter and Marian Fortune."

"Great-aunt Mabel and Edith Head did some of the costumes for the 1949 film *The Flame and the Moth* that they starred in," Elle said. "I even have a dress from the movie." Elle's deceased great-aunt had been an assistant to the famous midcentury costume designer Edith Head. When Aunt Mabel passed away she left tons of clothing, sketches, and movie memorabilia to Elle.

Excitement flushed Elle's cheeks. "Aunt Mabel told me Arden Hunter and Marian Fortune loved to fight in front of the press but were really best friends on set. Like Bette Davis and Joan Crawford."

"Well, best friends don't murder each other, do they? I wonder what went wrong?"

"You know, on second thought," Elle said, "keep the gory details to yourself. I don't like the look of that sky. Let's keep focused on our task at hand so we can catch the four o'clock ferry back to Sag Harbor."

"Don't you want to know what happened?"

"Oh, go on. I'm sure if you don't, what my imagination could come up with would be worse than what really happened." She let out a full-body shiver.

"Dr. Tobias Nightingale was in the middle of Arden Hunter's lobotomy, ice pick in hand, when Marian Fortune, also a patient, grabbed it from his hand and stuck it straight in Arden's heart."

"How barbaric! What happened to Marian Fortune?"

"She was sent to a state mental hospital shortly after, and the Nightingale Manor Sanitorium closed its doors for good."

"A lobotomy. That wasn't common practice, was it?"

"I researched it, President Kennedy's sister Rosemary had one in the forties. The procedure quickly lost favor after numerous deaths and no proof it helped the patient's mental state."

"Ugh. Time for a change of subject. Thankfully we're pulling into shore. It seems crazy they'd pick the middle of winter to film a miniseries. And of all places, on an island. They must have a big budget."

"Now that the Hamptons season includes spring, summer and fall, it was probably the only time they could shoot without fanfare. Most other movies and series that film out here are also filmed in late fall, winter, or early spring."

"That reminds me. Did I tell you they want to use one of Cole's yachts for filming in the early spring? I called him. He seemed skeptical but willing. I'm sure you can convince him. They're offering a bucketful of cash for just a couple weeks of shooting."

"Cole doesn't need money. He's a Spenser. Remember?" Cole Spenser and I had been dating on and off for over a year, trying to keep our long-distance relationship going. I'd fly down to North Carolina when I could, and he would fly up to New York. Cole owned a company called Plantation Island Yachts. He refurbished vintage sailing yachts, many of which had won the America's Cup, then brokered them to wealthy clients around the world. Usually, when one of his clients purchased a yacht, Cole and his first mate,

Tripod, his three-legged dog, would hand deliver the yacht to whatever location the buyer desired.

"Well, it will keep him nearby for at least a few weeks. Maybe he'll pop the question and you can join me. We can plan our weddings together." She flashed me her left hand, showing a dazzling engagement ring.

Last month I'd met Detective Shoner at an estate jewelry shop on Madison Avenue and helped him pick out a ring for Elle. Elle would never go for something new, as proven by the assortment of costume jewelry brooches left to her by Great-aunt Mabel that she wore every day.

"Cole and I are nowhere near that stage in our relationship," I said. "Have you set a date?" I was trying to distract Elle from the now-thick flakes of snow whiting out our view.

"No, I only got the ring a week ago. But I thought the walled garden at your cottage might be a perfect place for a May wedding?" For the first time since we'd driven onto the ferry, Elle wore a happy face.

"Indeed, it would," I said, grinning back at her.

The ferry pulled to the dock on the south shore of the island. We waited until the ramp was lowered, then Elle drove off. I waved at Captain Chris, who stood onshore wearing a puffy down-filled parka, snowflakes gathering on his bushy white Fu Manchu mustache. He resembled a walrus as he tipped his captain's hat in our direction, and we set out for Nightingale Manor.

I gazed to my right at the water as lightning ripped open the dark sky. Thunder soon followed. Mother Nature seemed resolute in unloading everything she had.

"Oh, no!" Elle screeched. "A sign. An omen. Should we turn around?"

I looked behind us at the South Shelter Island Ferry pulling away.

"Too late. At least the snow stopped falling," I said in a hopefully upbeat tone.

Concentrating on the slick road, Elle kept silent as we headed west along the shoreline. We passed by quaint restaurants and small shops, all closed for the season. I'd tried to distract Elle by telling her about the Shelter Island clambake I'd gone to with Cole and Tripod last summer. "Who would have thought a dog would love smoked oysters?"

Dead silence. She kept her white-knuckled grip on the steering wheel, her focus on what little there was to see of the narrow two-lane highway through the now-pounding rain. When we reached the entrance to Nightingale Manor the thunder boomed so loud the vibration traveled up my spine. I worried Neptune's lightning-charged trident might zap the pickup into the bay.

In retrospect, maybe Mother Nature had been giving us a warning . . .

Chapter 2

We turned onto the long drive that fronted Nightingale Manor, passing a small gatehouse that was still three times the size of my cottage. Elle had been right, Nightingale Manor looked nothing like it had in the online black-and-white photographs taken at the time of the murder. It seemed friendlier, except there was still something creepy about the numerous mullioned casement windows that made me wonder if at one time they'd been reinforced with steel bars. I counted four chimneys and numerous spires. The stone façade gave the mansion the look of an English manor house. Most of the homes and buildings in the Hamptons area, Shelter Island included, used early colonial architecture in the Federal style. I was sure Elle was right—in the spring the green landscape would soften the look of the cold stone building. For now, I tried to wipe out the old images of what the private sanitorium had looked like. Here I'd been trying to spook Elle about Nightingale Manor's past and instead I felt apprehension about our upcoming assignment. It wasn't the first time we'd be inventorying the contents of a Hamptons mansion where a murder had taken place.

Elle pulled the pickup behind a black limo that was parked near the main entrance. As if by magic, the rain, thunder and lightning dissipated, leaving behind dark storm clouds. Someone must have been watching for us because the massive double-hung front doors opened, and a pair of black scotties ran onto the covered portico. They bounded by two huge cement dogs with empty flower baskets in their mouths, then they scampered down the stone slab steps and headed in our direction.

"Aren't they adorable!" Elle called out in glee. "They're the dog actors for the miniseries. I met them the last time I was here."

Both dogs came to my side of the pickup and barked up at me, their tails wagging in concert.

Elle said, "You go on ahead, I'll grab the hanging bags and train case." The hanging bags she mentioned held vintage evening gowns and the train case was filled with exquisite costume jewelry from the time period *Mr. & Mrs. Winslow* was supposed to take place. The production company had been the ones to contact Elle about helping after they'd hired the insurance company Elle occasionally worked for. First Fidelity Mutual paid it forward by telling the producers about Elle's expertise with antiques and her vintage clothing and jewelry collection.

"Sure I can't help?" I asked.

"Just wait at the door so I can run inside."

I got out and both scotties yipped and yapped in a welcoming chorus. All thoughts of mental asylums and murders vanished as I bent to scratch under each dog's straight-clipped beard. "Are you guys twins?" I asked the pair.

Someone spoke from behind me, but I couldn't make out their words. I ripped off the knitted hat muffling my hearing aids. One of the dogs grabbed the hat from my hand and went prancing away toward the wooded area on the western side of Nightingale Manor. The sweeping lawn and bare magnolia and cherry trees were snow-free. But white blanketed the ground in the thicket of pines where dog number one had disappeared. "Drats!"

A young woman dressed in a long sweater and jeans and wearing round black glasses touched me on the sleeve. Her glossy blue-black hair was cut at an angle to just below her chin. Two dimples crowned when she smiled. "You must be Meg. I'm Felicity, the set designer. The pups don't belong to me but came with their trainer, along with our producer, director, and the two lead actors who're waiting inside." She looked over to where dog number one disappeared. Dog number two sat patiently at my feet, looking at me expectantly through shaggy brows. I knew that look. My cat Jo had perfected it. Felicity extended her small hand and we shook. The dog's stare remained focused on my coat pocket.

"They're brothers from the same litter, Murphy and Max," she said. "They'll be playing the Winslows' dog, Whiskey."

"Like the Olsen Twins on *Full House*."

Felicity laughed.

"How do you tell them apart?"

"Max is the one with the red collar who ran into the woods. And this here is Murphy. He wears a white collar."

The dog yipped, sat on his haunches, and extended his front paws in a begging position. "I think Murphy wants a treat," she said. "I've used up all the ones Bob, their trainer, gave me. Bob's inside trying to find an unused room to use as a place for him and dogs to bunk down once the production company arrives."

"Will the entire crew and actors be sleeping here during filming?" I looked up at the cold stone mansion. There seemed to be enough room, that wouldn't be a problem. And it would be easy to get to the quaint town of Sag Harbor and Southampton from the south ferry.

"Yes. We'll all be bunking here. I guess we could have done worse, although, fair warning, it's awful cold in there. Even the interior of a castle where we once filmed in Cornwall for another series seemed toastier."

My mind immediately went to one of my favorite PBS series, *Poldark*. Cornwall had been calling to me since I'd first read my mother's collection of Victoria Holt romantic suspense novels. To me, Montauk was a smaller version of Cornwall. Cole and I had a trip scheduled to England in the summer. It would be our first one together and we'd be bringing along his first mate, Tripod. He'd asked me a couple other times to go with him to deliver one of his vintage sailing yachts and I'd always been in the middle of a project. Knowing we were going to Cornwall, I had no problem blocking out my calendar for mid-July, the height of the Hamptons tourist season and the perfect time for escape.

Felicity rubbed her hands together for warmth, her breath coming out in icy puffs. "The Nightingales will be staying in the gatehouse." She nodded her head in the direction of the stone structure we'd passed on our way in. "But the good news is they're leaving Willa Sullivan, the Nightingales' housekeeper, at the main house to cater to us. It will be a lot easier than having craft services come to the island every day we're filming."

Murphy tapped his paw gently against my shin, hope shining bright in his dark eyes. I reached into my coat pocket and took out a handful of fish-shaped treats. "You think it's okay if I give him a cat treat?" I'd recently tried to take my twenty-three-pound Maine coon for a walk on a leash. *Tried* being the key word. Sedentary was Jo's favorite position. Not even the lure of her favorite cat treats could get her off my porch.

"I don't see a problem. I better go get Bob to see if he can corral Max."

"He's adorable," I said.

Grinning, she said, "Isn't he?" I loved Felicity's easygoing nature and could see that in the next few weeks we'd all get along. A crack of thunder made us jump. "Does Elle need help with anything?"

I looked over at Elle, who was still inside her pickup, talking on the phone. Worry lines creased her forehead. The exhaust from her decades-old turquoise pickup spewed fumes of smoke into the frigid air, matching the color of Felicity's lips. I said, "We're good, Felicity. Get inside before you freeze to death."

"Okay. I'll make sure Willa has some hot tea waiting for you. Come, Murphy. Let's go find Bob."

The terrier looked at me, then Felicity, then back at me. I handed Felicity a handful of cat treats. "I think these might help get him inside."

Sure enough, as she walked away she dropped a trail of fish treats in her wake. Murphy followed, lapping up the treats with his cute pink tongue.

I glanced over at Elle, who was still on the phone. The thunder and lightning had stopped and once again snow started falling. I wore my thick down coat and faux-fur-lined boots that made me impervious to the cold. I was born and raised in Michigan, so I had a high tolerance to the cold. It didn't bother me to stroll the beach in front of my cottage no matter what the weather. Especially when scouting out poetry etched in the sand. My former next-door neighbor, Patrick Seaton, was a bestselling author of corporate thrillers who'd moved to Montauk after his wife and daughter were killed in an automobile accident. It had been a year and a half since I'd first found his melancholy prose in the sand in front of his cottage. Soon after, I'd left my own verses for him to read. Last September, after I'd moved into my new cottage, a mile east of my old rental, we'd met face-to-face on the beach. It had been a slightly awkward moment because Cole had found us holding hands, looking into each other's eyes. Since then, I'd only seen Patrick once at Old Man and the Sea Books. He'd been with his stunning-looking New York publicist, and it took him a moment before he recognized me. I guess I hadn't made the impression on him that he'd made on me. I shrugged at the memory. What did it matter? I had Cole . . .

My thoughts were interrupted by Max, who came crashing out

of the woods like he was being chased by someone. Or something. He charged in my direction. Dangling from his mouth was something tan. It wasn't my blue hat, and I prayed it wasn't a defenseless bunny or squirrel. He stopped short at my feet and presented me with his find: a crude cotton doll with a stitched face wearing a stained apron. Soggy stuffing oozed from the area where her arms should have been. Max looked expectantly at me. "Uh-h-h, good boy," I praised him. "Thank you." I bent to pick the wretched thing up, then reached into my pocket and gave him a treat at the same time someone, who I assumed was Bob the trainer, called to the dog from under the portico.

The pup scampered away, and I was left holding the unfortunate doll.

Could it have belonged to a former Nightingale Manor Sanitorium patient? My hand trembled as I stuffed it into the large interior pocket of my North Face jacket.

Someone had to rescue it.

Chapter 3

Elle and I were seated on a modern Deco-style sofa facing a fireplace big enough to throw a party in. Felicity had been right. As soon as we stepped inside the stone-floored foyer, a chill set into my bones, causing me to reflect that Elle and I would be spending a lot of time in this ice palace. No doubt the twenty-odd rooms were too expensive to heat. Too bad the wool sweater I'd been attempting to knit was months, maybe years, from completion.

I thought a palace was a good description of the interior of Nightingale Manor. As far as twentieth-century insane asylums went, the place had a certain *je ne se sais quoi*. The furnishings were opulent, a mixture of Edwardian, Nouveau, and Deco. It was a marriage of styles that somehow worked. It would be the perfect late-1930s setting for *Mr. & Mrs. Winslow*. Of course, we'd only seen the grand hall, the dining room through an open doorway, and now the grandiose drawing room with its high ceiling and carved crown molding.

Felicity entered the room, walking across the Persian rug with quick, energetic steps. She took a seat on a raw silk upholstered club chair and said, "Well, that seemed to go better than expected. Elle, what do you think?" she asked, her brown, almost-black eyes large behind her round-framed glasses. She was referring to the fitting session Elle had just had with the lead female actress playing Lara in *Mr. & Mrs. Winslow*. The goal had been to find the perfect 1930s gown for the opening scene in the pilot—Christmas with Jack's family. Zoe Stockton and Dillon King had left Nightingale Manor minutes before. They seemed the perfect choice to play Jack and Lara. They had a chemistry that reminded me of famous screen legend couples like Katherine Hepburn and Spencer Tracy, Lauren Bacall and Humphrey Bogart, and Myrna Loy and William Powell. While watching them I'd thought I'd stepped back in time to the golden age of Hollywood. Elle hadn't been shy about getting autographs and a couple of photos taken. Sadly, Elle and I wouldn't be around when the actual filming began. Unless things changed and Felicity decided we were indispensable, demanding we become part of the crew. One could always hope.

Murphy and Max and their owner and trainer had also left

Nightingale Manor at the same time as Zoe and Dillon. Somewhere in the mansion were the director and producer, but we hadn't met them. Felicity had told us they'd all come on the north ferry, which ran from the town of Greenport on the North Fork of Long Island to the northern top of Shelter Island.

"The emerald satin Worth gown fit Ms. Stockton in all the right places." Elle giggled. "I mean Zoe, as she asked me to call her. She seemed thrilled with it, and also the rhinestone jewelry."

"It was perfect," Felicity said. "I sent the photos to our costume designer. I know she'll be thrilled to make a copy."

"A copy?" I asked.

"Yes, it's important to have more than one dress in case it gets damaged. Plus, Elle, she'll be able to return your dress to you afterward."

"But Zoe will wear my dress for the actual filming, right?"

"It's up to you. If you want to take the chance that something might ruin it?" Felicity answered.

"Oh, I'll take the chance. Just to see it on the screen." Elle's grin went from ear to ear.

"You might want to reconsider, Elle," I said, teasing, "I always wondered if the squibs holding fake blood stain clothing."

"I don't think Zoe gets shot in the pilot," Felicity said. "Not so sure about Dillon." She smiled. "Costume is just as important in a period piece as the set design." Felicity passed Elle her phone to show her how Zoe had looked in front of the baby grand piano in the corner of the huge room they were sitting in. "I thought she looked stunning. When our costume designer, Pat, returns from maternity leave, she told me to tell you, Elle, that she plans on coming to visit your shop and rent a few more articles of clothing from your collection."

"That would be fabulous. Anytime. I have to admit, I'm surprised that Zoe would travel this far to try on a dress. I could've brought a few selections to Manhattan, as I told you."

"To be honest," Felicity said, lowering her voice and leaning closer, "I've heard it through the grapevine that they weren't too happy about filming in such a secluded location in the middle of winter. Originally an estate on the mainland in Southampton had been chosen. At the last minute the director changed his mind and switched it to Nightingale Manor. He doesn't want anyone coming on set and passing on any spoilers to the press."

"I know a few canines that will be thrilled to be on Shelter Island," I said.

Felicity laughed. "You got that right. Murphy and Max, along with their trainer, have been following Zoe and Dillon around for the past month. Bob told me it's very important that the dogs get familiar with the actors. Especially for a miniseries that might go on for multiple seasons."

Before leaving, Bob and the pups had given Elle, Felicity and me a small preview of the dogs' range of acting. Starting with the simple act of rolling over and playing dead, all the way to fetching a newspaper and a pair of slippers for Dillon/Jack Winslow. The best part was to see the affection the dogs had for their trainer. I'd always wondered if animal actors enjoyed their jobs. In Murphy and Max's case, the answer was a resounding Yes! The excitement about what went into a project like *Mr. & Mrs. Winslow* was contagious. I said, "You must love your job, Felicity. By the way, who is writing the teleplays?"

"I'm sure you've heard of him. It's his first television miniseries, but he's done adapted feature film screenplays from his bestselling novels before. Even won a few awards."

Why did I know what she was going to say next?

"Patrick Seaton."

My hand trembled and my cup clattered against its saucer.

Elle said, "Meg, what's that weird look on you face?" Then it hit her. "Patrick Seaton is your poetry on the beach pen pal!"

I gave her a piercing look. Which she ignored.

Elle furrowed her dark brows. "Wow, that's crazy."

"So, you know him? I met him once," Felicity said. "He seemed very quiet and unassuming. And very attractive. But I'm happily married," she added, holding up her left hand.

"Do you think he'll come out here? Uh, while we're working?" I stammered.

"Don't think so. At least not until we start filming. Once a screenplay is written we have to wait to see how it goes. I've sent him pictures of the interior spaces we're using, so he might want to come check it out in person."

I coughed, feeling like I'd swallowed a bitter pill that went down the wrong pipe. While Elle and Felicity talked about how hard it was for newlywed Felicity to go away on location without her husband, I thought about what would happen if I ran into Patrick at Nightingale Manor. And why did I feel like I was betraying Cole just thinking about it? Only a few months ago, I'd dated Byron Hughes and Cole at the same time and hadn't felt remorse. Well, perhaps a tad.

When I'd moved to Montauk, on my first morning walking the beach, I'd found melancholy lines from classical poetry written in the sand in front of Patrick's oceanfront cottage. I still remembered the passage from Emerson that he'd left, *Sorrow makes us all children again. Destroys all differences of intellect.*

I forced myself to return to Elle and Felicity's conversation but found my mind wandering back to Patrick Seaton. His sandy-blond tousled hair and changeable green eyes had made their impression on me. Another thing that added to his attraction was the scarred greyhound that he'd recently rescued named Charley. Giving myself a mental slap, I said in a too-loud voice, "These cranberry muffins are to die for."

"You're right," Felicity said. "Willa makes a mean muffin. Wait until you try her orange Christmas scones, she adds just a hint of clove."

"I've already had two muffins," Elle said. Proof was in the large muffin crumb nestled on top of a rhinestone pin on her chest.

As if the housekeeper knew we were talking about her, she bustled toward us carrying our coats in her ample arms. "Here you go," Willa said, placing them on top of a huge ottoman fronting a wing chair near the fireplace. "It's stopped snowing, but the wind's picked up and is howling like a banshee." Willa was short like Felicity and Elle, but probably weighed fifty pounds more. She had short auburn hair that fell in relaxed curls. Her alert hazel eyes stood out in her round, rosy-cheeked face. I guessed she was somewhere in her early forties. Her best feature was an easy smile that made her immediately likeable.

I stood, then went over to the ottoman. Before grabbing my jacket, I asked Willa, "Could you please direct me to the restroom?"

Elle gave me a questioning look and pointed to her watch.

I pantomimed drinking a cup of tea to reiterate that I *really* needed to use the bathroom. It wasn't a ploy to check out the rest of the place. But now that I thought about it, I wouldn't mind opening a few doors for a quick look-see.

"Of course, Meg. Follow me," Willa said.

Felicity had told us that when the cast and crew came for the filming, they planned on shooting in the east wing and kitchen only. The west wing had been shut off, and that's where we'd be digging out items to inventory and use on set. The second-floor bedrooms in the west wing would be where the cast and crew stayed. It seemed our job not only entailed inventorying the items in the west wing but also organizing and redistributing items in the bedrooms to make room for the crew.

We exited the drawing room, as Willa called it, and turned right. I followed Willa down a carpeted hallway. For only being about five feet tall, she sure walked at a brisk pace. She stopped and pointed. "The second-to-last door on your left."

"Thanks, Willa. Are you prepared for the barrage of film crew and actors that will be arriving after the holidays?"

"I look forward to the commotion. We're pretty isolated out here. Blake and Sabrina are usually in Palm Beach for the winter, but this year, um . . . they've decided to stay. I always have my son come for winter break, but this year her highness has forbidden him to come." She'd gritted her jaw and a vein at her temple became visible. I assumed *her highness* must be Mrs. Nightingale, Dr. Blake's wife.

I didn't have a response, so I said, "Thanks," and continued down the hall. I wanted to question her further about why the Nightingales would give up Palm Beach. But it was none of my business. I could only conjecture that it had something to do with the loss of cashflow after the good doctor's TV show, *Bungled*, was canceled. I could think of one person who didn't think of Blake Nightingale as a good doctor, the maimed woman who'd called him a charlatan.

I started toward the door she'd mentioned. When I looked back, I saw Willa had disappeared. I kept walking. Passing the bathroom, I stopped at the last door on the left. Something about a door at the end of a dark hallway intrigued me. I turned the doorknob and opened the door to find cement stairs leading downward.

The basement.

Chapter 4

I broke out in a sweat. I knew Elle was waiting and we had a ferry to catch. Plus, we'd be coming back the day after tomorrow to start our inventorying and staging. I'd learned from my online search of Nightingale Manor and the murder of Arden Hunter that the operating rooms were in the basement. I had no desire to scout out the long-ago murder scene. I wasn't the type to slow down to look at car accidents on the side of the road; I'd just say a prayer and move on. What I wanted to see was a preview of the antiques we'd have the privilege of inventorying to use on the set of the miniseries.

Or so I told myself.

I crept down. Near the bottom of the steps was a gray metal door with a glass window enmeshed with crisscrossed steel wire. I pressed my nose against the glass. My reflection was as frightening as anything I might find on the other side of the door: shoulder-length blonde hair spiked out in all directions except on top, where it was flattened from my knit hat. Frankenstein's monster had nothing on me. My face and pale blue eyes looked ghostly. I could easily fit in as a mental patient of yore, reminding me of the poor rag doll Max had presented me earlier.

Centering my gaze between the wire in the glass, I saw a cement-floored room. Florescent lights flicked on and off, revealing two metal gurneys laying on their sides. Black cushions that must have gone with the gurneys were stacked inside a huge metal bathtub-type contraption. Against the far brick wall, where sickly yellow paint peeled into curling shards, was a hospital bed. It looked like it was waiting for its next customer. On top of the bed's striped mattress were thick leather straps arranged in neat horizontal lines at three strategic places: chest, waist, and ankles. The buckles on the restraints were rusted with age, the rust resembling dried blood. Was that the exact bed where Arden Hunter's attempted lobotomy took place? Ending with her murder by her frenemy Marian Fortune? My hand automatically reached for the doorknob, half hoping it would be locked to keep the modern-day world, myself included, away from the horrors beyond.

I put my hand on the knob and took it off a dozen times. I

rationalized that I'd just take a quick peek and head back upstairs with no one the wiser. I turned the knob. The door didn't budge.

Relief set in, but curious cat that I was, I tugged harder. The door opened, and I went barreling backward. My tailbone hit the lip of the bottom step. I screeched, "Son of a biscuit eater!" One of my tough-cop father's favorite expletives.

I didn't have to turn to read the lips of the person standing at the top of stairs. His voice, amplified by my hearing aids, reverberated with, "What the hell are you doing down there! And who the hell are you?"

I managed to pull myself up with the help of the steel banister. I turned slowly, pain shooting up my spine. I bit my bottom lip, not wanting to complain to the person with the menacing voice. Climbing halfway up the stairs, I finally lifted my head to see a tall man with slicked-back salt-and-pepper hair. He wore tan pants, a crisp white button-down shirt, and a navy blazer with a silk pocket square. Even in the dim light, his amber eyes reminded me of a wolf's. I'd seen his face in a few Southampton society photos and in the trailer I'd watched on YouTube of *Bungled*. Staring down at me was Dr. Blake Nightingale. And he wasn't a happy camper.

I brushed off his insolent stare and climbed a few more steps, the pain excruciating. What was the big deal? Soon Elle and I would be checking out the whole house for period items to use on the show's set. I had every right to look around the place. Didn't I? But something about Blake Nightingale made me feel uneasy and very small. Did I think the doctor took after his grandfather and was planning to perform secret lobotomies on his cosmetic surgery patients? Or me?

Maybe I did. Because when I said to him, "Sorry, Blake. Thought Willa told me the last door on the left was the powder room," my hands were shaking so violently that I had to put them behind my back. I took the remaining steps to meet him face-to-face. Or face-to-chest.

"Call me Dr. Blake," he admonished, "and why would you think we would have a bathroom, or powder room, as you call it, in the basement? Try again."

He wasn't my doctor, I thought. Why did I have to call him Dr. Blake? Contrary to my shaky knees, we were equals. I giggled then stammered, "I was surprised, but you never know in old mansions like these."

He continued to hold the door open. There was a cruel turn to his mouth, nothing like how he presented himself on the clips from *Bungled*. "Are you going to pass through? Or just look at me. This door should have been locked."

My lip already bruised, I bit the inside of my cheek, literally, to keep from giving it back to him. *This job is my bread and butter, this job is my bread and butter,* I kept repeating to myself.

There was silence, but I got his drift. I hadn't made a good first impression. But I'd done worse.

I hurried away, following the hallway that led back to the foyer. Elle was probably having a conniption about how long I'd been gone. The walk down the hallway seemed miles longer than when I'd followed it earlier. I felt *Dr.* Blake's sharp gaze burning into my back like a branding iron. One disadvantage to having a hearing loss was even with my hearing aids turned on to their highest volume, I couldn't hear anyone sneaking up behind me. I turned my head slightly and saw out of the corner of my eye that he was catching up. I walked faster. Right before I made the left turn into the foyer, I looked behind once more, just in time to see him disappear inside a room only a few feet away. I froze when I heard loud voices.

Snoop that I was, I turned and doubled back.

The door was ajar. I saw the doctor with his back to me. He was standing in front of a man who looked familiar. Then I got it. The man was Langston Reed. He must be the director of *Mr. & Mrs. Winslow.* I almost didn't recognize him from when we'd met at the Hamptons International Film Festival. A *Where's Waldo* red-and-white scarf was coiled around his neck, covering his trademark beard. His shaggy dark hair was peppered with gray and almost fell to his shoulders. It was his frosty blue eyes behind horn-rimmed glasses that gave him away. They were almost the same shade as Cole's. The only difference was Langston's eyes were smaller and he had numerous laugh lines etched next to them. Cole rarely laughed, which didn't bother me because when he did, you knew it was genuine. Just like Cole's admission the last time we'd been together that he'd thought he was falling in love with me. I hadn't known what to do with that and had responded with a quick, "I feel the same way." I really did, but we barely saw each other. Plus, when he'd said it, it was almost as if he'd done it grudgingly. Maybe it had to do with Cole refusing to move from the North Carolina coast where his yacht company was located, and me not wanting to leave Montauk and my Cottages by the Sea business. We were two stubborn idiots. I'd worked hard for my serenity and didn't plan to change my life for a man. Even if he was the most attractive, albeit moody, dark, and mysterious guy I'd ever met. When we were together it was good. Better than good. I didn't want to jeopardize it with resentments — either his or mine. "If it was meant to be, it will happen. And you'll have no doubts." Words that Georgia, the proprietor of Old Man and the Sea books, said to me while we were reclining in warmed salt chairs at the Montauk Salt Caves. "You ever see the movie *Sleepless in Seattle*?" Georgia had asked. "The scene in the attic with Meg Ryan's character and the actress playing her mother? 'You'll just know.'" Had Georgia been kidding? I remembered watching *Sleepless in Seattle*, first on VHS tape at age seven with my mother. Now, I owned it on Blu-ray. If it came out in 3-D, I would buy that too.

I inched closer to the door and saw Langston had his hand resting on an open filing cabinet drawer. I stepped back and flattened myself against the wall. In the same overbearing tone as he'd used with me, I heard Dr. Blake say, "Mr. Reed, what are you doing in here? This office is off limits. And what the hell are you doing riffling through my filing cabinets? I said you can rent the house and the furniture; however, I didn't say you could go through my personal files."

I heard Langston's calm voice, "I was under the impression that the entire main house was at our disposal. Excuse me if I'm off the mark on that. I was looking for old files from back when this house was a mental hospital. Thought it might give us a feeling for the time period of the miniseries. Don't worry. Not looking for anything about the old murder. The time line is all wrong, although it would make a great documentary, maybe combine it with your bungled career. Two medical tragedies involving grandfather and grandson."

"A what? Are you crazy? A documentary? And why would I have anything of my grandfather's in *my* filing cabinets. I haven't seen anything of his in ages. Yes, you might get full use of the house, but when your crew arrives, and I move to the caretaker's cottage, I plan on taking everything in my home office with me. Obviously."

Peering in, I wanted to view the expression on Langston's face to see if he was intimidated by the doctor.

Nope. He didn't appear frightened at all. Especially after he sidled up to Dr. Blake and said in a threatening tone, "Well, Doctor, if my presence in the house is not going to work out we can tell Mr. Prentice, who holds the purse strings, and see if we can't find another location for our little project. Whaddya say? Should I call him in?"

"That won't be necessary. Just find another room to do your research. You won't find anything else in my office relating to your time period. We deserve our privacy."

I took off for the foyer, skidding on the tile, then stumbled into the drawing room.

Elle looked at me like I had two heads. She had on her coat and her face was either red with heat or anger. I couldn't tell which.

"Sorry, had a hard time finding the loo," I said, panting and bending at the knees.

Willa, who'd been staring into the fire, still holding my coat, turned and brought it to me.

"No worries, darlin'. But you gals better skedaddle. The ferry waits for no one."

After what I'd witnessed in the basement and meeting Blake Nightingale, I didn't relish spending a night in the old mental asylum, antiques or not.

Chapter 5

As the four o'clock ferry pulled from the dock, I saw a relaxing of Elle's shoulders.

"See," I said to a glum-faced Elle, "everything's turned out okay and we made it onto the ferry. No problemo. And the roads weren't that bad, either. I, for one, am looking forward to going back on Wednesday, even after my run-in with the owner."

She groaned. "He was just standing there? Looking down at you?"

"I would say lurking. Definitely lurking."

"Wonder why he didn't come into the drawing room to introduce himself? Do you think we'll be fired? I hope you didn't blow it. Then again, if it's meant to be, it's meant to be. I had a bad dream last night that snow was falling from my bedroom ceiling. Then the snow turned into tiny emerald-cut diamonds. Right before they reached my face, the diamonds turned into pieces of glass from a broken mirror."

"Mirror, mirror, *off the wall* . . . How could that be a bad dream? I could use some falling diamond dreams."

"To see snow in a dream signifies feeling alone, neglected, and inhibited. Sure, diamonds mean riches and good luck, but the idea that they turned to . . ."

"Pieces of a broken mirror. Seven years of bad luck. Got it. Don't need a dream dictionary for that one."

"Whatever. I just hope we still have a job on Wednesday."

Already on Elle's bad side, I decided to keep mum about the exchange I saw between Dr. Blake and the director.

"Aren't we getting paid from two sources?" I asked. "First Fidelity Mutual and then the production company? So technically, we'll only lose half if the doctor feels like kicking us out for me sneaking into his basement."

"There's no *us* in this scenario," Elle said. "Speaking of which. What the heck were you thinking!"

"Oh my gosh!"

"What?"

"Look next to us."

Parked alongside Elle's pickup was a black Mercedes. The person in the driver's seat was none other than Dr. Blake Nightingale.

"Who? I can't see," Elle squealed.

"Dr. Blake."

"Duck. What if he sees you and tells us never to come back?"

"I don't think he's paying much attention to us. Looks like he's screaming at someone in the passenger seat and banging the steering wheel.

"Do you think it's about you?"

"I doubt it. He couldn't be that upset." I was thankful it wasn't snowing so the air was as clear as my vision. I watched Dr. Blake's lips, praying I could make out a few words, but I could only see the corner of his mouth. Once, he turned his head toward me and I made out, "Not one penny." Then I missed the beginning of his next sentence, but clearly saw him say the word *blackmail* before turning his head to his companion. All I could make out was that his companion was a female with long blonde hair and a perfect profile. *Mrs. Blake?*

"He just said the word *blackmail*," I told Elle.

"You shouldn't eavesdrop. And you better not let him see you."

I supposed Elle had a point. I laid on the seat, while Elle pulled her brimmed hat lower on her face.

After ten minutes of silence, I said, "Am I being punished?"

"No," Elle replied. "But you should be. I want to enjoy our time at Nightingale Manor."

"So do I."

"Then let's make a pact. No more snooping around."

"Gladly," I said, thinking of Dr Blake's ire. "So, who do you think is blackmailing the Nightingales?"

"Meg!"

"It was a joke."

Twenty minutes later we drove down the ferry's ramp. On Sag Harbor's Main Street, there was no mistaking what holiday was around the corner. The charming New England storefronts were adorned with greenery and white twinkling lights. The wreathed and ribboned lampposts looked like they'd walked off the front of a Christmas greeting card. Last week, Elle and I had attended the holiday festivities in Sag Harbor. Santa had arrived to a cheering crowd of waiting children trailing wish lists. He hadn't come by sleigh and eight prancing reindeer. Instead, he rode on the back of a Sag Harbor Volunteer fire truck that dropped him off by the windmill near the bay. There had been the tree and menorah lighting at the foot of Long Wharf, along with carolers dressed in nineteenth-century garb. Steaming cups of hot chocolate were passed out by local high school students raising money for their spring sports programs. Elle had even gotten an autograph in front of the Bay Street Theater from one her favorite movie actresses who was playing a female Scrooge in a new-millennium version of Dickens's *A Christmas Carol*. For the most part the Hamptons were empty of celebrities in December and January. Occasionally, the winter holidays brought back a small flock of Manhattanites who yearned for a white Christmas out their frosty window instead a dirty, charcoal-gray slushy one.

The lighting of my beloved Montauk Point Lighthouse was slated for tomorrow, and I couldn't wait to partake in the festivities. Cole promised he'd try to make it. He was as excited as I was about viewing the ceremony. It was a ritual he remembered as a child, growing up in nearby East Hampton. I was all for tradition and I was more than ready to decorate my own, *finally my own,* cottage with heirloom, vintage, and artisanal decorations. This time, I half believed Cole would make it because he'd sent me of photo of his plane ticket to LaGuardia. He was still in the doghouse for missing Thanksgiving. My father and his wife, Sheila, had traveled by car from Michigan. A gourmet home cook, my father had prepared a fried turkey and fixin's worthy of any Michelin-star chef. My contribution had been doctored-up Stove Top stuffing with fresh herbs from my windowsill and pumpkin ice cream—I just added canned pumpkin pie filling to top-shelf vanilla ice cream. It would have been the first time my father and Cole met.

Sadly, my father and Sheila wouldn't be able to make it for Christmas because they planned to visit Sheila's relatives. Not afraid to admit I was a terrible cook, I'd already made reservations for Christmas dinner at my favorite Montauk eatery, Pondfare. I'd invited Elle and her fiancé, Detective Shoner. Also promising to attend was Doc, my father's retired coroner friend and my surrogate uncle, and Doc's lady friend, Georgia, the owner of Old Man and the

Sea Books. Now that I'd met Felicity, if she didn't already have plans to fly home for the holidays, I'd add her to the mix. I voiced my idea aloud to Elle.

Elle, who was driving at a slug's pace toward Mabel and Elle's Curiosities, said, "It's a great idea. This is only the second time I've met her, but I felt a rapport immediately. I think she shares our passion for vintage décor."

"We are a passionate bunch, aren't we?" I grinned at the thought.

After Elle turned onto Sage Street, we pulled into the driveway in front of her carriage house. She put her hand on my arm. "I think we need to talk about what happened at Nightingale Manor. If you have any qualms about working there, I'm sure I could turn things over to Maurice."

"Why? Because I was spooked by a hospital bed with bloody restraints?"

"Bloody what!"

"Just kidding. But our Dr. Blake reminds me of *The Abominable Dr. Phibes*."

She gave me a look that after all our years of friendship should have been patented. "That's who Dr. Blake looks like? Vincent Price?"

"No. But he sure sounds like him. And when you think of it, the movie and its follow up, *Dr. Phibes Rises Again*, fits the scene in the basement."

"You and Dr. Phibes!" she said in exasperation. "Granted, both movies are hilarious, but I don't think you should compare Dr. Blake to a deranged fictional Dr. Phibes until we get a chance to know him better."

"True. Now that I think about it, both movies had great Deco sets. Maybe we could get some ideas for staging *Mr. & Mrs. Winslow*? The movies were cult favorites when I attended NYU. Just like we did with the movie *The Rocky Horror Picture Show*, we'd watch *Dr. Phibes* then throw things at the screen. The items thrown were related to the imaginative way Dr. Phibes killed the doctors responsible for his wife's death. Let's just say, once, my roommate brought a sausage she'd taken out of its casing."

"Gross!"

"Good times."

"You're incorrigible," Elle said, adding a laugh. "Now get out, before the weather changes. And call me when you get to Montauk."

I hopped out of the pickup and hurried to my Wagoneer. The smell of leather seats and the immediate warmth from the heater were a better welcome than my ancient Wrangler, which I'd said farewell to last September. My custom-created Woody Jeep Wagoneer had been purchased after I received a surprise windfall of cash. Currently, I was back to broke status, but happy as a Montauk clam in my new/vintage one-of-kind vehicle, which my father had hand-delivered direct from a factory in Detroit. My hometown.

A few minutes later, I was cruising down dry roads on Highway 114, thinking about my encounter with Blake Nightingale. At the intersection of Montauk Highway and 114, I reached into my coat pocket and pulled out the forlorn-looking rag doll and placed it gently on the seat next to me. The doll reminded me of the velveteen rabbit my grandmother had given me as a child that still had a place of honor at the top of my bedroom closet. Missing ear and all. I doubted there were any children admitted to Nightingale Manor Sanitorium in its day. I also knew that Dr. Blake and his wife didn't have children and he was an only child. I'd never admit it to Elle, but this was the one time I planned on letting the story of Arden Hunter's death stay where it belonged—in the past. If the doctor didn't fire me when we showed up on Wednesday.

I made a pact with myself that I'd never go near that basement of horrors again.

From my lips to God's ears.

Chapter 6

Tuesday morning, a matted chunk of cat fur had found its way into my mouth. I grabbed a tissue off the bedside table and spit into it. "Ick! Josephine Eater Barrett!" The cat feigned innocence, but given her early morning disposition before mealtime, I wouldn't have put it past her to have used her two meaty paws to stuff the furball into my mouth. When you owned a Maine coon you were in for a lot of cat hair. Everywhere. On every surface.

Glancing at the clock, I saw it was an hour after feeding time. Jo never meowed at mealtime. Maybe she was cognizant I wouldn't hear her nagging without my hearing aids. Instead, she gave me her one-eyed stare, because that's all she could give, occasionally swatting me on the cheek. Her insinuation was clear. I was a lazy bum. Which I occasionally was. That was the price one paid for tranquility. Living and doing exactly what I wanted with no one looking over my shoulder. Except Jo.

"All right. All right. Let's go down for breakfast."

Jo moved up to my cheek. Instead of hitting it, she nuzzled it. It was rare that she showed affection and I reveled in it. I scratched behind her ears, then jumped out of bed. After putting on slippers and a fleece robe, I walked to the French doors that opened to my small Juliet balcony. Snow was falling in thick flakes, obscuring my view of the Atlantic. The thirty-six steps leading down to the beach were covered in white. It would be a slippery descent, but since moving in I hadn't missed one day of walking the shoreline. And even though it was snowing, today would be no different. I could tell the wind was fierce because of the drifting snow and choppy waves, but I couldn't hear it howling without my hearing aids. And that's the way I liked my mornings—quiet and peaceful. Especially now that I owned my dream house and the land it stood on.

Jo head-butted my shin. "Okay, let's go." I followed her wide rear down the narrow staircase, realizing this was the first time in a while I'd felt settled. I owned land, my cottage, and a business. I never once regretted leaving my old life in Manhattan, even though I'd loved working at *American Home and Garden* magazine. But I hadn't loved the pressure of running a magazine owned by my former fiancé's twisted ex-wife's family, the Whitneys.

It seemed, even though I was only thirty-three, I had the makings of becoming a Miss Marple–type spinster with my one-eyed cat, a basket of knitting by my *New York Times* reading chair, and an occasional murder investigation. Like Jane, I seemed to be a murder magnet.

After serving Jo breakfast and grabbing a cup of coffee and my cell phone, I went into the great room and struck a match to the waiting kindling. I'd had my handymen reproduce the flagstone fireplace and thick wood-plank mantel to match the one at the cottage I'd previously rented. I'd also made a few other changes to the structure of my bungalow copied from my old rental—like adding a balcony off the attic bedroom and tearing down the wall between the living room and kitchen. Sadly, the four-room rental cottage had been demolished last month to make way for a new mega beach house slated to break ground after the thaw. *Throw out the old, bring in the new* wasn't a motto I adhered to. But then everyone had a choice on what resonated with them when it came to home design. When it came to personal style I made sure to follow my clients' directives, not my own. However, a little bit of vintage or antique melded well with even the most modern of design. Adding one-of-a-kind items and art that couldn't be replicated from an online catalog or a home goods store was one of the things I lived for.

There was something I'd added to my cottage that hadn't been in my rental—a hidden room. While Jo munched away in the kitchen, I padded toward the wall of bookcases in the great room and pressed against a small rectangular section of wood molding. Presto-chango, the bookcase opened, revealing a narrow room. I stepped inside, then placed my coffee cup and phone on the small table next to a thick-cushioned window seat. The window seat had been built into a bowed window, giving me 180-degree views. Morning magic included sipping coffee as I gazed toward the Montauk Point Lighthouse. When spring came, I changed my routine to sitting on the huge rocks jutting out from my beach at low tide, while gazing to the east at the sun rising out of the Atlantic. Life didn't get much better.

After pulling a velvet crazy quilt over my legs, I picked up my phone. Cole had left a voice mail that had been transcribed into words. The problem with the phone app for the hearing impaired was that things tended to get lost in translation. I didn't think he'd called to say, "All kites are canceled." I took a deep breath and shelved my disappointment when I read he wouldn't be attending the holiday festivities at the lighthouse. And this time, Mother Nature was the only one I could blame. Breaking me from my woe-is-me thoughts was a loud pounding that vibrated the windows. If I'd been in the great room or the kitchen a light would blink when someone rang the doorbell.

I trotted into the great room to find my neighbor Claire standing at the door with her pink nose pressed against the glass. I quickly opened the door and motioned her in. "Claire! What are you doing out in this weather?" Claire had moved into Little Grey last October and was clasping a handful of seaweed in her gloved right hand. "And what the heck's with the seaweed?"

"Kelp," she said, frosty vapor billowing from her mouth. The deep green kelp matched the color of her eyes as she held it toward me. Her long, dark curly hair was mixed with strands of silver and glistened with melting snow.

I grabbed her elbow. "Hurry inside before you freeze to death."

She stepped onto the plastic mat by the door and kicked off her boots. She switched the kelp from hand to hand as I helped her out of her thin raincoat. Then I draped it over the arm of my *New York Times* reading chair. No matter what the weather, she always wore one of her long gauzy skirts. Weighted down by a band of ice, the hem dragged to the floor.

"I read the most wonderful thing about the healing properties of kelp when made into a poultice for your skin," she said in her soft, lyrical voice. Then she pushed the slimy thing closer to my face and I caught a whiff of briny ocean. "Helps remove toxins and provides a moisture barrier for scarred tissue. Do you mind fetching a baggie I can put this in? I want to retain the seawater."

"No problem," I said, scurrying to the kitchen, where I retrieved a Ziploc bag and brought it back to her. She dropped the kelp inside and closed the bag. The scars Claire talked about were on her right leg. She'd once told me matter-of-factly that in her twenties she'd gotten a ride home after a performance of *The Nutcracker* on her boyfriend's motorcycle, they'd slid on a wet road and the bike had tipped over, trapping her right leg between the pavement and the tailpipe, causing third-degree burns. After she recounted the story, she'd picked up her long skirt and shown me the damage to her leg, saying, "So, my career at the San Francisco Ballet ended, and my true calling began." The way she talked of the incident that had changed the direction of her life had been one of acceptance. Void of pity seeking.

I remembered trying not to wince after viewing her scarred leg. Then she'd lowered her skirt and never mentioned it again. She didn't have to. All I had to do was read her early poetry to learn about the pain she carried with her after that fateful day. The loss of her ballet career didn't stop her from pursuing another. Claire Post was a renowned American poet. Her bound poetry collections had been reprinted and translated worldwide. *Tiger by the Tail*, the first book of poetry she'd published, in her late twenties, was still in circulation today.

"Want me to throw your skirt in the dryer? Now that the fire is cracklin', I can loan you my robe."

"Sounds like a plan," she said, laughing, holding up the bag of kelp. "You must think I'm a nutjob."

"Of course I do. That's why we get along so well."

I took off my robe and handed it to her. She didn't mention my *I've been to Hell, Michigan*, jammies, but I saw a slight upward curve to her lips. She slipped on my aqua fleece robe, took off her skirt, then handed it to me. While Claire took a seat at the card table, I went to the kitchen and opened a pair of louvered doors that hid my washer and dryer. I put her skirt in the dryer and closed the doors. When I turned, Jo was still lapping at her spotless plate. "Give it up, Josephine. Go say hi to Claire." For once she listened and waddled out of the kitchen, her bushy tail in the shape of a question mark.

When I came around the open counter area that separated the great room from the kitchen, I found Jo sitting at Claire's feet with her head tilted upward, her nose twitching as if she could smell the kelp inside the bag at the edge of the table.

Claire grinned. "I think she wants to eat some."

"She wants to eat everything. Everything but pet food with the words *healthy, lo-cal,* or *weight-management* written on the front. I swear, she can read."

I looked over at Claire's still-pink nose and thin frame. I was surprised she'd made it over in one piece and wasn't blown off the cliff into the Atlantic. Looking over at her raincoat on the chair, I said, "Think it's time we went shopping for warmer clothing. Long Island winters are a far cry from California's."

"Deal. It is a little colder than the Northern California town I grew up in. I just wanted to check on you."

"What's that look in your emerald eyes, Ms. Post?"

Glancing around the bare surroundings, she chastised, "When are you going to start decorating this place? I know you told me you want to savor every detail. But it's time, young lady. My attic is waiting. What you haven't used in Little Grey is all yours."

Claire's beach house, Little Grey, got its name after it was discovered that the original architect had been the same person who'd designed the famous Grey Gardens in East Hampton—the former home of Jackie Kennedy Onassis's cousins big and little Edie Beals.

"I forgot to tell you that Dave's Hamptons wants to shoot Little Grey in April, so get ready for Cottages by the Sea to have more clients than you know what to do with." When Claire talked she always used her arms and hands in big sweeping gestures, her hands cupped ballerina style.

When I'd first viewed it, Little Grey had been in deplorable condition. Since then the entire two floors had been renovated by D&D Construction. The only space that hadn't seen the ravages of time was the watertight attic filled with antique and vintage goodies dating back to the early 1900s. On my initial visit and every time thereafter, its contents had made me swoon. Claire's son-in-law, the owner of Little Grey, had given me carte blanche to decorate using what I wanted from the attic, but only after I talked to his mother-in-law, who would be living there. Claire's aesthetic leaned more to the organic side, so I'd used the items from the attic sparingly. Luckily for me, I was promised the remainder of what was left to decorate my seven-room cottage—or eight-room, if you counted my hidden room. Seeing that Duke and Duke Jr. had only just completed our last construction project, I hadn't had a chance to begin bringing in furniture and accessories. In the meantime, I'd been living with the bare necessities — my bed, dresser, sofa, a card table, two folding chairs, and of course my *New York Times* reading chair.

"Yes, ma'am. I'll get on it," I said. "As soon as I finish with the Shelter Island project, you won't be able to get me out of Little Grey's attic. It'll be just me and the bats. Coffee? Donut?"

"Bats? What bats?"

"Just the ones in my head," I joked. Stepping behind the counter, I took out a plate and mug from the overhead cupboard. I snatched the last Dressen's donut from a covered glass cake stand, put it on the plate, and filled the cup with French roast.

She laughed and said, "I'm dying to know how yesterday went. In grad school, I once attended a writing sabbatical on Shelter Island sponsored by UCLA Berkley. We stayed at the old slave plantation Sylvester Manor. Even slept in the slave quarters to get an idea of what it must have been like. There were slaves at the manor until 1820. We always think of the South when it comes to slavery, not the Northeast. Some of my best poetry came from that sobering experience."

"Now, with the help of the Land Trust, Sylvester Manor is an educational farm."

"That's wonderful."

"You went to Berkley? Don't tell me you were a hippie back in the seventies. When you came to the Hamptons, did you hang out with all the bohemian writers and artists?" Claire was in her late sixties, so I knew the timing was about right.

"No. We spent most of our time on Shelter Island. But I did spy Truman Capote and Kurt Vonnegut once in front of Bobby Van's restaurant in Bridgehampton. We called ourselves the Nature Conservatory Poets Society. We were a very select group of poets, each writing our college thesis. NCPS still meets every couple of years. We use our poetry as a voice in stopping the development of land in secluded small oceanfront towns like the one I grew up in in Northern California."

"That's one of the things I love most about our tiny hamlet of Montauk. It boasts six state parks and isn't overdeveloped like the rest of the Hamptons."

"You're lucky. My book *Seldom Tweets the Bird* might have won prizes in England, but alas, it barely made a dent in keeping the developers at bay in Southern California," she said wistfully. "The good news is my Northern California hometown of Whitethorn remains untouched due to its remote location on the Lost Coast. The town is so isolated the government had to give up their plans to build roadways through the rocky terrain. Too expensive."

"Why'd you move to L.A.?"

"After Berkley, I met my late husband and moved to Santa Barbara. We lived there for most of our marriage."

"I love Santa Barbara," I said from the kitchen. I'd been to Santa Barbara a few times and always loved its cliffs overlooking the Pacific Ocean, similar to the view off my Montauk deck. After adding milk to her French roast, I brought the plate and coffee to her and took a seat at the card table.

Claire took a sip of coffee, then continued, "When Brad got sick we sold our oceanfront house, packed up the contents, and put them in storage. Then we left Santa Barbara and rented a furnished one-bedroom apartment in Century City so Brad could get top-notch medical care at Cedars-Sinai. All our retirement money went to his health care. They were able to prolong his life, so it was worth it. But I never got used to L.A.'s freeways. Not to mention the smog, overcrowding, and no water view. That's why I was so excited when my son-in-law handed me the keys to Little Grey. It's so beautiful here. Reminds me of Santa Barbara, and I'm happy conservation seems to be a top priority. With my new gig as an editor and contributor to *Prose & Poetry* magazine and my small social security checks, it'll be a struggle, but I should be able to make ends meet."

"And what about all the royalties from your books?"

"Dearest Meg," she said with a wry smile. "Poets make the least amount of money in the writing arts. We do it because we have to. Never for the money. Now, tell me about your assignment on Shelter Island."

"We haven't started going through the contents at Nightingale Manor, but it was an interesting couple of hours."

"Nightingale Manor?"

"The name of the house where they're filming the 1930s period mystery series I told you about. It was a former sanitorium for the mentally ill."

"Oh. You've got my poet's blood buzzing. There's nothing like the tales an old insane asylum can tell."

I filled her in as best I could, making a quick mention of the old murder.

Claire didn't own a TV, so she'd never watched *Bungled*. She popped the rest of the donut into her mouth. After licking her fingertips, she wiped her hands with a napkin and said, "These donuts are so good." Claire reminded me of Jo after a satiating meal. "I curse you for turning me onto them. I think I'm beginning to see a paunch." She rubbed her hand across her flat stomach.

"Please, you have a perfect dancer's body." I realized what I'd said might come off the wrong way because of her accident, so I quickly switched gears. "Cole finked out. Again. So, it looks like it's just you and me for the holiday festivities at the lighthouse tonight."

Claire leaned across the table and gazed into my eyes. In case I wasn't wearing my hearing aids, she always made sure I was facing her when she talked so I could read her lips. My ex-fiancé, Michael, had tried to get me to wear them during my every waking hour. It was hard to explain how irritating they could be. Not that I wasn't grateful for the wonderful hearing-aid technology that every couple of years made my hearing even better. My new aids were even Bluetooth capable. Someone could call me on the phone and the call would go right into my ears. Streaming music and audiobooks were another perk. I'd been lucky, because my hearing loss wasn't progressive. It was caused by an ear infection in my early teens.

"I know you're disappointed. But I'm sure if Cole could be here, he would."

"You're right." Claire had only met Cole once, but they'd gotten on well with each other, seeing Claire was an avid sailor. Mention sailing to Cole and you'd see his blue eyes, the color of the Caribbean on a cloudless day, light up.

"Looks like I might get a walk in yet," I said, glancing out the window that looked to the south. The snow had stopped but the wind still rattled the cottage's frame.

"Yes, walking is great. I see a big difference since moving in. Before, I only did yoga. I feel years younger since walking the shore. So, when do you go back to Nightingale Manor?" she asked.

"Tomorrow. Hold that thought." I went to the storage closet

under the stairs and took out the armless doll Max, or was it Murphy, had given me. I'd wrapped it in tissue paper. As I handed it to Claire, I explained how I'd gotten it.

After unwrapping and examining the doll for a few minutes, she said, "Now you've really got my imagination boiling."

I watched her finger the area where an arm had broken off.

"Wait! I think something's inside." She tried to stick two fingers in the left arm hole, but the opening was too small. "Do you have something like a barbeque skewer? Maybe I can push it out the other side? I know you're allergic to cooking, but I'm also aware you have a built-in outdoor grill inside your walled garden."

"Ha-ha. My father insisted. I am able to do chicken and vegetable skewers marinated in my herbal vinaigrette. I may be a poor cook, however, I make a mean salad dressing with fresh herbs from my garden."

I got up and went to the kitchen, where I found a metal skewer in the drawer under my small center island. I brought it back to the table and passed it to her.

"Thanks," Claire said, then laughed. "I'm not a great home chef by any stretch, nothing compared to your father."

"Nobody can compare to him," I added with a grin.

I watched as she gently stuck the skewer into the arm hole. Once inside the doll's torso, she carefully moved it around until a folded piece of paper poked out the other side. I took my thumb and forefinger to remove it as delicately as possible. The paper was thin, yellowed onionskin, like the paper secretaries used in their typewriters in the fifties and sixties. I fingered the folded square and felt a lump. "Looks like there's something inside," I said excitedly. Unfolding the paper, I exposed two vintage-looking train tickets from the Long Island Railroad. Both read *Montauk to Pennsylvania Station*, with a date of December 23, 1950. They were one-way tickets. On the onionskin paper was a short note written in pencil, the writing so faded all I could make out was the date of December 22, 1950, and a name.

The note was addressed to — *Marian.*

As in Marian Fortune? Arden Hunter's killer?

Chapter 7

"I don't like the look of that sky," Elle said Wednesday morning after I parked my car in her driveway and hopped into her pickup. I was thrilled the heater was on full blast. Before pulling out, she moaned, "Just got a major weather alert on my phone. Not from weather.com but FEMA. FEMA! As in the government!"

I pooh-poohed her misgivings after she told me about another one of her prophetic doom-and-gloom dreams, promising I'd talk to Captain Chris about the weather after we boarded the ferry. If anyone knew the dangers of a winter storm it would be him. Ten minutes later, when Elle had pulled up to the ferry, Captain Chris hurriedly beckoned us on board. He directed us to the same spot we'd parked in on Monday. I lowered the window to talk to him, but he was already scurrying to pull up the ramp.

It seemed we were the only vehicle on the ferry, and for a moment I had my own misgivings about traveling across the water in a nor'easter, even if it was only a quick ride. Then I thought of the doll and the train tickets. Had Arden planned on giving the note with the train tickets to Marian? And if she did, it didn't sound like they'd been enemies. Were they planning to flee Nightingale Manor together? And if so, what had happened to stop them? The hairs on the back of my neck stood at attention like the area at the base of Jo's tail when she saw a real, or *toy*, mouse. I was being ridiculous. Marian was a common name in the time period Arden and Marian were at the sanitorium.

Not that common, the irritating voice in my head said.

Elle nudged me on the shoulder. "Hurry. Get out of the truck. You promised to ask Captain Chris about the weather." The ferry started moving. "Go! Before it's too late to go back."

It was a feat just to open the passenger door. Fighting the wind, I made my way toward Captain Chris. His long beard and mustache were flattened against his neck and face like a dog's when sticking their head out a car window. He assured me the ferry would arrive at Shelter Island to pick us up at four on the dot. "I've told you before, Meg. We have a perfect record. Not once did we cancel because of the weather." His words made me feel secure, but at the same time he kept glancing toward the horizon at the huge waves and black clouds, something I didn't pass on to Elle when I got back inside the pickup. I was too excited about getting to work at Nightingale Manor to let a little wind ruin things.

Luckily, I hadn't received a call from Dr. Blake telling me to stay away from Nightingale Manor. I promised myself if we came face-to-face, I'd keep my chin up and avoid his gaze.

Once upon the open water, Elle was too busy looking at the weather app on her phone to notice the snow that started to fall. Not light, fluffy flakes like Monday. Instead, the view in front of us was so opaque I couldn't see two feet off the starboard bow. Buffeting gale-force winds caused huge white-capped waves, mimicking the ones I'd seen many times out my cottage window during a nasty nor'easter. But my cottage was on the ocean. We were on the bay.

The ferry swayed, the pickup tilted, and my stomach lurched in unison. I seriously thought I might lose the Belgian waffle, egg, brown-sugar-crusted slab bacon and cheese sandwich I'd had at Paddy's Pancake House with Doc only an hour before. Doc Heckler was my father's best friend, who'd moved to Montauk after retiring from his job in Detroit as a Wayne County medical examiner. Doc was also my surrogate uncle and always had my back. However, he tended to be a bit overprotective when it came to me and my *shenanigans*, as he called them. That being said, I'd purposely left out any discussion at breakfast of old murders, madhouses or maiming doctors. Plus, he and his gal-pal Georgia, the owner of Montauk's only bookstore, were leaving a few days after New Year's for a serenity cruise. Whatever that entailed. Since meeting well-read and enlightened Georgia, Doc had changed from an occasional stick-in-the-mud to an adventurous reincarnated teen.

We arrived at Nightingale Manor forty minutes later than scheduled because of the near-blizzard conditions. I'd taken over the wheel of the pickup when the roads became too slick for Elle to handle. She'd wanted to stay on the ferry and wait until it headed back to Sag Harbor but changed her mind when Captain Chris told her he had to stay at the dock until he fueled up and fixed a minor problem in the ferry's engine. Not to worry, he'd assured her. Elle didn't believe the *minor* part, and after I encouraged her that everything would be fine, she'd thought she'd chosen the lesser of two evils.

She hadn't.

Nightingale Manor didn't look as dark and brooding under a mantle of white snow. If it wasn't for the tombstones I noticed adjacent to the gatehouse when we pulled into the driveway, I'd say I'd been foolish to have any trepidation about working at the estate.

I parked the pickup in the circle drive in front of the main house. It looked like someone was on top of plowing the now-accumulating snow. The next ferry wasn't for three hours so we had to make the best of it.

"See, they have a snowblower, no problem, Ms. Worrywart," I said to Elle and saw an immediate relaxing of her shoulders. Secretly, I knew if the snow kept falling at the rate it was, we'd be hard-pressed to make it back to the main road, snowblower or not.

Elle stuck out her bottom lip. "Said she, who almost skidded into a hundred-foot elm a few seconds ago."

There were four other vehicles parked in front, a black Range Rover, a white Mercedes, a navy BMW and a silver Prius. It seemed we weren't the only crazy ones visiting Nightingale Manor in a blizzard. "Not even close to losing control," I said, "And remember, if Dr. Blake answers the door, try to have my back. I was just looking for the bathroom on Monday. Wink. Wink."

"If you weren't so curious, I wouldn't have to have your back. But of course, I'd support you 'til the end of time."

We got out and fought our way up the front steps. As I reached for the intercom button, Elle grabbed my wrist. "Maybe it would be smarter to head back to the dock and wait for the ferry?"

"And run out of gas, sitting there for three hours?" That shut her up.

As I reached again for the button of the intercom, the door opened. Felicity stood in front of us dressed in layer upon layer of clothing—turtleneck, pullover sweater, cardigan sweater, fleece pants and fleece-lined boots. She motioned us inside, pressing a finger to her lips, shush-style. Loud male voices echoed down from the high-ceilinged foyer. I recognized one as Dr. Blake's.

"You have no room to criticize me for unpaid bills, knowing what I know, partner. If I tell her lawyers about your little secret, that will be the end of your career forevermore. Don't make threats you're not willing to carry out, Doctor." Dr. Blake's voice was deep with a raw edge, sending goose bumps up my spine. His tone reminded me of a towering male substitute teacher I once had in elementary school, who'd asked, "I don't know, Megan, *can* you go to the bathroom? Are you able? Is everything in working order? Or do you think the proper way to ask would be using the word *may*?" The whole class had laughed as I'd hurried out of the room. Afterward, I had to write the word *may* fifty times on the blackboard.

"Come this way," Felicity whispered. We left our boots at the front door, wondering if we shouldn't have entered through the servants' door. Felicity led us through the grand foyer and into a back hallway. She opened a closet door and we handed her our coats.

After we were safely out of earshot of the arguing from the drawing room, Felicity said, "I've been waiting for you. Couldn't stay in that room with them for one more minute."

I thought I'd dressed appropriately in a long-sleeve white T-shirt and red wool cardigan, but it was so cold, I swear I could see my breath when I asked her, "I recognized Dr. Blake's voice. Who else is in there?"

"Dr. Blake and his partner at the practice are the ones arguing. They're being sued, and their malpractice insurance has expired. It was Dr. Blake's job to keep it current, and he hadn't. I've met his partner, Dr. Lewis, before. As sweet as they come. Not today." Felicity laughed but it wasn't a ha-ha laugh, more of a nervous laugh. "I'm not a gossip, it was really uncomfortable. That's why I snuck out and waited at the door."

"There are a lot of cars parked out front," Elle said. "Anyone else here from *Mr. & Mrs. Winslow*?"

I could tell Elle had forgotten her fear about the storm and was focused on the chance of meeting more actors from the series.

"Yes, the show's producer, Jeremy Prentice, and Langston Reed, our director. I could tell they wished they could escape the room like I did. Between you and me, I think Mr. Prentice was unhappy with the location Langston chose to film the series. Our lead actors, Zoe and Dillon, must have complained."

Maybe someone found out about the murder and the fact the

mansion had once been a mental hospital? I knew Langston had many quality films to his credit and was a big supporter of local Hamptons charities. It was surprising the lead actors in the series would complain about the location. I said, "When Elle and I met the two leads, they seemed genuinely happy with the Nightingale estate. I even overheard them talking about how nice it would be to be incommunicado from the paparazzi and other voyeurs that came as the price of being famous. I know the pups, Murphy and Max, loved the open outdoor spaces."

Elle wore a pout. "Tell me they aren't going to change location."

"Thankfully, no," Felicity answered. "At least that was confirmed before Dr. Blake's partner showed up and the fireworks began. Earlier, Dr. Blake begged our producer to use the estate, even lowering the agreed-upon rental fee."

It seemed the Nightingales didn't want to jeopardize their contract with the production company, especially if they were being sued and needed the money. I couldn't guess how much they'd be paid for use of the estate, but I'd bet it was a bundle.

Felicity motioned us to follow her. "Whatever we find to use on the set has to be inventoried, assigned a value, then a percentage of the value will be added to the location fee."

"Looks like we lucked out," Elle said. "First Fidelity Mutual is paying Meg and me for doing the inventory, and the producers of *Mr. & Mrs. Winslow* are paying us for helping you stage the rooms before filming."

"Believe it or not, it's still cheaper than renting everything for the set and having it shipped to the island. And we're saving on not having to pay you guys union wages. Something I'm not supposed to know but I heard Langston and Jeremy discussing. And when I say *we*, I mean Prentice Productions. Now, let's go get some coffee or hot chocolate to bring to the attic. Heat rises so I'm hoping it will be warmer up there. Maybe the Nightingales also forgot to pay the electric bill." She smiled. "I'm dying to find items for the opening scene, which takes place on Christmas Day, 1935. Dr. Blake said the attic is where his family had been storing Christmas decorations since the turn of the last century. We plan on flying in a huge live tree by helicopter to decorate." She rubbed her hands together, either in excitement or for warmth.

The damp and coldness from the drafty hallway left my bones and were replaced by a flush of heat that filled my veins after I heard the word *attic*. *Attic* equals *treasure* in an old house like this. Obviously, I couldn't take anything home with me, but it would be a hoot to find treasures circa 1900 to 1940 that could be uncovered, dusted off, and seen on the set of *Mr. & Mrs. Winslow*.

"But what about the weather? Shouldn't we be more concerned about that?" Elle said. She must have been worried. Elle loved a good attic as much as I.

Felicity shook her head. "I overheard Dr. Blake say he has a generator. So, no worries on that score. I plan on making the three thirty ferry to Greenport." She pulled out her phone and looked at it. "We still have two good hours of work." She tapped the screen and said, "Darn!"

"What's wrong?" Elle asked, panic clouding her brown eyes.

"No wifi. Not surprising in this weather."

A woman's voice came from inside an open doorway next to them. "Girls. Come inside. You'll freeze to death out there."

Felicity laughed and called out, "Be right there, Willa." Then she turned to us and said, "I don't know where Dr. Blake found Willa, but she's the best. Never seems put out when you ask for anything and always anticipates your every whim. I wouldn't mind living in a mansion on a beautiful island with someone who's as good a cook as Willa. It's a shame she and Mrs. Nightingale don't get along. Come, let's get inside. There's a fireplace in the kitchen that Willa always keeps stoked."

I wanted to grill Felicity more on Mrs. Nightingale, remembering Monday on the ferry when Dr. Blake had been pounding the steering wheel and using the word *blackmail*. I'd looked online for photos of Dr. Blake's wife and found quite a few of them attending social events in the area. The blonde woman next to him in the car on the ferry had been his wife, Sabrina. The doctor could be quite intimidating, and now to hear his wife didn't get on with the housekeeper made me curious as to the type of woman he'd chosen to marry. It was none of my business, seeing I doubted we'd have contact with anyone but Felicity while we were at the estate. At least, I hoped that was the case.

When we entered the kitchen, Willa was standing in front of a double farm sink looking out at the winter scene. Unlike Monday, the snow was sticking, flying vertically and horizontally, depending on the wind gusts. She turned, arched her thick brow and said to Felicity, "You must be happy to escape the fracas in there. Dr. Lewis is a good man. I've never seen him in such a tizzy." She went over to a large coffee urn and filled a thermal pitcher. I inhaled the rich scent of French roast. We all gravitated to a small fireplace in the corner of the room. In front of a blazing fire was a braided rug and two rocking chairs. All that was needed to complete the scene was either a dog or a cat, snuggled on the rug. As if part of the movie set, a red tabby's head crowned from a basket near the hearth. It looked us over, then snuggled back to sleep.

"Tabitha only leaves her basket to eat," Willa said, going over and scratching the top of the cat's head.

Another feline obsessed with food, I thought, thinking of Jo.

"Of course, at sixteen, she leads quite the sedentary life."

There was a whistling up the chimney that my hearing aids picked up. It sounded like a wolf howling or the moaning of a ghost — Arden Hunter's?

The room was huge, but at the same time warm and inviting. There was a square wooden table and chairs in the center and the walls showed exposed brick. Copper pots and pans hung from an iron rack over a professional-grade six-burner gas stove. The two large wall ovens looked like they were from the fifties or sixties. The refrigerator and dishwasher looked new. I couldn't help but think that this kitchen would have been the only one serving meals to patients when Nightingale Manor was used as a boutique sanitorium. Willa was too young to have been around during the infamous murder, and depending on when Dr. Blake's grandfather died, it was doubtful she'd met him. I couldn't stop myself and said, "Willa, how long have you been working for the Nightingales?"

She turned her kind hazel eyes in my direction. After swiping a short auburn curl off her forehead, she said, "Fifteen years. Blake took pity on a single mother and gave me a job. I started here after his father passed away, before he married Sabrina." Even though she spoke fondly of her employer, I noticed her hands clenched into fists and the light had left her eyes. I didn't know if it had something to do with Blake or his wife, Sabrina.

Elle interrupted my thoughts. "We better get going up to the attic if we're going to make the four o'clock ferry."

"The attic?" Willa gasped, sucking in her full rosy cheeks. "Why would you ever want to go up to that dusty thing? Fair warning, I don't clean up there. You better take paper toweling and a broom."

Little did she know she was making the attic sound even more appealing.

Elle laughed. "No worries, Willa. Cleaning will be part of the fun."

The housekeeper gave Elle a skeptical look.

"Has anyone ever told you that you look like Mrs. Padmore from *Downton Abbey*?" I blurted out before I realized that Willa might not take what I said as a compliment.

"You're not the first," she answered, smiling.

My shoulders relaxed. Willa filled a bucket with cleaning supplies and handed the bucket to Elle, saying, "Have at it." She handed Felicity a wicker basket lined with a napkin and a slew of orange-cranberry muffins—her mother's recipe, she told us. I was awarded a sterling silver tray upon which we placed our mugs and the large thermos. As I tried to balance the heavy tray, the mugs went sliding. "I'd make a terrible waitperson," I said, righting the tray just in time.

"Oh, my." Willa took the tray and placed it on the table. "I think I have a solution." She went into the pantry and came out with a rolling tea cart. "Here. Place everything on the cart and then you can take it to the elevator. I don't know what I was thinking." She went to the Sub-Zero refrigerator and took out six large water bottles and placed them on the cart.

"Thanks, Willa," Felicity said.

"You're more than welcome. I'm looking forward to some activity in this old manse." Glancing toward the crackling fire, she added, "Hold one sec. You might need something else." She opened a door next to the pantry and stepped inside. A few minutes later she came out carrying two space heaters in her ample arms. "I'm sure you'll need these." She put the heaters at the bottom of the cart, then directed us to the elevator that would bring us to the attic.

The elevator was a couple doors south of the kitchen. When we reached it, Felicity pushed the button on the wall. Nothing happened. I'd seen a similar elevator in an old house Elle and I had inventoried in East Hampton. I stuck my fingers between the crack separating the two doors and pulled them apart. Voilà. In front of us was an old-school accordion-gate elevator cab. I grabbed the latch and opened the brass gate. Elle and Felicity walked inside. I followed with the tea cart.

"This is serendipitous. It looks to be of the same time period as *Mr. & Mrs. Winslow*," Felicity said, getting out her cell phone and typing something. "What a wonderful place to shoot a scene."

"Hope it doesn't stop mid-floor," scaredy-cat Elle answered in a shaky voice.

As if the elevator heard her, the light above our heads flickered. "If it did get stuck," I said, "someone could climb inside from that hatch up there"—I pointed to the ceiling—"murder us, then escape with no one the wiser."

Felicity put her phone away and grabbed the handle of the gate, then slid it across. A loud reverberating clank shook the cage. For a moment, it felt like we were in a jail cell. "Floor, please?" she asked with a laugh.

As Felicity went to push the button for the third floor, a giant stick figure of a woman passed in front of the gate. She backed up, then looked down at us. I felt like a caged bird as she peered in.

"Felicity," she said in a clipped tone. "This must be the team you talked about. Where are you starting?" The woman was almost six feet tall. Her frame was on the emaciated side. Long, perfectly styled blonde-highlighted hair framed a heart-shaped face accented with high cheekbones and full lips. Her eyes were a light gray, framed with lush lashes that had to be fake.

I wasn't surprised when Felicity said, "Mrs. Nightingale. We're heading up to the attic to check for vintage holiday decorations."

"Please, call me Sabrina. There isn't that much of an age difference between us." She laughed and waved her left hand. A huge emerald-cut yellow-diamond engagement ring and matching wedding band were on the ring finger of her left hand. On the pointer finger of her other hand was a ring encrusted with pavé diamonds forming a wave pattern, topped with a single South Sea pearl. Mikimoto, I assumed. Glancing at her perfect features and knowing she was a cosmetic surgeon's wife, I'd gamble Sabrina

Nightingale was older than Felicity. The only thing giving away Sabrina's age were her crepey hands.

"Mrs. Nightingale. Sabrina. This is Meg Barrett and Elle Warner."

Before we could respond with a nice-to-meet-ya, she said, "Well, carry on. I need to talk to Willa about something. Again!" She turned abruptly and clip-clopped down the hallway toward the kitchen in her red-soled heels. The strong scent of her perfume lingered, and I sneezed.

"Bless you," Felicity and Elle said at the same time.

I took a tissue from my pocket and put it to my nose. A loud pounding made us all jump. It came from the direction of the kitchen. Shouting soon followed—Sabrina Nightingale's and Willa's. I had no problem hearing Sabrina yell, "One more time, Willa Sullivan! One more time and you're outta here. No matter what my husband says. What you did today was unconscionable."

Elle went to push the button for the third floor. I tapped her on the shoulder. When she turned, I put my finger to my lips and whispered, "Shush."

After giving me an eye roll, she lowered her arm. Felicity leaned forward, her head tilted to the left, trying to catch the heated exchange. It seemed she was just as interested in Sabrina's and Willa's conversation as I was.

"How dare you add your two cents in front of Greg. If it wasn't for you, he wouldn't have gone off the deep end. How embarrassing in front of our director and producer. What are the chances I'll get a walk-on role now?"

"I couldn't stand to hear the lies," Willa said in a loud but controlled voice. "I had nothing to do with the practice's malpractice insurance lapsing. Wasn't that boy-toy you talked Blake into hiring in charge?"

"You have a lot of room, talking about a boy-toy. You had an affair with my husband when he was much younger than you. Plus, Rob is gone, we have someone new. Not that it's any of your concern. Keep to your housekeeping duties like a good servant."

"Blake and I are the same age, Sabrina. And it was one time. Way before you came into the picture."

"Well, that's the only reason he hired you. He felt sorry for you and your son. Then you betray him by throwing him under the bus in front of our guests."

"Maybe you're right. There's nothing for me here. I know it was you who told Blake Donnie had to leave."

"The kid's eighteen. Time for him to leave the nest. Our nest. The kid was always underfoot, especially when we were entertaining."

"You've had it out for Donnie ever since you came here," Willa said, her voice a little lower than before, and I had a hard time making out the end of her sentence.

"What did she just say?" I asked Elle.

"Willa said Sabrina's had it out for her son from the time she moved in five years ago."

A few seconds later, I had no problem hearing Willa's raised voice. "Now that that's in the open, like the other thing, you're right. There's no reason for me to stay. You two deserve each other."

There was a clattering of pans, then silence. Sabrina went barreling by us, calling out, "Greg. Greg. Can I have a word?"

I whispered to Felicity, "Who's Greg?"

"Greg is Dr. Lewis's first name. This is very concerning. Willa's on contract to feed and take care of the cast and crew. If she leaves, it could be a deal breaker for us setting up production here."

Elle waited until we no longer heard Sabrina's high-heeled footsteps and asked, "Am I allowed to speak now? What do you think all that was about, Felicity?"

"All I know is what I overheard earlier. Dr. Blake blamed Willa for not giving him the bill for the malpractice insurance policy and she claimed she'd given it to him. Along with many other past-due notices. Willa told me during one of our chats that sometimes she'd filled in as office manager and nurse at the office in Southampton when they were short-staffed."

"Nurse?" Elle asked, a puzzled look on her face.

"Years ago, Willa worked at the practice as Dr. Lewis's and Dr. Blake's RN. That was before Dr. Blake thought of bringing high-profile celebrity clients to Nightingale Manor to convalesce, guaranteeing they'd be far away from the prying eyes of the press. He convinced Willa to move here with her son and be his private nurse and housekeeper. I don't know exactly when Sabrina came into the picture, but from what we just heard it sounds like five years ago." Felicity laughed. "I think we might have a whole new miniseries to film."

"Something to replace *Bungled*," I said.

Felicity gave me a knowing look.

"Willa seemed excited about the filming," Elle said. "She must be getting a good stipend for working on the set. And, as you told us, Dr. Blake and his wife will be staying in the gatehouse. It would be a shame if Willa left before filming even started."

Felicity looked alarmed. "I sure hope she doesn't leave. I better go talk to her. Convince her she's indispensable. Plus, I know Jeremy will be very upset if she leaves. We'd need to hire Craft Services at the union rate. Our producer is very frugal, probably why he's one of the richest men in the industry. You guys go on ahead. I'll meet you up there." She slid open the gate and went in the direction of the kitchen.

Once again, I closed the gate, then pushed the button for the third floor, noticing that under the button for the first floor was an unmarked button. It must be for the basement. I shivered and wondered what it must have felt like for former Nightingale Sanitorium patients to descend to the bowels of the mansion on their way for shock treatment, or worse yet, a lobotomy. Like Arden Hunter . . .

Chapter 8

Our cage shook and we started our ascent. When the elevator finally reached the attic level, the doors opened. Elle stepped out and I followed with the tea cart. It rattled down the long carpeted hallway, the sound jarring in the eerie silence. The six electric sconces that lined the hallway had been left on. Their low-watt candelabra bulbs cast little light, adding a spooky ambiance, perfectly fitting for the attic of a sanitorium.

There were two doors for us to choose from. Elle opened the first door and flipped the light switch, illuminating a small bathroom with just a toilet and pedestal sink. The mirror over the sink was shattered, little fissures traveling across the surface like the threads of a spider's web.

"Wonder if the plumbing's in working condition?" Elle asked.

I was too excited about what might lay behind the next door to answer. I left the cart in the hallway and jogged to the door.

"Hey," Elle called after me, "not fair!"

"You got the first door. This one's mine." I turned the glass doorknob and walked in.

Someone had left two floor lamps on. Elle came and stood next to me. In the dim light we saw a single set of small footprints stamped on the dusty floor. Felicity had told us she'd been up here before us. It appeared that no one else had entered in decades. I rubbed my eyes to find what appeared to be a hologram of my recurring attic dream. The attic's depth and breadth were that of Noah's Ark. Every junk picker's and antique connoisseur's happy place. Including mine.

"And to think," Elle said, adding a whistle, "they had to transport all this stuff by ferry or boat."

I pointed up to the buttressed ceiling. Hanging from a beam on long chains were three Tiffany dragonfly lamps. Yes. Three. All in different shades of colored glass. Even under eons of dust, they seemed to glow. Having worked at Sotheby's in their Americana division prior to coming to *American Home and Garden* magazine, Elle had given me a crash course on all things Tiffany when we'd inventoried Caroline Spenser's legendary collections at her

Hamptons estate. I also learned from watching *Antiques Roadshow* how to spot a fake Tiffany lamp. "Those seem to be the real deal."

"Looks like it to me," she whispered, as if afraid she'd wake the other goodies before we got to them.

Next to me was a lacquered bar cart topped with a chrome cocktail shaker in the form of a dumbbell.

Elle followed my gaze. "Definitely in our *Mr. & Mrs. Winslow* wheelhouse." She moved next to the traveling bar and ran her finger through the dust on the shaker to reveal shiny chrome. "Amazing. It's from the Jazz Age. Deco. I'd guess around the early thirties. I sold a similar one in my shop for twenty-six hundred dollars and it didn't even have a chrome stand like this one does."

"Wow. Can't you picture suave Jack Winslow shaking a cocktail while holding a roomful of suspects captive as they waited for the great reveal? Wonder if the miniseries will have as many references to booze, like they always show in hard-boiled detective films?"

"You'll have to ask the screenwriter, your tortured poet, the reincarnated John Keats, aka Patrick Seaton," Elle teased.

I ignored her comment, even though it made for an interesting scenario. Me, strolling down Montauk's shoreline, looking for writing in the sand on Patrick's beach, then climbing the steps to his cozy little snow-covered cottage, knocking on the door, being greeted by his dog Charley, then asking him if there was going to be a lot of drinking going on in the miniseries he was writing . . . I screeched on the brakes in my addled brain. Patrick Seaton's wife and daughter were killed by a drunk driver.

"Why's your face so red? Thinking about Patrick? You naughty girl."

I didn't answer Elle and tried to steer the conversation in a safer direction. "Remember when we watched that Thin Man movie marathon at Maurice's? The thirties time period of the films was the same as *Mr. & Mrs. Winslow*. I hope the Lara Winslow character is like Nora Charles. Nora could hold her own not only in the liquor department compared to her boozer of a husband Nick but also in the sleuthing. Female detectives were rare in film and literature back then. Nora wasn't afraid of danger and was always a good sport, no matter what her better half was up to. Didn't even blink a lush eyelash when some thug aimed a gun at her and called her a dame."

"Great-aunt Mabel was a big fan of Myrna Loy, who played Nora Charles," Elle said as she examined a set of chrome martini stemware.

"My father told me my Nana Barrett read hard-boiled detective stories. Not just by Dashiell Hammett, but by Raymond Chandler and Mickey Spillane too. And she loved Ross Macdonald. My dad has all her books in his study."

"Might have had something to do with his becoming a homicide detective," Elle added.

"Possibly."

"You've got some role reversals going on in your family. Your gram read detective novels, and your gramps owned a restaurant. Maybe that's why your dad went into the police force and he's the best home chef I've ever met. What happened to you, Megan Elizabeth Barrett?"

"I can hard-boil an egg," I said with a grin. "If not for moi, *we* wouldn't have figured out what happened to Randall McFee last October."

"It seems in all three instances of your hard-broiled detecting, you were as surprised as everyone else about whodunit. And, you almost got killed in the process."

"Back to *Mr. & Mrs. Winslow*. I think Zoe will handle playing the female lead perfectly. Just hope they don't decide to find another location."

We heard a clattering and Felicity charged into the room, pushing the cart I'd left in the hallway. She paused, then bent over and grabbed her knees, gasping for breath. When she stood she gave us the biggest smile. "Think I've placated . . ." She grabbed a water bottle from the cart, chugged the whole thing, then said, "Willa into remaining, no matter what the Nightingales say or do to make her want to leave. Ran up the stairs . . . wanted to see the looks on your faces when you saw the space. Plus, I wanted to get away before I got embroiled in another spat between Dr. Blake and his partner. They were really going at it." Sweat beaded on her forehead.

"At least you've warmed up," Elle said. "Maybe that's what we all should do, run up and down the steps to keep warm."

"I grabbed our coats," she said, motioning to the bottom of the cart. "After we plug in a couple space heaters that should do it."

"Seems like Dr. Blake attracts controversy." I walked to the cart, grabbed my jacket and zipped it up. "What were they arguing about? The unpaid malpractice insurance?"

"I don't think so," Felicity said, going over to Elle, "this time it was Dr. Blake who seemed to be threatening Dr. Lewis with something. All I heard him say was, *You make a stink about the insurance and I'll tell our lawyer about your part in our little television drama.* I took off before I heard any more." Felicity picked up a stuffed toy dog from a built-in shelf. "Told you guys the attic was amazing. Look at this little guy, he's the same kind of dog they're using in *Mr. & Mrs. Winslow.*"

"It's a Steiff," Elle said. "Scotty, the black Scottish terrier."

"He'd look adorable under the Christmas tree in the first scene," Felicity said, excitement showing in her sparkling eyes illuminated by her glasses. She handed the stuffed dog to Elle.

"I'm afraid he dates from the early fifties, not the right date for the miniseries. There were some made in the thirties, but I can tell by the eyes this one is much later. One of my customers collects Steiff. She already owns Scotty, but if you find a Steiff Titanic Mourning Bear, she'll pay a pretty penny to add it to her collection. Only eighty-two were made and the last one at auction went for more than a hundred thousand dollars."

"Wow! I don't think that would fit in our budget," Felicity said.

"I'm sure my customer wouldn't mind loaning you her huge stuffed bear on wheels that I sold her a year ago. It even has a growler." Elle placed Scotty back on the shelf and went over to the north side of the attic to a cupboard under the eaves.

"Growler?" I asked.

"It was actually a rattle they added to a tin box in the bear's throat so when you shook him, he growled."

"G-r-r-r! What fun. Better than a video game, I'm sure." I went to join Elle at the cupboard door, excited by what we might find. "I know Teddy Roosevelt was the inspiration behind stuffed teddy bears after a cartoonist in the early 1900s drew a picture of Roosevelt letting a baby cub free because he said it was unsportsmanlike to shoot it."

Felicity joined us and Elle pointed up at the three lamps. "We believe those are real Tiffany."

"I'm ninety-nine-point-nine percent sure they are," Felicity said. "The attic is just a preview of the rest of the house."

"That guy over there might fit in, too." I pointed to my left. In the corner was a skeleton dangling from a metal stand. That wasn't what gave me the heebie-jeebies, it was what was on the top of a double-tiered bookcase next to him — four human skulls. Lobotomies gone bad? It seemed the southeast corner of the attic stored items from when Nightingale Manor was a sanitorium. Human body charts hung from a hook on the wall. Under the quadruplet skulls were microscopes, Pyrex lab beakers, even a metal syringe with a huge plunger. It looked like it might be perfect to baste a fifty-pound turkey. Someone had placed a Santa hat on Mr. Skeleton. "Was that your handiwork, Felicity?"

She grinned. "Maybe . . . Dr. Blake told me his grandfather was a doctor. We can't use any of it, because most of those medical items look like they're from after 1940."

"Aren't skeletons timeless?" I asked, watching her closely for a tell that would let me know if she knew about the murder.

"You have a point."

She hadn't reacted, so I guessed she knew nothing about Nightingale Manor's murky past. Which was just as well.

"First things first," Elle said. "Sustenance."

Elle went over to the cart and filled our coffee mugs, put some muffins on napkins, then handed them out. I found outlets to plug in the space heaters, hoping they were up to code. If not, I'd get fried and end up like Santa Skeleton. Felicity rooted through a closet packed with Christmas ornaments, oohing and ahhing as she uncovered more tissue-packed boxes. "Check out these babies," Felicity said, showing us a cache of exquisite Victorian handblown glass ornaments.

After chugging down our coffee and under Felicity's tutelage, we set up a grid system similar to what an archeologist might do on a dig site. I rolled up the beautiful twelve-by-twelve-foot Aubusson rug for a dustless space and then we placed items according to decade in their proper grid, combining anything prior to 1940 in the largest square.

"How big is the Christmas tree you're bringing in?" Elle asked Felicity after we'd finished clearing the closet.

"Huge. It will go in the drawing room and almost touch the twenty-foot ceiling. So, a guesstimate would be just shy of that."

After scouring the attic for every last Christmas-related item we could find, we perused our bounty.

Elle left to wash up. When she returned she said, "Meg, I think we should leave soon. Who knows how long it will take to get to the ferry. I couldn't see much out the small bathroom window. Only white and the sound of ice hitting, along with a rattling wind so loud I thought the glass might crack."

I glanced up at the fan-shaped windows under the pitched ceiling on the east and west ends of the space. We'd been so immersed in our work, we hadn't a clue as to what was going on outdoors during the past two hours.

Felicity took out her phone and glanced at the screen. "We better get going. We can finish tomorrow."

"Wish we could have gotten to that last set of closets under the eaves," I said, "the ones across from the closets we've already pillaged."

"Meg, we need to go *now!*" Elle ordered. "We'll have plenty of time tomorrow. Remember, I have that appointment."

I knew she had an appointment, but I doubted the other party would make it during a blizzard. Elle just didn't want to get stranded at Nightingale Manor. Neither did I.

A man's voice boomed toward us from the hallway, "So, this is where you've disappeared to . . ." Langston Reed walked in, a huge grin on his face.

When I'd met him at the film festival, I'd immediately liked him. He was a big supporter of Hamptons charities and had been a pivotal figure in the creation of the film festival. I also knew his mega estate in Bridgehampton had been featured more than once in *Architectural Digest.* But after the exchange I witnessed between him and Dr. Blake in the doctor's home office, I could see there might be a less amiable side to him.

Felicity bounded up to Langston. "We're finding lots of good things for the pilot," she said, spreading her arms in a sweeping motion to show him our handiwork.

"Fabulous," he said, glancing around the space. His gaze stopped where the skeleton and skulls were housed in the corner. He walked toward them.

"Do you think we can fit a skeleton into one of our episodes? Halloween at Jack and Lara's," Felicity said, laughing.

At first, Langston didn't answer. He went behind the skeleton and viewed the tattered pull-down chart of the human body. Then he turned to the bookcase and bent to the lower shelf and picked up the huge syringe, examined it, then tossed it back on the shelf like it was alive and ready to infect him with a deadly poison. "No," he finally answered, "I haven't read any scripts that might have the use of a skeleton. I suppose we could always add one."

At the mention of a script, I once again thought about Patrick Seaton, my pen pal in the sand and *Mr. & Mrs. Winslow*'s screenwriter.

Langston kept poking around the area littered with mad-scientist odds and ends. Finally, Felicity said, "Langston, I'd like you to meet Meg Barrett and Elle Warner. They've been a great help."

He looked toward us and smiled. "Ms. Barrett, you look familiar. Have you worked on any of my other projects?"

I went over to him and extended my hand. "Please, call me Meg. I think we were introduced at the international film festival. I was with Byron Hughes. This is my first time working on a set and I hope it's not my last." I flashed him my best smile, excited about what the future may hold. The Hamptons were notorious for being the perfect location for filming movies and television series.

"Of course. I rarely forget a face. A name, yes. And Ms. Warner," he said, nodding in Elle's direction, "I saw the photos of the items you brought for Zoe to wear. Perfect in every way."

She giggled. "Please, call me Elle."

A plump man in holey jeans and a fisherman's sweater walked into the room, followed by perfect-postured, reed-thin Dr. Blake Nightingale.

Elle nudged me and mouthed, "That's Jeremy Prentice, the producer."

Jeremy seemed close in age to Langston, the show's director, but instead of salt-and-pepper hair, his was pure white and pulled back into a short ponytail. The good doctor or bad doctor, depending on who you talked to, was dressed similar to when we'd met on Monday. He wore a baby-blue button-down oxford under his navy blazer.

"Langston, I'm leaving for the North Ferry," the producer said, chewing gum as he talked. "The snowplow has come and gone, and I've been informed it won't be coming back until tomorrow morning."

From what Elle had told me, Jeremy Prentice was close to being a billionaire. He sure didn't dress like one, then I remembered Felicity saying he was as cheap as they came.

"Nightingale," Jeremy said, turning to address Blake, "you know we could have picked a million other locations for this project. Now that we've chosen your home for filming, I hope you'll accommodate us by getting some heat in this monstrosity. I don't want any union complaints. Any whisper of one and we'll have to change the filming location. I'm sure you *understand*. Look at these people. They're wearing their winter coats."

I noticed Dr. Blake didn't tell Jeremy to call him doctor. He kept his mouth closed like it'd been wired and gave us a dismissive gaze. Something about him rubbed me the wrong way. I wasn't too enamored with Jeremy Prentice's poor manners either, billions or not. He'd looked over at us without introducing himself.

Friendly Elle had no qualms about walking up to them. "Dr. Nightingale, it's such a pleasure to meet you. You have an amazing home." She extended her hand. "I'm Elle Warner, you have my assurance we'll handle everything with the care it deserves. You have my oath."

"Please call me Dr. Blake. I'm sure my family's treasures are safe in your hands." He gave her a smile, but when he looked over a me, it faded.

I averted my gaze. There was an awkward silence. Again, Elle came to the rescue. "And you must be Mr. Prentice. I'm Elle Warner, and this is my partner in crime, Meg Barrett," she said, laughing.

Jeremy gave Elle a weak smile, then looked across the attic to where Langston was perusing an old leather journal he'd pulled out from the shelf under the skulls. "Langston, I need to speak to you about something of the upmost importance. Give me a call as soon as you get home."

Had the show's producer just learned about the old murder and didn't want any stigma attached to the miniseries? Or, like his director, did he already know about it?

Langston placed the journal back on the shelf and picked up one of the skulls. He held it in the air, examining it like he was in a Shakespearean play . . . *Alas, poor Yorick!* For a minute, I didn't think he was going to answer his producer. Finally, he put the skull down and said, "Fine, Jeremy. I'll call you as soon as I reach Bridgehampton."

"Don't forget," Jeremy said, "this was your idea for a location. Felicity, can you please step out in the hallway for a minute? I need to talk to you and Nightingale." He sounded like a stern high school principal. For some reason, I didn't think it would be a good idea to get on his bad side. Jeremy Prentice might have dressed in a down-to-earth pedestrian style, but something about the sharp way he took in his surroundings and the way he glared at Langston made me want to morph into the shiplap walls. Before leaving the attic, Dr. Blake glanced my way. His hypnotic amber eyes caught mine. I glanced away. He would always win in a staring contest.

After they left, I glanced over at Elle. She had a stricken look on her face. I didn't think it had to do with the miniseries's rude producer, but more to do with the weather outside. Also, hearing that the snowplow wouldn't be coming back wasn't a good sign.

I recalled the downtrodden look on Felicity's face when she'd left the attic, trailing behind Jeremy and Dr. Blake with her head down. She hadn't appeared happy and I realized how hard it must be to work on something of this scale. When the rest of the set department arrived with the crew and the actors at the beginning of January, things would be easier, making me more resolute for us to help her as much as we could.

Felicity reentered the room, her cheeks flushed either from the cold or embarrassment. Langston went up to her and whispered something I didn't hear. She laughed and said, "Let me walk you to the elevator." Langston thanked her. At least it seemed she and the director had a good relationship. I could tell by the way Langston compatibly put his hand on her shoulder, talking softly in a father-like manner as they left the room.

"We need to listen to Mr. Prentice and get downstairs," Elle told me. She began organizing the top of the tea cart. "I'm going to take the cart to the bathroom and rinse the cups. I'll meet you and Felicity at the elevator. No dawdling, Meg Barrett."

Once I had the attic all to myself, I rebelled against Elle's directive to hurry. Plus, I knew Langston was taking the elevator, and it moved at a snail's pace. It might be awhile before it returned. I sidled up to the storage space next to the attic boneyard, moved an old machine on wheels whose function I could only guess at and didn't want to know, then opened the small closet door under the eaves. Getting down on my knees, I stuck my head inside. It was too dark to see much of anything. I got out my phone and tapped the screen for the flashlight function.

In front of me were at least two dozen suitcases in all shapes and sizes. I pulled one toward me. It was an oldie. The caramel-colored leather had started to peel and crack. It had a worn hangtag with a name and date, followed by a six-digit number written in script. The date was 1950. I pushed it back inside and went to grab another. I heard Elle screech from the hallway, "Meg! We're waiting for you!"

I quickly closed the door and stood. The discovery of the suitcases caused an empty feeling in the pit of my stomach. Had the suitcases belonged to patients of Nightingale Manor Sanitorium? The ones who'd checked in but never checked out? Their families and loved ones anxiously waiting for them to be "cured" so they could come back home, but never would?

"Another time," I said to Santa Skeleton. He gave me an evil grin. I must have been on his naughty list. I scurried out of the attic—not quite as excited about it as when I'd entered.

Chapter 9

Felicity and Elle were at the elevator waiting for me. I hurried inside, ready for Elle to give me the third degree. She remained silent. I looked from her face to Felicity's. "What's up? You two look like you've lost your best friend. But you haven't, 'cause here I am. Ta-da!"

They remained sullen. Felicity closed the accordion gate, then turned to me. "I just told Elle what Jeremy told me. They still plan on shooting the pilot episode here, but they might change things up and move to another estate after that."

"They can't do that, can they?" I knew of course that they *could* do it. "I thought this estate was supposed to be where the couple moved after Jack was left everything in his great-uncle's will?"

"I really don't know what's going to happen. We're in such early stages and I'm lucky Jeremy shared any information with me. He said they might have the script rewritten. Jack comes to visit his great-uncle for Christmas and then he's murdered, and of course Jack is the lead suspect because he inherits his estate. Instead of moving in for the next episode, they buy a new mansion, making filming at Nightingale Manor a one-episode shoot."

It was obvious the Nightingales were in financial difficulty. Dr. Blake wouldn't be pleased, that I could tell. Not my worry, I told myself as Felicity continued.

"Usually the set designer is the last to know what's going on. I guess I should be thankful Jeremy told me that much. We're to keep working as planned. Langston promised to get ahold of the new script if there is to be one. In the meantime, I have the script for at least the first episode. I've gone through and made notes in the margins with some ideas of props we need, inspired by the rooms and dialog."

No one responded, as we were each lost in our own thoughts. Mine centered on seeing screenwriter Patrick Seaton showing up to go over the script he wrote, rewriting it for a new location.

"Is there any chance we can see the script?" Elle asked. "It would make good bedtime reading and then we'd have a better idea of how to edit the items as we inventory." She gave me a nudge, knowing I would love to see Patrick Seaton's teleplay.

"Of course." Felicity reached inside her duffel bag and pulled out a rolled sheaf of papers. Then she handed it to Elle. "If you want, you can bring it back tomorrow. And if you wouldn't mind, make a couple copies for you and Meg. But don't let anyone else see it. I would be in the doghouse for sure if Langston found out."

Elle took it. "No problem. How exciting. It will also help me see the costume changes, in case there's anything I left at home that might work for Zoe's character."

Felicity smiled. "That would be wonderful, Elle."

"Great. We better get going, I don't want to get stuck here overnight in an old insane asylum where a murder took place." Elle realized what she'd said and looked at me. "Oops."

Felicity pushed the button for the first floor. After the doors closed she turned to Elle and me, put her hands on her small hips and said, "Murder? Insane asylum?"

After giving Felicity a brief synopsis of the old murder, I tried to spin it in a more positive light. "It gives the place more color, don't you think?"

I waited for her to moan and complain, as Elle had done. Instead she said, "A sad tale. But that was almost seventy years ago. I never would have guessed this had once been a mental hospital. I suppose that's a good thing."

"I think it was more of a boutique hotel–type sanitorium. A celebrity hideout," I explained.

The elevator started to move, the pulleys grinding as we made our descent.

"I think we should forget about murders and crazies and concentrate on getting back to the mainland alive," Elle said. "And back to our other subject, if *Mr. & Mrs. Winslow* is moved to another location in the Hamptons, it's not that big of a deal, is it?"

"You have no idea," Felicity said. "It will mean I have to set up two different sets and we might need to call in a staging company from Manhattan, when everything we need for the proper time period is right here under our noses. Plus, everyone from crew to actors planned on staying here. A nice affordable hotel in the Hamptons, even off-season, will really cut into our budget."

The brass floor indicator over our heads moved lower toward the number two. The cab stalled for a second, then continued. The overhead lamp flickered like it had when we'd taken it up to the attic.

Suddenly, we jerked to a stop. Between floors.

Elle squealed, "Oh, no!"

Then the light went out.

Chapter 10

It seemed my earlier comment about climbing out of the hatch at the top of the elevator for an easy escape was wishful thinking. Being the tallest at five foot seven, I'd gotten on Elle's shoulders and tried to push it up. It didn't budge. Then Felicity had given it a try. She'd determined the hatch was bolted in place from the other side. I wondered if it might have been a safety measure implemented years ago to keep sanitorium patients from escaping Nightingale Manor. It didn't matter because I wasn't too keen about what would happen if I did have access to the elevator shaft. I pictured myself shimmying up a steel cable to the third floor, the generator Willa had mentioned kicking in, and me getting electrocuted, or worse yet, crushed if it moved up instead of down.

We'd eaten the rest of Willa's muffins, but no one wanted to drink the remaining coffee or water in case we had to use the bathroom. Elle's pickup and Felicity's car would still be outside, so we'd remained hopeful of rescue. We had screamed and pounded. No one came. We'd tried sending text messages and emails from our phones, but there was no signal. The only smart thing I did, anticipating our cell phones dying, was to tell Felicity to change her greeting to say we'd gotten stuck in the elevator at Nightingale Manor, giving our address and ending with "We're okay." It was something my father had told me to do after the last hurricane hit the East Coast. Even if our phones were dead, when someone went to leave a voice mail they would hear our greeting. Elle, in her haste to leave the attic, had left her cell phone behind. I'd tried to reassure her that if Detective Shoner called her phone and didn't get an answer, he would call mine.

The first hour was spent naming places or things we wanted to see before we died. I listed a couple — Cornwall, the Northern Lights — but basically all I wanted was to see my small cozy cottage in Montauk and my kitty cat Jo one last time. We then moved on to our best-ever restaurant meal, which was a big mistake because at that point we were all starving. The conversation eventually switched to all the terrible things our exes had pulled over the years. Elle only had one ex and they'd parted amicably. Compared to

Felicity's and mine, he didn't seem terrible at all. My cheating former fiancé, Michael, won the blue ribbon, especially after I told them about the time I found him in a compromising position with his ex-wife, who was now his current wife once again. I'd been invited to their big Hamptons wedding but hadn't attended. It wasn't because of Michael's and my past, we seemed to have come to terms with that. It had to do with Byron Hughes, who I'd recently dated. I knew he'd be attending with my replacement and everyone's favorite award-winning actress, Nicole Wolfstrum. Byron and I were still friends, but two exes at one wedding was a little much. Plus, Cole hadn't been able to attend, per usual, because he was delivering one of his yachts to the other side of the world. For Michael's and Paige's wedding present, I'd regifted them an ice cream maker, still in the box from Michael's and my engagement party. I hadn't felt the least bit guilty giving it to them, seeing the Whitney family was one of the richest in the Hamptons. I was sure they owned everything money could buy, but I doubted they had an ice cream maker.

While held captive inside the elevator, I kept reassuring Elle we would be saved, though as the hours ticked by, I began to doubt my own words. The longer the night stretched on, the colder the cab got. Thanks to Felicity we all had our coats. There were no emergency call buttons because the elevator was too old for such a modern convenience. The only noises we heard were Elle's occasional sobs.

At one point, Felicity had said, "Did you hear that? It sounds like the scream or howl of a wounded animal."

I had heard it and I could tell by the panic in Elle's eyes when I'd shone my light on her face that she'd also heard it. "Probably the wind whistling up the elevator shaft," I'd said, more as a comfort for myself than them. My teeth were chattering. Not from the cold—my down jacket kept me warm enough. The scream or guttural howl I'd just heard wasn't from a draft. It was the shriek of a human in pain. Finally, somewhere around three in the morning we called it a night. I curled up on the floor in a fetal position, trying to reassure myself that even if Jeremy and Langston had left for their ferry, Dr. Blake, Sabrina, Willa, and possibly Dr. Blake's partner, Dr. Lewis, would come to our rescue. Sleep hadn't come easily. Shortly after my phone battery died, so did the batteries in my hearing aids. I'd reveled in the silence and finally fell asleep, my head resting on Elle's left thigh.

Sometime later, Elle kicked out her leg, waking me as the overhead light flickered on and the elevator started moving. Wiping the drool off my chin, I shot up. Felicity checked her Fitbit for the time. It was noon. We'd been trapped in the elevator for nearly twenty hours.

The three of us held hands as the cab slowly descended. We watched the dial on the floor indicator, holding our breaths, praying it would stop when it hit one.

We were disappointed.

The elevator continued past the first floor. We huddled closer. The cab stopped. The doors opened.

In front of us was Dr. Blake Nightingale, strapped to the same hospital bed I'd seen on Monday when I'd snuck down to the basement.

His pale blue button-down shirt was soaked in crimson. An ice pick was sticking out of his chest.

We screamed.

But not loud enough to wake up the dead.

Chapter 11

Since I was the only one with hands-on experience with dead bodies, I was chosen to confirm that Dr. Blake Nightingale was indeed dead. Wisely knowing not to contaminate a crime scene, the only thing I touched was the side of his cold, blue neck to verify there wasn't a pulse. Next to the bed was a rusty metal cart with drawers. The middle drawer was open; inside was an assortment of surgical tools, something that might be found in Dr. Frankenstein's workshop. And, no doubt, where the ice pick had come from.

The temperature in the basement had to be in the upper twenties, and we realized why. On the opposite side of the room were cement steps. At the top of the steps was an open door. Light filled the doorway with such dazzling brightness that I had to turn away. When I turned back I saw what was going on. Outside, the sun reflected on layers of snow that had spilled onto a cement landing. Someone had either come in from outside or left through the door. Judging by the accumulation of snow, it must have been hours ago that the door had been opened. Was this the exit Blake Nightingale's killer had taken? Or had the culprit opened the door as a red herring to throw off the CSIs? We didn't have time to contemplate the scenario in case someone still hid inside, lurking behind a rusty electroshock machine or hiding in the bizarre bathtub contraption.

"Let's get the heck out of here," Felicity shouted. We ran toward the open door leading outside but realized there was no way to get through the deep snow. With their short statures, Elle and Felicity would no doubt suffocate in a high drift.

"This way," I shouted, pointing to the door I'd peeked through on Monday. I held open the door and they galloped through. I took up the rear. Five steps from the bottom of the stairs, something caught my eye. A pen. I told Felicity and Elle to hold up. They ignored me and ran up the flight of stairs like they were being chased by an apparition. Whose ghost, I wasn't sure. *Eeny, meeny, miny, moe*, pick one, Dr. Blake Nightingale's or actress Arden Hunter's? I couldn't blame the others for not waiting. I crept back down until I reached the step with the pen. I didn't touch it in case it had prints on it and I didn't have a camera to take a photo. The pen had advertising on it: *Nightingale and Lewis Dermatology*, then in small print, *Free Consultations*, with an address and phone number. The most disturbing thing about it was the area near the point, where I saw brownish red spots. Blood? Proud of myself, I left it alone for the powers that be and went scurrying after Elle and Felicity.

Minutes later, we found Langston Reed, Sabrina Nightingale, and a man who I assumed was Dr. Lewis crowded around a crackling fire in the drawing room, joking as if they hadn't a care in the world. There was a look of shock on their merry faces as we charged in. They froze in place like a flash mob getting ready to break into a choreographed dance. It seemed obvious they'd thought we'd left the estate the day before. Glancing out the windows facing the front of the mansion, I realized why. They were covered with thick sheets of ice, blurring the view outdoors. Even from an upstairs window, I knew Felicity's car and Elle's pickup would be buried under mountains of snow — erased from the landscape.

Willa stood near the man who I assumed was Dr. Lewis, a teapot in hand. If someone hadn't just been murdered, I could picture Tiny Tim walking in without his crutch, grasping Scrooge's hand, Christmas pudding smeared all over his chin.

"Oh, my Lordy!" Willa exclaimed. "What a scare you've given me. I thought you were long gone on the ferry yesterday! Your coats were missing from the closet." She backed up until she felt a chair. Then she sank into it, fanning her flushed face with her hand.

Glancing at Dr. Lewis, I saw concern on his face for Willa. He stood and went to her side. "Are you okay, Willa?" He spoke in a soft tone with lots of bedside manner. The doctor was the antithesis of his former partner in looks and it seemed demeanor. Where Dr. Blake had been tall and well dressed, sporting a ten-thousand-dollar Rolex, Dr. Greg Lewis was short. He wore baggy khakis and an oversized dress shirt. I wondered if he recently lost a lot of weight or bought his clothes from Goodwill. I wasn't knocking shopping at Goodwill, especially after I'd once found an oil painting by a listed artist that worked perfectly in one of my client's cottages. Due to his lined face, shaggy white hair and bushy eyebrows, I'd guessed Dr. Lewis's age to be somewhere in the upper sixties. If Albert Einstein was still alive, I would have bet he and Dr. Lewis would have shared the same barber — or a pair of dull scissors. There was one feature on his face that stood out from all the others: his large beaklike nose, which looked sharp enough to open a can of soup. I gave him kudos for not getting a nose job, especially since he'd been the partner of a celebrity cosmetic surgeon and could've gotten it for free. I also understood Dr. Lewis's looks must have been the reason he had such a small part on *Bungled*. Dr. Blake might have been a jerk in person, but he definitely had charisma onscreen.

"Dr. Blake is dead!" Felicity burst out.

"Dead? What do you mean dead!" Sabrina shouted.

Elle moved to Sabrina's side and took her bejeweled hand in hers. "I'm afraid he's been murdered." Tears trailed down Elle's face.

Sabrina didn't shed one. Instead, she stood, almost knocking petite Elle over, and spat, "Who would dar-r-r-e kill my Blake!" She looked at each one of us full in the face, moving her head from left to right. Analyzing us like she was a human lie detector looking for a tell.

Wouldn't the natural reaction be, *How? Where?* Even, *Are you sure?*

In her defense, I'd learned there was no natural way to handle death. I'd been known to laugh at funerals and cry at weddings. When Sabrina's gaze met mine, I said, "Don't look at us. Felicity, Elle, and I were trapped in that old elevator for the past twenty hours."

Sabrina's mouth opened, then she sat back on the sofa, defeated, realizing what everyone else was thinking.

Someone in the room might be a cold-blooded killer.

Chapter 12

It was funny how even after a night spent in the dark elevator of a former insane asylum, and then discovering a body killed the same way Arden Hunter was murdered almost seventy years ago, we still had an appetite.

Willa removed the most amazing version of shepherd's pie from the oven. It was the best I'd ever tasted or smelled. She backed it up with a croque-en-bouche that rivaled the one my father made each Christmas. The name, when translated from French to English, was *crunch in mouth*. The pyramid of choux pastry balls held together with threads of spun caramel disappeared twenty seconds after she'd placed it on the kitchen table.

The cozy kitchen vibe was the polar opposite of the scene in the basement below us. We all needed showers and sleep but agreed we wouldn't sleep for a second in Nightingale Manor. Someone who *hadn't* been trapped in the elevator had murdered Dr. Blake Nightingale. I wondered how long he'd been dead and realized it would be hard for a coroner to tell because the temperature in the basement had been like a meat locker's—or a medical examiner's cadaver drawer.

I studied Willa, knowing I had to add her to our suspect list. Even if one of the others alibied her, they'd both be suspects. And if everyone said they were together during the window of death then this might turn into a Dame Agatha Christie murder mystery. Or a Sherlockian conundrum, the snowstorm turning Nightingale Manor into the locked-room scenario—a dead body with all the windows and doors bolted from inside. But there had been an open door leading outside . . .

Glancing at Willa scurrying around the kitchen, anticipating our every need, it was hard to picture her dragging Dr. Blake to the basement, strapping him to the hospital bed, then stabbing him with an ice pick. I'd done a cursory scan of his body and saw no other trauma, but I hadn't turned him over. Obviously, whomever killed him wouldn't have been able to use the elevator because we'd been inside. It was plausible he could have walked down to the basement on his own for some kind of assignation. But with whom? The billion-dollar question.

I thought back to yesterday and Willa's argument with Dr. Blake's wife, along with knowing Felicity had to convince Willa to stay for the filming of *Mr. & Mrs. Winslow*. You would think my lack of sleep and the trauma of our discovery would stop me from grilling, or should I say lightly sautéing, the kind-faced housekeeper. "Willa," I asked as nonchalantly as possible, "where was everyone when the power went out?"

Elle threw me one of her looks. Maybe she hadn't grasped the situation—or maybe she had and didn't want me to tick off whoever killed the doctor.

At first, Willa acted as if she hadn't heard me. She went near the fire and picked up a snoozing Tabitha and cuddled her in her arms. Then she whispered something into the cat's twitching ear, brought her to the table and sat down. It seemed all the composure and sunny disposition we'd been witnessing in the past hour had been a shield, because she broke into hiccup-like sobs, tears flowing as if from a geyser.

Felicity jumped up and handed Willa a box of tissues. Elle gave me another look, similar to the last one, only this time, knowing I could read lips, she mouthed—*Now look what you've done!*

After a few minutes, Willa stopped crying. She stroked Tabitha's back in short frenetic strokes. I was worried the fluffy thing might need some Rogaine to replace the flying fur.

"I apologize," Willa said, still sniffling. "It's just . . ." She looked at each of us. "Well, you know."

We shook our heads in the affirmative.

Continuing, she said, "When the power went out I was at the bottom of the main staircase, cleaning the foyer floor from Hector's snowy boot prints. I waited a few minutes for the generator to start. But it never did. Blake called to me from the drawing room to get candles and flashlights ready. As if I wouldn't think about it."

Which meant Dr. Blake had been killed in the hours following the power outage, when we were in the elevator. That left a lot of time for one of the others to have killed him. Then I remembered the wounded animal howl we'd all heard. Was that when he'd been stabbed with the ice pick?

Willa stopped for a minute and looked down at the tabby, then continued, "After the power went out, I hurried to the butler's pantry to get everything together."

"Was anyone else in the drawing room with Dr. Blake when it went out?" I asked gently. "And who's Hector?"

"Yes, Dr. Lewis and Sabrina were there. I don't know where Mr. Reed was. Hector is a sometime handyman who works over at Sylvester Manor as their gardener/yardman. A couple hours earlier, he'd come to the door saying he'd plowed the front circle and wanted to see Blake to give him his bill. It was past due."

"Did he see Dr. Blake?" I asked.

"No. I didn't want to bother him, especially after what happened earlier when I became Blake's scapegoat. So, I took the bill from Hector and said I would give it to Blake when I saw him."

She didn't elaborate on the "what happened earlier" and must not have known we'd overheard her arguing with Sabrina about the practice's unpaid malpractice insurance.

"How about Jeremy," Felicity asked. "Was he here when the power went out?"

She continued, "No. When I went to retrieve Mr. Prentice's coat from the closet and saw your coats were missing, I assumed you'd all left for the ferry. That's why we were all in shock when you walked into the room a little while ago. Before leaving, Mr. Prentice seemed visibly upset about something and had me confirm that I'd remain at Nightingale Manor for the duration of the filming. He even asked if he brought a contract to that effect, would I sign it. I told him I would. When I opened the door and saw all the snow and ice, I tried to talk him into staying, but he refused, saying his Range Rover could make it through anything."

Elle was listening, wide-eyed. "Oh, I hope he did."

"So," I asked, "how long after he left did the power go out?"

"I would guess about ten minutes. I remember saying a prayer he would make it safely to the North Ferry. After the outage, I was pretty busy getting everything ready. I apologize for not knowing you were still here."

"I'd brought the coats up to the attic," Felicity said, "in case the space heaters didn't do their job."

"That explains it," Willa said, sitting a little straighter, obviously feeling better than a few seconds before. "It must have been terrible being locked inside. The generator was still out when I got the rooms ready for Greg and Mr. Reed on the second floor. We stayed in the living room in front of the fire until it was time for bed. We were all there, including Blake, even though Sabrina kept on him to go check why the generator wasn't working."

"Let me guess," I interjected, "the generator's in the basement?"

"Yes. But Blake didn't go. He's not the handiest when it comes to things like that. Dr. Lewis went, but he couldn't get it going, either."

Well, somehow Dr. Blake ended up in the basement.

We heard Sabrina's heels clicking and clacking down the hallway. She entered the kitchen wearing a full face of makeup, dressed in silky loungewear more suitable for beachside on the Riviera than a freezing-cold mansion. "Langston, I mean Mr. Reed, wants to know if anyone got through to the authorities on their cell phones. The wifi is naturally out but we can't understand why we can't get a satellite signal. It's imperative that we let the outside world know we're okay. I mean . . . mostly okay." She turned her pert nose in Willa's direction. "Now that the power is on I think it would be prudent of you to whip up as many cooked meals as possible in case we lose it again. There is no way that generator should have gone out. When Blake brought the occasional patient here to recover from surgery we had to have the generator up to code."

"Maybe Blake didn't pay the gas bill," Willa mumbled under her breath. If Sabrina heard her, she ignored it.

Sabrina snapped her fingers, inches from Willa's face. "We need nourishment brought into the drawing room. Pronto! Felicity, maybe one of your girls could bring us some coffee and something sweet. It's so important to keep Langston happy after the tragic circumstances of my loving husband's death."

Everyone heard Willa's "Hmph!" after Sabrina said the word *loving*. Willa handed Elle a carafe of coffee, saying everyone already had cups. Then Willa turned to Sabrina, her pale skin in sharp contrast to the bright pink of her cheeks. "Don't you want to go down and see him, Sabrina? You act like his death is of no consequence and that you're oblivious to knowing one of our little party might be guilty of murder."

Sabrina didn't let us see her sweat. "I don't believe he was murdered. I'm sure there will be a rational reason for his untimely death at such a young age. Plus" — she pointed at me — "you said that door leading outside was wide open. An intruder or vagrant might have come looking for shelter from the storm, Blake caught him and he was killed." She swiped at her cheek theatrically. Her makeup stayed intact because there hadn't been any moisture to dampen it.

Perhaps Sabrina was as good of an actress as Zoe Stockton. She of all people must know the history of Arden Hunter's murder and how she'd been murdered with an ice pick. I observed her gestures, looking for a clue as to how she could remain so cold to the death of her husband. Maybe it'd been a relief. Or maybe she'd had a hand in it.

"What about these two?" She nodded her head at Elle and me. "What do we really know about them? I plan to hire a private investigator to find out what happened to Blake. In the meantime, do your job. Looks like no more favors from Blake for you, Willa Sullivan. You're on your own. That ship has sailed. And I'm sure you're wondering if we had a prenup. Well, we didn't. Boo hoo."

"Sabrina, I guess you don't know," Willa said. I could tell she was angry by the way she was arranging cinnamon rolls that were still warm from the oven. Half had come unrolled and resembled snails looking to escape the plate. "I've been hired by Prentice Productions to be housemother for the actors and crew during filming. I'm no longer under Blake's control. And Lord knows, I was never under yours. And never will be."

Sabrina must've been caught off guard because she didn't have a good retort. She grabbed ahold of Elle's elbow and steered her out of the kitchen. Elle looked back at me and mouthed, *Go get my phone from the attic.*

Chapter 13

I exited the kitchen, passing the cursed elevator, and went in search of the servants' staircase that would lead me to the attic. Although I'd made jokes yesterday about Elle being a sissy and squeamish about anything related to the old murder, this new murder had me looking over my shoulder as I climbed the dimly lit staircase. No more elevators for me. I'd take the stairs for the next twenty years.

I'd found an extra hearing-aid battery in the bottom of my handbag, so I only had hearing in one ear. Enough to hear the howling of wind and icy sleet hitting the window at the end of the third-floor hallway. Rubbing a spy hole with my coat sleeve, I pressed my nose against the frosted pane of glass. The sun had disappeared from when we'd been in the basement, and the entire landscape was covered in mountain ranges of white. In the distance, I saw that a light was on in an upstairs room of the gatehouse. As far as I knew, the gatehouse was unoccupied until it came time for Dr. Blake and Sabrina Nightingale to move in while *Mr. & Mrs. Winslow* was filming. Felicity had even told us that Sabrina wanted her entire bedroom suite and the contents of her huge walk-in closet transferred there when the time came.

So why was there a light on? I didn't see any footprints in the layers of white. A moot point, since if someone had gone there during the storm, their tracks would have been covered with layers of snow by now. Maybe Jeremy Prentice hadn't made it off the estate and had taken refuge?

Again, I reviewed the entire cast of murder suspects: Willa, housekeeper and nurse; Sabrina, wife; Langston, director of the miniseries; Jeremy, producer of the miniseries; and finally, Dr. Greg Lewis, Dr. Blake's partner.

I jumped back from the window. Something moved behind the snow-laden pine trees in the thicket where the rag doll had been found.

There it was again. Something beige and alive.

A human?

What I saw wasn't the boogeyman or Blake Nightingale's ghost. It was a wide-eyed doe whose neck and head were the only things visible behind a bank of drifting snow. She glanced up at me, then, as if spooked, turned tail and leapt deeper into the woods. I couldn't blame her for her instinct to run away from Nightingale Manor.

When I stepped into the attic and flipped the switch for the lights, all our previous work was illuminated. I'd forgotten how far we'd gotten after just a few hours of toil. Elle's cell was on a window ledge. It was dead. I pocketed it and then felt the skeleton's eye sockets aimed my way. The Santa hat that he'd been wearing yesterday was lying on the floor. Next to him, the door to the closet under the eaves was slightly open. I remembered latching it yesterday. Someone had been up here after we'd left, and it hadn't been Felicity, Elle, or me.

I went to investigate. The wide floorboards creaked as I slowly made my way to the shadowy corner. Getting down on my knees, I switched on my phone's flashlight and peered inside. Almost all of the suitcases were lying flat on the floorboards, not upright as I'd seen them yesterday. Most were open, exposing their private contents. I crawled inside and moved to the highest point, then stood and pulled a string hanging from the chain of a fixture with an exposed bulb. The space filled with soft light.

Even though the closet glowed brighter, the sadness and loneliness emanating from the suitcases filled the cramped space. I saw silver women's vanity sets tarnished by years of oxidation. There where old Broadway playbills and other ephemera. A few suitcases had old bisque-faced dolls and stuffed teddy bears nestled inside flannel receiving blankets; others held men's toiletries, straight-edge razors, Brylcreem hair dressing and shaving brushes. But the saddest of all were the family photos, mostly old cabinet cards in black and white or sepia. They were like eyes looking out after being shut away for so many decades. The suitcases must have belonged to former sanitorium residents who either left Nightingale Manor without their belongings — or as my melancholy mind guessed . . . never left at all. I remembered the old cemetery that I'd seen behind the estate's gates. For some unknown reason, I got down on my knees and methodically closed all of the suitcases, not wanting to invade their owners' privacy. All except one. The reason I didn't close it was because it was empty. Had someone taken the contents? I pulled it closer, searching for any clue to its owner. Then I found it.

The old luggage tag at first glance didn't display a name, initials or a series of numbers like I'd seen on the suitcases yesterday. I slid the oak tag paper from its sleeve and aimed my light on it. It was blank, but when I flipped it over, I saw *A. Hunter* written in script. Arden Hunter.

Arden Hunter never left Nightingale Manor with her suitcase because she'd been murdered.

Who'd been inside the closet? And what were they looking for? Was the carnage related to Blake Nightingale's murder? And what happened to the contents of Arden Hunter's suitcase?

These were all questions I was determined to find answers to. But first I wanted to get out of Nightingale Manor and back to my cozy Montauk domicile and my cranky fat cat. I needed to analyze things from a distance. A far distance.

I pocketed the tag from the suitcase, and before closing it I felt along the satin liner to see if I'd missed anything, but the interior was clean. I closed it, then stood it upright. Underneath, stuck in the space between two wide floorboards, was an envelope. Only a small portion was visible. I tried to pull it out but couldn't get enough of a grip. My nails were clipped short because of all the woodworking, painting, and staining I did on my projects for my Cottages by the Sea clients. I tried once more unsuccessfully, then tried again. "Ouch!" Instead of the envelope, I came up with a huge splinter that protruded from my pointer finger. Blood gushed as I pulled to remove it. But only the tip broke off, leaving a good portion wedged under my fingernail. I was no stranger to pain, but this was up there in my top ten.

Now it was a question of woman against envelope. I was determined to get the darned thing out. I opened a few suitcases, trailing blood as I went. Finally, I spied some rusty tweezers and used them to remove the envelope from between the floorboards. I'd had half a mind to use the tweezers on the remaining part of the splinter but knew I hadn't had a tetanus shot in the last decade. Stowing the envelope in my pocket, I pulled the string to the light and crawled out, backing straight into Santa Skeleton, causing a clattering of bone against bone. When I stood, the skulls on the bookcase next to me grinned at my theatrics. I felt like I'd just been on a trip to another dimension, one beyond the twilight zone.

I booked it out of the attic and flew down three flights of steps like I was being chased by the specters of Dr. Blake and Arden Hunter. When I reached the first floor I ran into, literally, Willa and Dr. Lewis. They'd been in a passionate embrace until I body-slammed them and they went catapulting backward onto the hall carpet.

All I could think of to say as I lifted my chin from Willa's back was, "Oops." There were a few uncomfortable minutes before Willa and I got up. We both pulled Dr. Lewis to his feet. He wouldn't hear of me apologizing for tackling him to the ground like I was a Giants linebacker.

Dr. Lewis was polite, and instead of getting upset that the blood from my finger with the splinter ruined his shirt, he spoke calmly, with a steady voice. His bedside manner instantly put me at ease. "Come," he said, "let's take care of that finger right away."

I followed him and Willa to the kitchen, where Willa fetched a first-aid kit and handed him a pair of tweezers. I noticed a slight tremor to his hand.

"Stress," he explained.

"Understandable. I seem to have gotten blood on your shirt."

He looked down at a spot near his pocket and shrugged it off. "No worries, my dear."

"I know how to get it out," Willa said. "Ms. Barrett just needs to spit on the stain and it will come right out."

"Say what?" I wasn't about to spit on someone.

"It's true. My mother taught me," Willa said. "Greg, hand me your hankie."

He did.

She held it up to my mouth and they both looked at me.

"Go ahead," Dr. Lewis prodded.

"I spit into the hankie, which was just as wrinkled as Dr. Lewis's shirt. The man needed a woman in his life or a good dry cleaner. Perhaps Willa planned on filling the first role.

Willa patted the moistened part of the hankie on the stain, explaining, "The enzymes in your saliva break up the stain, but it can't be someone else's saliva, only the person whose blood it is. Of course, hydrogen peroxide works just as well or immediately soaking it in cold water."

After all the talk of blood, there was an awkward pause. I told them that Elle was waiting for her phone and I'd better get going, then took off for the drawing room.

Instead of walking in, I lingered outside the open French doors, seeing if I could do some lip detecting. I shimmied behind a fake potted tree and peeked in. The person facing me was Langston. I made do with what I got and was able to decipher most of what he was saying, something to the effect of, "Why wouldn't the police let us go? *Mr. & Mrs. Winslow* has nothing to do with what happened to your husband, Mrs. Nightingale. Not to sound callous—at first, I'd thought he'd mouthed *jealous*—but you, the housekeeper, and his partner are the only ones with ties to the man. I've only met him a total of three times."

Elle came toward me from behind the staircase, coffeepot in hand. "What are you doing?" she whispered. "Where's my phone?"

"Shhh, no need to get in a tizzy, I have it right here." I handed it to her.

She took a charger out of her pocket and plugged it under a reflectory table. Once it came on she changed the greeting to say where we were. I was confident her fiancé detective would be knocking at Nightingale Manor's door any second. Especially now that I noticed through the window by the front door that the snow had stopped falling.

"Why were you hiding behind a tree?" Elle asked. "Let's get inside. Don't you think it's important we keep track of everyone? One of these people could be the lunatic that killed Dr. Blake."

We walked in and found Sabrina standing near the floor-to-ceiling windows, waiting for rescue. Willa, Felicity and Dr. Lewis entered and took seats flanking the hearth. For a moment we were all silent.

The realization Sabrina's husband had been murdered must have finally sunk in because Sabrina asked, more like demanded, we remain together, even for bathroom visits. If Sabrina hadn't suggested that we stay together until the police arrived, then Elle or I would have, especially after my visiting the attic and finding the murdered actress Arden Hunter's empty suitcase, along with the knowledge that Willa and Dr. Lewis were romantically involved.

Minutes ticked by like hours. Finally, Dr. Lewis took things in hand, insisting we follow him to the basement to view his partner's body. All for one, one for all.

We trudged out of the drawing room and into the hallway, following behind Dr. Lewis like we were in a funeral procession, a dirge echoing in my head. When we reached the basement stairway, Dr. Lewis held the door open. Sabrina, who was second in line, said, "Please, you go first, Greg, I might faint at the sight." As we went down the stairs, I was the only one who noticed the blood-spattered pen on the fifth from the bottom step. Using what I hoped was a slight-of-hand move, I took a clean tissue from my pocket, swiped up the pen, and stuck it up the sleeve of my jacket. I reasoned it was better that I took it instead of Dr. Blake's killer.

When we reached the body, we all watched Dr. Lewis turn Blake Nightingale's body on its side to see if there were any other wounds besides the ice pick protruding from his chest. As we'd stood around the hospital bed, Agatha Christie's *And Then There Were None* came to mind. Perhaps if the characters in the book had stuck together things would have turned out differently. Just to be safe, as we were leaving the basement, I quickly snapped a dozen photos on my phone to share with Doc, my surrogate uncle and former Detroit PD coroner.

That's if I ever got out of the house alive.

• • •

Back in the drawing room, after taking a long swig of brandy, Sabrina said, "I think it would be prudent of you, Dr. Lewis, to share your findings on the cause of my husband's death." We were huddled around the fire. All eyes were fixed on Sabrina's face.

No one answered Sabrina's stupid question. She said, visibly upset, "Well, I hope everyone noticed the door and cement steps leading outside. Someone could have come in and killed him, then left out that door. It doesn't necessarily mean my Blake was killed by one of us. How about that ugly woman and her phony lawsuit? I bet we'd find she might have snuck in and killed my Blakie." She then turned and sent Felicity, Elle and me a formidable accusatory look. "And even though the three of you *claim* to have been stranded in the elevator, how do we know you aren't in it together?"

I blurted out, "What would our motive be? I've only met Mr., I mean Dr. Blake, twice, Elle just met him yesterday, and Felicity, well, why would she want to kill him knowing her job as set designer depends on filming at Nightingale Manor?" I looked around at the faces of our killing pool and didn't see any blinking neon signs pointing to whodunnit. And, for the life of me I couldn't see how a murder that happened over sixty years ago had anything to do with Blake Nightingale's murder. However, there had been an obvious connection because Blake had been killed the same way Marian Fortune had killed Arden Hunter.

I couldn't wait to leave the estate and dig into the murder and any connections there might be from a distance. The key words being *from a distance*. The elephant in the room was not only who knew about the old murder, but what the killer's message was in using the ice pick.

Dr. Lewis cleared his throat. "It seems obvious he was killed with an ice pick, however, until the medical examiner does a full tox screen and removes his clothing, we won't know if he'd been drugged first or has other injuries."

"It wouldn't take much to strap him down," Langston Reed said. "Earlier, he'd finished a whole magnum of Dom Perignon that Jeremy and I had planned to serve to everyone to kick off the production of *Mr. & Mrs. Winslow*." He glanced around and caught Felicity's eye. They exchanged a look that only I'd noticed. It seemed improbable newlywed Felicity and Langston, one of her bosses, were having a fling. Then again, I still had a hard time picturing Dr. Lewis and Willa together because of their age difference. I checked Dr. Lewis's left hand for a wedding ring. Nothing. Up until now, Langston had remained silent, following Sabrina's directives and looking a little green around the gills when we'd traipsed down to the basement as if we were on a school field trip.

After five minutes of silence, I broke the ice. "How many of you know about the murder at Nightingale Manor?"

"What kind of idiotic question is that? We all do," Sabrina said, standing up.

"Not your husband's murder. Arden Hunter's?"

She sat back down and gave me a piercing look. "That has no bearing on today."

"I think the ice pick gives it bearing," Felicity said. "Meg told me about it when we were trapped in the elevator. Langston, did you know that Nightingale Manor was a former sanitorium and an old-time movie actress was murdered here in the basement? The same way Dr. Blake was?"

Langston shifted uncomfortably in his high-back wing chair. "I had no idea. I would have never chosen Nightingale Manor as a location if I'd known."

Liar, I thought. He gripped the arms of his chair like he was on a roller coaster waiting for the big plunge.

Dr. Lewis spoke up. "Blake had shared with me about the murder, and we agreed it wouldn't do our practice any good to talk about it. Not that plastic surgery and psychiatry are related."

Sabrina pointed a finger at me. "I don't see your point, um . . ."

"Meg."

"Meg. Anyone could look up that old story. I still say that woman that forced the cancellation of Blake's show is to blame for his death. Her and her ambulance-chasing lawyer, Margulies."

"Justin Margulies?" I knew him, and he wasn't an ambulance chaser, more like a competent attorney well known in the Hamptons.

"I suppose that's his name. Wait!" Sabrina shouted and ran to the snow-covered window. "I hear something! It's gotta be a snowplow. Thank God." Everyone stood. "Oh, no, you don't," she said, gritting her teeth. "Everyone stays put until the police arrive."

Elle ignored her and ran into the hallway. She grabbed the door handle and opened the front door. We watched as an avalanche of snow buried her. She sputtered and flailed before I could reach her.

The snow parted like the Red Sea. A short man, pushing a snowblower and wearing a head-to-toe snowmobile suit, complete with helmet, came into view. He switched off the engine and hurried to Elle's side. He picked her up and cradled her in his arms like in the famous last scene of the movie *An Officer and a Gentleman*, and carried her to the sofa in the drawing room. I didn't have to wait until he removed the helmet to know who it was.

Relief set in.

Detective Arthur Shoner from the East Hampton Town PD was in the building and I couldn't have been happier than if he was my very own fiancé, not Elle's.

Chapter 14

After the pickup was unearthed from a gigantic snowdrift, we left for the ferry. As soon as I got in my car, I called Claire to make sure Jo was okay and fed. I had no idea if the rest of the people/ suspects had to stay at the estate or were free to leave. And frankly, it wasn't any of my business — unless I made it my business. Which knowing me, I probably would.

When I reached home, the first thing I did was run down the steps to the ocean. Well, maybe not run because the snow on the steps was so deep that halfway down my rear end became a toboggan and I landed face-first in the sand. It always amazed me that no matter how much snow accumulated offshore, the beach only got a dusting.

It was a homecoming nonetheless.

Once upright, I took deep inhales of the cold, salt-scented air and glanced toward the horizon. Thoughts of Nightingale Manor crept in with each incoming wave. I tried to push them out with each outgoing wave. I had nothing to do with Dr. Blake Nightingale's death. Knowing Detective Shoner wasn't allowed access to the case because he was on the East Hampton Town PD, I'd decided to let the Southampton and Suffolk County authorities take the case and run with it. In the meantime, I planned on staying put in Montauk. My touchstone.

Elle, Felicity and I were scheduled to go to the Southampton Police outpost in the morning to give our statements. When the ambulance and three police cars had arrived earlier, everyone had been taken to a small study off the drawing room and interviewed by a team of four shivering Southampton PD inquisitors. How many times I wanted to tell them what I knew about the old murder. But I kept my mouth shut. All I had was an armless doll, old train tickets and a name on a luggage tag. No doubt they'd figure it out themselves. Plus, Blake Nightingale wasn't even born when Arden Hunter was murdered. If she'd been twentysomething when she was murdered, and Marian Fortune had been a similar age, that would make Marian somewhere in her nineties now. *If* she was still living. I couldn't picture her in her walker dragging Dr. Blake to the basement and strapping him to a hospital bed. One thing for sure, whoever did the nasty deed knew about the murder and that Nightingale Manor was at one time a private sanitorium. It shouldn't take the police that long to make a connection with so few suspects: Willa, Langston, Sabrina, Dr. Lewis and Jeremy Prentice. I'd included the show's producer until we had definite proof that he'd left Shelter Island and was nowhere near Dr. Blake at the time of death. What would be Mr. Prentice's motive? I was betting it was either Dr. Blake's wife or his business partner. A sharp gust of wind paddled me from behind, making me realize that I was postulating again.

The waves were getting closer, and I was getting colder, but I couldn't pull myself away from the shoreline. A lone gull divebombed my head, no doubt scavenging for something that wasn't frozen solid to sink his beak into. Many a day and night I turned to the sea for answers and I always got them—*Go slow, take it easy, steady as the tide. Live for today's sunrise, not in fear of the next storm.*

Wrapping my scarf around my face, I took off toward the lighthouse. When I reached a secluded section of the beach I found a large boulder to sit on. In twenty or so minutes the rock would be swallowed by the sea and me with it. The sun came out for a moment, then hid behind a cloud. The brief kiss of golden light gave me hope of a brighter future, not a continuation of the last twenty-four hours. A future that included furnishing my cottage with things from Little Grey's attic, bonfires on the beach at twilight, hot cocoa with a dash of cayenne pepper on my deck and knitting. Yes, I, Meg Barrett, was finally getting the hang of knitting. Thanks to Claire, who'd talked me into taking lessons at Karen's Kreative Knitting. I'd just completed the project I'd gotten as a gift for my birthday, a fluffy throw whose rows widened and shrunk in odd places but still looked good folded and draped over a chair, away from Jo's errant claws.

The wind was picking up, raw and unrelenting. I fumbled in my pocket for my gloves and only came up with one. I felt something else in my pocket and realized what it was. The pen I'd found on the basement steps still wrapped in a tissue. I'd forgotten to turn it in. Understandable with everything going on. I put my right glove on then searched my left pocket for the other. Not there. But the envelope I'd found wedged between the floorboards was. I'd not only forgotten about the pen but also about the envelope from the attic. I sat as long as I could before feeling the fingers on my left hand getting numb. I couldn't wait to see Jo, knowing she would probably ignore me because I'd missed a few of her feeding times. I was sure she could go a month or two living off the fat stored in her huge belly. I stood, glanced once again toward the healing sea, then trudged west. Toward my beach. Toward Home.

As I walked, I thanked my lucky stars that the police had let Elle, Felicity, and me leave Nightingale Manor. Detective Shoner had vouched for us all. At first, he'd only planned on letting Elle and me leave, but after tons of begging from his fiancée, he'd included Felicity, provided she stayed local. Elle had insisted Felicity bunk at her house in Sag Harbor.

It was almost high tide, the waves encroaching closer to the twenty-foot cliffs. Halfway home I found a perfect piece of driftwood for writing in the sand. I grabbed it and continued on, the waves licking at my boots. In front of my cottage, I placed my hand on my hips and looked down. A blank slate. Now that Patrick Seaton's and my new cottage were almost a mile apart, there'd been no more playing pen pals in the sand, trading lines from classical eighteenth- and nineteenth-century poetry. Even if no one else would read it, I needed to think of a verse that would anchor me after the tragedy at Nightingale Manor. I figured it was a cathartic way of journaling my feelings, then letting them go — washed away by the next big wave. I chose something by Keats, my favorite go-to poet:

Do you not see how necessary a world of pains and troubles is to school an intelligence and make it a soul?

I felt a large paw on my back and heard a male voice say something I couldn't make out. *Cole and Tripod?* Earlier, I'd removed my hearing aids because they were no match for the buffeting wind. Turning slowly, ready to jump into Cole's arms, I found Patrick Seaton and his greyhound Charley. In her mouth was my missing glove.

Before I could thank her, Patrick looked behind me at what I'd written in the sand and said, "Did you know Keats only wrote fifty-four poems in his short lifetime?"

"Actually, I did," I said, adding a nervous schoolgirl giggle.

Charley dropped the glove on the wet sand and left in search of more treasure. For a minute there was an awkward silence, then I figured out why: with my hat and scarf almost completely covering my face, he hadn't recognized me from the time we'd met on this same beach last September or later at Old Man and the Sea Books. I unwound the scarf and said, "Patrick, right?" Then stuck out my ungloved hand.

He took it and said, "Your fingers are blue, Meg. Looks like Charley found your glove just in time." The corners of his mouth turned up in a grin that transformed his face into someone unrecognizable. Many times in the past I'd watched his dark shape from the deck of my rental cottage as he traversed the shoreline in one of his melancholy sojourns. His body always hunched, head held down, the only facial feature visible under his hoodie—a frown.

I'd felt a connection when we'd first met, and I felt one now. "More of a puce, I think." Just that he remembered my name had my heart doing jumping jacks. Something I needed to analyze later. Today, his changeable eyes were a dark green, like the ocean behind him. His tousled, sandy-blond hair was highlighted with sun streaks of gold, his strong jaw was covered in a couple days' beard, and his ears were almost the color of my left hand.

"You're correct," he said, "your fingers are more of a purple brown. However, if you stay any longer in this subzero weather, they might turn white and you'd be in danger of losing a few."

Only a writer would know what color puce was, making me think of the bad movie I'd just played as an extra in—*Nightmare at Nightingale Manor*. Knowing he was *Mr. & Mrs. Winslow's* screenwriter, I didn't see the point in filling him in on the murder until we learned more. Maybe it wouldn't affect him at all. I couldn't see the production continuing on Shelter Island after what had happened, plus I wasn't a fan of dumping torrential rain on anyone's parade. Especially the man who'd held my curiosity ever since I'd first found writing in the sand in front of his cottage. The press would be all over it soon enough.

"Are you left-handed?" he asked.

I laughed. "Yes." I bent to pick up the glove, then stowed it in my jacket pocket. I pulled out the envelope I'd found in Nightingale's attic, not wanting whatever it was to touch the sandy drooled-upon glove.

"Was that something you found inside a bottle, washed ashore? It looks old," Patrick said, glancing at the envelope.

Unfolding it, I saw a name written in flowery script, *Arden*. I stuffed it in my opposite pocket. In the attic, I'd only glanced at it quickly, not noticing the faded writing under the closet's dim light. "No," I answered. "But I like your thinking. The beach holds many treasures, doesn't it?" I pointed to where Charley, dressed in a rainbow-striped knitted sweater, came bounding toward us with a dead crab dangling from her mouth. She laid it at Patrick's feet.

He patted her dark gray head and reached for the stick I'd used to write my quote, then threw it to her. "She does have a penchant for finding treasures that are extremely odorous," he said, then put two fingers in his mouth and whistled, shouting for her not to travel too far away.

Charley looked back at him and moved closer to us.

"What a well-behaved pup. I know when we met on Labor Day weekend you said you rescued Charley from a greyhound racetrack that was forced to shut down. She sure looks happy enough now."

"She's thriving."

There was a small gap in the conversation while I once again mulled over letting him know about the murder. Instead I said, "I've been out of the loop. Any more surprise nor'easters or blizzards heading our way?"

Before he could answer, a figure appeared at the top of Little Grey's steps. Claire glanced down at us and waved. Then she shouted something, but it got lost on the wind. She started down the snowy steps, grabbing the handrail like a lifeline. We really needed to go shopping; she was dressed once again in a thin raincoat. When she reached the sand, Charley galloped toward her. Claire reached in her pocket and gave the dog a treat. It seemed they were old friends.

Out of breath, she joined us. She gave me a huge hug. "I'm so happy you got rescued. I've never seen so much snow. But, then again, I lived in California."

When I'd called her, I hadn't told her about the murder, just that we'd been snowed in at Nightingale Manor and to please feed Josephine.

Claire turned to Patrick. "I didn't know the two of you were acquainted."

I laughed. "This is only our third face-to-face."

"But we've known each other for over a year in a deeper and more visual way. Your sand-script is quite distinctive." He pointed at the Keats verse I'd left and winked.

I felt my face heat. It was as if he knew about my hearing loss and the importance of words in my life. It seemed the cat was out of the bag that I was the one responding to his verses with my own.

Claire made things awkward when she said, "Oh-h-h, Patrick, your poetry in the sand . . ."

I gave her a dirty look and cut her off. "Claire, how do you and Patrick know each other?"

"Patrick and I are part of a small poetry book club that meets once a month for dinner and wine tasting. We alternate homes. Patrick can make a mean beef bourguignonne," Claire said, raising an eyebrow. "Meg, join us! I know you love poetry."

"Yeah, but I can't cook a lick."

"Don't worry," Claire said. "There's another in our group who's culinarily-challenged. She just picks up something from one of our fabulous Montauk eateries and pretends to have made it herself."

"No one will call her out on it because we love everything she serves and can only imagine what she'd make on her own," Patrick added. "Come. Our next poet is Robert Frost."

"Please do," Claire said excitedly. Then she sneezed.

"Bless you!" Patrick and I said.

I glanced at Claire's long skirt pressed against her legs from the blustery wind. "Speaking of frost, not the poet, but frostbite"—I put my arms around Claire's frail shoulders—"we should probably go up and thaw out before a warm fire."

Patrick glanced up to the top of the dune. "Is this where you live?"

"Yes, just moved in," I answered. "Claire and I are neighbors."

"Thought you lived closer to town?"

"I did, but that was a rental. My lease was up."

"The cottage that was just bulldozed, right?"

"Sadly, yes."

"Well, your new quaint cottage looks similar. Not ostentatious like some of the newer ones going up."

I loved that he used the word *quaint*. I'd always suspected

Patrick had been the good Samaritan who'd done kind acts when I'd lived in the rental. Like adding kindling to my pile of firewood and cleaning up after someone had pulled a prank on me with a bucket of fish guts.

"You two go," he said. "Charley needs a bath and a warm-up in front of a fire, also. Nice seeing you again, Meg. And Claire, I'll see you at Kevin's next week. Try to talk Meg into coming. Old Man and the Sea still has some copies of the Frost book we'll be using. It has discussion questions at the back of the book we loosely follow." Then he turned toward the ocean and whistled for Charley to follow him west.

Claire and I watched the pair until they were out of view. As we walked toward the steps leading up to my cottage, my thoughts were on Patrick. I was struck by how different he was from when I used to see his melancholy figure walking the shore. Always during or before a storm or at nightfall, never during the day. Perhaps he'd learned how to better handle his grief over losing his wife and child. Time didn't heal all wounds, as I learned after losing my mother, but it did push you toward a new normal.

When we reached the top of the steps, Claire interrupted my musings. Turning toward me so I could read her lips, she said, "I have a fire waiting for you, and Jo is fed and satiated until it's time for her snack. I want to hear all about Nightingale Manor. I could tell from your voice on the phone there was more going on than just getting snowed in at a former mental asylum. I want all the details. And the scoop about you and the gorgeous Patrick Seaton, but I can see you're exhausted. Stop over tomorrow, if you're up to it."

I welcomed having a new friend to share with and help me sift through what happened on Shelter Island, but she was right, I needed time alone to digest the past twenty-four hours, including my feelings for author-screenwriter Patrick Seaton. It might be too late to untangle my mixed emotions when it came to Cole and Patrick. It's only as complicated as you make it, my mother always said. She might have been right, but I knew from the past, simple was a path I rarely followed.

After Claire left, I hurried inside to my chair by the fire and extracted a fat lump of cat, then sat to read the letter I'd found in the attic at Nightingale Manor. Jo looked at me, turned down her nose and slunk off to the kitchen to see if I'd replaced her dry food with wet. I hadn't.

"Missed you too, but I know Claire fed you. Don't try to pretend she didn't. Eat the dry food." The vet said she needed it to keep her teeth sharp. I'd told him my foot kept them sharp enough. Whenever I'd mistakenly kick her in the middle of the night, she'd turn into Vampira and take a blood-letting nibble.

I glanced out the cottage's side window that faced my walled garden to the right and the ocean to the left. I never wanted to leave. I had a brick fireplace in my walled garden and loved spending time outdoors in the early evening, reading mysteries on my ebook reader and toasting my toes along with a marshmallow or two. Winters on Long Island were fickle: you could have a day in the fifties one day and twenty below the next. Growing up in Michigan had been a different story, tons of snow and always cold enough to make it stick until at least the end of March. And then there was always the surprise April snowstorm. Memories of building snow forts with my dad and skating on the river made me smile as I scratched behind Jo's ears.

I laid the luggage tag from Arden's suitcase, the onionskin paper with the old train tickets folded inside, and the envelope on the tray table next to the chair. My hand shook as I picked up the envelope. The suspense had been killing me, but instead of ripping it open, I got up and went to the kitchen, opened a drawer and got out a knife. My antique scrimshaw letter opener, a gift from a previous Cottages by the Sea client, was still packed in a box in the guest bedroom. Soon, I thought, maybe even tomorrow, I would start the task—well, not really a task—of decorating the cottage. It was time and it would keep my mind occupied with something besides the murder. I went back to my chair and carefully used the knife to make a clean slit in the thin envelope. With trembling fingers, I extracted the delicate paper inside. It was of the same onionskin as the one with the train tickets that Claire had taken out of the doll. Glancing over at the table with the luggage tag and paper holding the train tickets, there was no doubt all three had been written by the same hand. Arden Hunter's.

I smoothed out the page, worried it might disintegrate in my hands.

Marian, I am not insane. And neither are you. You lost a baby, you didn't lose your mind. And I lost the love of my life to the ravages of polio. I plan to leave this place before my scheduled operation and I think you should go with me. I am afraid. I know Dr. Tobias has been a good doctor to us both, but I fear this upcoming operation that he proposes will be the end of my identity, if not my life. Nurse Mary has been kind enough to procure two tickets on the Long Island Railroad to Pennsylvania Station for our escape. I feel if we travel together maybe one day we can return to the big screen in a comeback picture, letting the past remain buried. I owe it to the memory of Fred and you have your son Grayson to think about. I've tried to tell the doctor of my concerns, but he seems confident the procedure will work. In my opinion he is overconfident. I've had Nurse Mary take out the seam in the arm of your Amanda doll and put the train tickets inside. Don't worry, you can't even tell that she has been disturbed. I know how much Amanda means to you, but it was the safest place I could think of to put them until it is time to leave, away from warden Louise's prying eyes. Lately, that is how I feel here. Like a captive without a voice. Please meet me under our pine tree after lights-out tomorrow evening and I promise all will be well. Don't we deserve happiness? Or at least our autonomy? I didn't know, and I'm sure you were also unaware, that Nightingale Manor isn't the sanctuary they'd promised us. It is more of a prison and I don't understand why they are keeping us separated. Why can't we be together, like when we arrived? Are you ill? Have I done something wrong? Just know my affection for you hasn't changed.

Your friend in pain and hopeful resurrection,
Arden

I placed the open letter next to the other two samples of writing. Yes. Arden Hunter had written all three. But did that change anything? Dr. Tobias Nightingale, Dr. Blake's grandfather, was talked of kindly in the letter. But I understood Arden's fear; it was doubtful she would have survived a lobotomy. Maybe there was another scenario to that day. Perhaps Marian went to save Arden and she and Dr. Tobias struggled. Or Marian got upset that Arden defaced the doll named after Marian's dead baby and was mentally incapacitated and grabbed the ice pick out of the doctor's hand and murdered Arden, just like the doctor had reported. But then why were the tickets still inside the doll and how had the doll ended up in the woods? Had Marian waited for her the night in question? It seemed Arden and Marian were friends, not enemies, just as Elle's great-aunt Mabel had told her. Did Arden and Marian choose to go to Nightingale Manor together to heal and lament their losses? Arden mourning the man who died of polio, and Marian her dead baby? I would probably never find out. And what did it matter? And what did it have to do with the modern-day murder? One final conundrum: who had been in the attic during the power outage and why? Too many questions and no answers. My mind was spinning. I glanced toward the hearth. All that was left of the fire were embers that blinked and spit sparks of red, yellow and blue. Tomorrow was a big day. Big in the sense that I would give my official statement about Blake Nightingale's murder. For the ease of it all, I'd been trying to talk myself into believing that Dr. Blake's former patient, the one who was suing him because of what he'd done to her on *Bungled*, was his killer. If you dug into the Nightingale family online, it wouldn't be hard to find out about the old murder. Maybe the woman decided to extract her revenge by doing a copycat killing? Farfetched but not out of the realm of possibility.

I stood and walked to the bookcase. Jo had long since gone to bed and I knew I should join her. Instead, I took the luggage tag, letter and tickets and pressed a section of molding on the bookcase. The door opened to my secret, hidden room. It really wasn't that much of a secret to everyone near and dear, and it was the opposite of a panic room; it was a place to shut out the world while still having a view of the lighthouse. Its light, a beacon of stability and comfort. Stepping inside, I randomly pulled out one of my nineteenth-century antique gilt books of poetry. *Wordsworth*. I put the letter, tag, and tickets inside and stuck it back on the shelf. Then I sat on the window seat and looked toward the light. Usually comforted by its sight, I shivered. What had Dr. Blake done to have someone do such a thing? To get my mind off my macabre thoughts, I reached for a book on twentieth-century poets and went to the index and found my favorite poem by Robert Frost, and probably the rest of the world's, "The Road Not Taken." An hour later I drifted off to sleep with thoughts of Patrick Seaton. Not Cole.

Bad Meg.

Chapter 15

Friday, I woke to a scratching and loud meowing from Josephine. I'd fallen asleep on the window seat in my hidden room and felt guilty that two nights in a row Jo had slept without me. Scurrying to the door, I pulled it open. "So sorry, my furry feline. Promise tonight we'll be bedmates. I'll even rub your fat belly until you fall asleep."

For only having one eye, she sure knew how to make it work. She looked at me with distrust and I knew the only way to placate her was to add a few stinky sardines to her morning meal.

After a quick cup of coffee, I showered, dressed and headed out to Southampton. The roads were better than yesterday when I'd driven home from Sag Harbor. The fact the sun was out and the temperature was in the upper forties had a lot to do with it. The only problem was that in certain places the melting snow was flooding sections of Montauk Highway. I was told to be at the Southampton Police Station at ten o'clock. It was only eight. Southampton was twenty-eight miles away, a no-brainer when the roads were clear, but who knew when I'd get there. Elle had left a message that she and Felicity would meet me at Priscilla's Tea & Toast at nine thirty. Not that we had to coordinate our stories, but it wouldn't hurt to do a quick recap. I planned to bring up the time line of when we'd heard the harrowing scream that might have come from Dr. Blake. My guesstimate would be around two in the morning because I knew it was shortly after my phone died.

My Woody made it through the water that had flooded the road in front of the Windward Shores Hotel. I continued west on 27A- Montauk Highway, passing snow-crested sand dunes backed by a sparkling Atlantic. The Seafood Shanty was boarded up with plywood, its roof covered with snow that was melting so fast it looked like the runoff from an infinity pool. When the Shanty opened in April, cars would line both sides of the highway for a chance to sample their famous lobster roll. On the outskirts of Amagansett, I opened my windows before reaching the East End Farmers Market, slowing as I passed to catch a whiff of pine from the Christmas trees stacked near the road.

In the seventeenth-century town of East Hampton, I saw only a few people mulling about, looking like extras from a Hallmark Christmas movie. Like most of the towns, villages, and hamlets that made up the Hamptons, the white clapboard Early American shops and small houses gave off a timeless New England feel. Even Starbucks, with its white façade and large plate-glass window decorated with evergreen boughs interlaced with red ribbons and blinking white lights, seemed in step with the cozy village ambiance. I knew from trying to get permits for my cottage that the Town of East Hampton Zoning Board of Appeals took their job very seriously, not allowing any riff-raff and very few chain stores into the area, Starbucks being one of the exceptions.

Next on my travels to Southampton were the villages of Bridgehampton, Wainscott, and Watermill. The snowplows had been busy during the night, the sides of the road piled with a thin layer of white slush that was starting to melt—a little different than the black-tinged sludge I remembered the trucks in Manhattan leaving behind that usually morphed into solid UFOs (unidentified frozen objects), never disappearing until late spring.

It was nine fifteen when I walked into Priscilla's Tea & Toast. Elle and Felicity had scored a private table in a little nook to the right of the barista bar. Their heads were bent, whispering like coconspirators. Felicity looked up and smiled, showing off her dimples. Elle followed her gaze and waved me over.

After sitting and ordering both a chai tea and a double espresso, the espresso something I rarely drank but needed, we discussed what we would tell the police. We agreed that for the time being we would leave out anything having to do with Arden Hunter's murder. We concurred that the loud howl we'd heard had come in the ballpark of two or two thirty in the morning.

Glancing around the tearoom, I saw that each teacup and saucer in Priscilla's had a different design. I recognized more than a few antique transferware patterns from Ansley, Coalport and Shelley. Coffee came in oversized white mugs with a large P monogram. They were so large they could double as soup bowls. A waiter brought over two platters of avocado toast and set them in the middle of the table, then he passed out small bread plates to each of us. Like the teacups and saucers, the plates were in mismatched patterns, making for a festive table. Each piece of toast had mashed avocado arranged inside a metal Christmas tree cookie cutter. I placed the toast on my plate and removed the cookie cutter. The tree in the center of my toast was almost too charming to eat. But I managed.

Elle stuffed half of a piece of toast in her mouth, mumbling as she chewed, "Arthur said he has a good buddy on the Southampton PD." She wiped her mouth with a napkin, then took a sip of Darjeeling and continued, "Because Arthur was the first on the scene, even though Shelter Island isn't in his jurisdiction, he might get special disposition to assist in the case."

"Well, that's great news," I said, raising my right hand to give her a fist bump that she didn't return. "Did he share anything about what happened after we left?"

"No. You know Arthur. He goes by the book." Then she added, "For the most part."

"No pillow talk?" I asked, giving her a wink.

"He won't share anything unless my safety's involved. He said he's already played every card he could when he allowed you, Felicity, and me to leave the estate before the CSIs processed all the evidence."

"What did you share with him?" I asked, trying to get a snippet of info from her.

"What could I? We were locked in that box during the murder," Elle said. "However, I did tell him about Sabrina and Willa not getting along and the thing about not paying the malpractice insurance. I'm happy he's not involved directly," Elle said wistfully. "He has a lot on his plate."

She didn't elaborate, just took a sip of her tea and gave me a mournful look. I'd tried earlier on the phone to get her to open up about what was going on besides the obvious murder at Nightingale Manor, but she'd been with Felicity and said she would share everything the next time we were alone.

Felicity added the contents of a wildflower honey stick to her cup of tea and stirred it. I could tell by the rising steam it was too hot to drink. "I love this place. It's so cozy. It's a shame we have to go to a police station and give our statements about a grisly murder." Felicity dabbed the corners of her mouth with a linen napkin. "I'm so grateful I got to leave the Nightingale estate. All thanks to you,

Elle, or should I say your fiancé. My husband wasn't too thrilled when I told him what happened. Wanted to fly out here. But I told him no. At least until we decide if the filming will stay here on the East Coast." She turned to me, cognizant even with my hearing aids that it was easier for me when I also read lips. "Meg, I have some news you might like. Elle told me your father is a homicide detective."

"Retired," I added.

"And that you've been involved in a few murder investigations." Felicity took a sip of tea and smiled. "Yum."

"And almost got killed each time," Elle scolded, sending me her motherly look.

"Anyway," Felicity said, placing her cup on its saucer, "I think you can eliminate one suspect from your list."

"List. What list?" I said in mock horror, throwing up my hands.

Felicity laughed. "Our producer. Jeremy Prentice. I talked to his production assistant, Roger, and he'd picked Jeremy up from the North Shelter Island Ferry dock on Wednesday, the afternoon of the snowstorm. They shared a room at a B&B in Greenport, then yesterday took a limo to Manhattan."

"So that narrows it down to Willa, Sabrina, Dr. Lewis and Langston. A short list." I was doing it again. Getting involved in something that wasn't my business. This time it felt less dangerous because I was away from the murder scene and had no connection to Dr. Blake Nightingale. I was willing to allow the authorities to handle it, if not for the nagging puzzle of how a murder from decades ago was mixed into the equation of Blake Nightingale's murder. "Felicity, you seem pretty close to Langston. Do you have any idea why he might have a motive to kill Dr. Blake?" Then I told them about what I'd witnessed on Monday in Dr. Blake's office. "Yesterday, your director knew all about the old murder and the fact the estate used to be a mental asylum and pretended he didn't."

"It's impossible to figure out why Langston would keep all that from me. As far as I know, he'd never met Dr. Blake until he saw an advertisement in the *East Hampton Star* offering to rent out the mansion for movies or television. It happens a lot out here. Or so Langston tells me."

I knew what she said was true. "There's always filming going on in the Hamptons. I have to give Blake Nightingale credit. Renting out the estate was a good way to make extra cash off-season." Not giving up on picking Felicity's brain, I added, "I know Langston has a mega mansion in Bridgehampton and has been a public figure in the Hamptons for quite a while."

"I've worked with him on two other projects. One in England and one in California. Never heard a bad thing about him. He's always treated the cast and crew with the utmost respect. He's one of those rare people who takes time to stop and listen to you. Eye contact and all."

"What about the woman who was suing Dr. Blake from the show *Bungled*?" Elle asked. "I'm sure she has to be on the list. At least we know Mr. Prentice is in the clear. And it's also hard to imagine Langston having a motive for murdering Dr. Blake. Willa, Sabrina, and Dr. Lewis, I would keep near the top of our list. Ugh, here I go, Meg. Getting sucked into all your hypothesizing. Let's get this interview over with and get back to some semblance of serenity. I have a new crate of goodies to unpack from that estate sale Maurice went to last weekend. Think I even spied an old Sag Harbor whaling captain's log book from the early 1800s."

"That's a rare find. It could be a fake though," I said.

"Why so distrustful? Think of all the treasures we've found in the past."

"Don't you watch the *Roadshow*?" I asked her. "It could be a facsimile."

"Yes, but even if it's a copy, I'm sure the Sag Harbor Whaling Museum would love to put it on display. Speaking of copies," Elle said, digging through her ginormous vintage handbag, "I made copies of the pilot script. One for you, Meg, and here's the original, Felicity." She handed me a sheaf of papers. "By the way, Meg, I looked it over. Patrick Seaton is a very talented screenwriter."

I grabbed it, excited to read Patrick's work. Felicity had been staring into space. She took the original script and stowed it in her bag. "Willa is so sweet. I would look into the other two first."

"Willa seemed mad at the doctor and Sabrina for sending her son away," I said. "Plus, she has to remain a suspect. Our pool is limited but the reasons for murder are limitless. Felicity, did she talk to you about Donnie? Maybe he did it." I said it as a jest, but now that I thought about it, he could have been hiding out in the mansion. A lot of schools had winter break. It would be interesting to see if he attended one of them.

Someone had cranked up the Christmas music, adding to the tea shop's holiday atmosphere but making it hard for me to hear. Background noise, even when wearing my top-of-the-line hearing aids, was one of my biggest challenges. I reached for my key chain in my handbag and pressed the up button on the fob that controlled the volume to my hearing aids.

Felicity noticed and paused until I gave her a thumbs-up. "All I know is Willa really misses her son."

"I wonder why Willa was so angry with Dr. Blake. His wife, Sabrina, I can understand. She seems a little one-dimensional. Not that I know anything about her," I added.

"Mrs. Nightingale's always running off to Southampton for shopping or beauty appointments or lunch at the country club," Felicity said. "I guess that does sound slightly shallow, but I get the feeling she's one of those people with a lot of nervous energy that needs to get burned off, and like Willa said, the Nightingales usually go away in the winter months to a more temperate climate. Langston told me she asked to have a walk-on part in *Mr. & Mrs. Winslow*, but now with the murder there's a good chance we'll be switching locations."

Elle's cup clattered against her saucer. "I think that will be a relief."

Felicity slapped her forehead with the heel of her right hand. "The logistics of moving to another location because of the murder are daunting. We'll have to bring in craft services. I know Jeremy. If the budget goes over the initial projections, he might cancel the whole thing. Or sell to another production company."

"He can do that?" Elle asked.

Felicity looked up at the glittering holiday ornaments hanging from the ceiling catching the light and reflecting off the walls in red, green, silver and gold. "Yes, it's done all the time. I don't know if you've ever stayed for the ending credits in a movie. Sometimes they have multiple producers and production companies listed. They each get a piece of the pie."

Elle grabbed a cranberry scone, took a bite, and said, "Yum," then asked, "Felicity, maybe they'll catch Dr. Blake's killer soon and things will go back as planned?"

"I doubt it. Too much bad press about the old and new murders. I'm low woman on the totem pole when it comes to decisions on that level."

Feeling the espresso coursing through my veins, amping up my already jittery nerves, I told them about the letter I'd found between the floorboards in the attic storage space and the empty suitcase that probably belonged to Arden Hunter.

"Wow. How sad," Felicity said, putting down her teacup. "I had a great-aunt who was put in an asylum in upstate New York because her husband said she was crazy. What husbands said back then, no one questioned. What we found out years later was she was just suffering from postpartum depression after giving birth."

"Mental health issues were dealt with differently back then," I said. "Epilepsy, seizures, blackouts, schizophrenia were all lumped together. From my research, even if you were born with crossed eyes, or your husband simply wanted to get rid of you so he could take up with another woman, you might find yourself admitted to a sanitorium with no chance of leaving. Last night, I found an article about a photo exhibit based on four hundred suitcases that were found in the attic of an old asylum ready to be demolished. Each photo showed the suitcase and next to it all the items that were inside, giving a voyeur's view into the type of people who were admitted to mental institutions during the middle of the last century before major reform happened. What struck me was how normal the contents were. It was like they were packing for a weekend in the country or a trip to the seaside. The photos from the exhibit reminded me of what I saw at Nightingale Manor. You can learn a lot about people from what they pack in their suitcases."

"Thankfully, we've come a long way in psychiatry," Elle added, stealing the top of my cinnamon-bun muffin, having already eaten hers.

"Hey, that's the best part!" I scolded.

Elle ignored me and put the whole thing in her mouth. After she swallowed, she said, "Let's focus on getting our interviews over with and enjoy the holiday season. I say we take a break from any talk of the murder. I need to start making the cookies for our weekend open house at the shop. I'm also doing something different this year, I'm bringing in local artisans who can sell holiday items that are handmade but still fit the vintage Christmas theme. One woman, who's in her nineties, makes these amazing wood and uncombed wool sheep that look like they came from an 1890s German Putz nativity scene."

We talked for a few minutes about childhood holiday memories and I invited Felicity and her husband to spend Christmas with us at Pondfare.

"With everything going on, I can say, if production continues, I would love to spend Christmas with you guys. My husband might be able to fly in. I have a feeling I'll be too behind schedule to fly home to California, even for a day."

I was facing the front window, which was fogged around the edges like a mirror after a hot shower. But in the center, I spied Sabrina Nightingale strolling by. She was dressed in fur, her matching hat like something from a Chekov play or the movie *Anna Karenina* or *Dr. Zhivago*. She appeared to have been crying. "Look who just passed by," I said, pointing to the window.

"Sabrina," Elle said. "Not a surprise, I'm sure everyone from Nightingale Manor has an appointment with the police."

"Hurry. Let's follow her." I stood and threw down a twenty.

"Why?" Elle exclaimed.

I didn't answer. I wasn't sure myself why we should follow the Widow Nightingale but something beyond curiosity spurred me on. I threw open the door, jingle bells jingling, and went crashing into Langston Reed's chest just as he'd called out, "Wait, Sabrina!"

Had they gone to the police station together? I opened my mouth to ask, but my boots hit a patch of ice and I went down butt-first on the slushy sidewalk. Langston chivalrously scooped me up and set me back on my feet. He was stronger than his thin frame suggested.

"Ms. Barrett, isn't it?" He kept his gaze toward where Sabrina disappeared inside a shop. The white sign etched with gold letters read *Beauty Bar Salon and Day Spa*.

"Yes, but please call me Meg. So sorry for almost knocking you over. Nothing like black ice to send you to the hospital with a broken hip."

He smiled. His face was so darn friendly. Judging by the casual way he was dressed in jeans, sneakers, wool sweater and down vest, it was hard to believe he had almost as much money as his producer, Jeremy Prentice. Langston was also one of the top philanthropists in the Hamptons area. I remembered reading about some local charity he'd started, I just couldn't remember what it was for.

Elle and Felicity trotted up to us.

"Nice tumble," Elle said. "Meg, are you okay?"

I nodded. "Nothing's hurt but my pride . . . and my tailbone."

"Felicity," Langston said, "I suppose you've been to see the police?"

"Not yet. We're going now."

"I just returned from giving my statement," he said. "What a sad state of affairs. Recapping the morning we found Blake Nightingale seems almost surreal. Although I don't think I had anything to say that would help the investigation, except that he was drunk as a skunk."

"Do you know if they've arrested anyone for Dr. Blake's death?" Felicity asked.

"I don't think so."

He unzipped his vest. The sun was doing a fast job of melting every patch of white. "I don't think I would be in their confidence if they had. I did see Willa the housekeeper inside, waiting her turn to be interviewed. I'm relieved the authorities promised they won't be sharing anything about *Mr. & Mrs. Winslow* at this time. The whole point of coming out to the Hamptons in the winter was to keep things hush-hush so the press wouldn't get in the way. And we sure don't need bad press preproduction."

"I thought any press is good press," I said.

"Not always."

It was hard to reconcile the man in front of me, who I'd immediately liked and Felicity admired, as the same person who'd gone off on Blake Nightingale with an almost venomous zeal.

He glanced at me and smiled, as if reading my thoughts. "The police seem competent and nothing like the good-cop, bad-cop scenarios you see on television. That is, until this huge man with a military buzz cut, dressed in a state trooper's uniform, entered the room. The two officers shrunk into their chairs and only repeated, 'Yes, Sir' and 'No, Sir.' Talk about being frightened."

"Chief Pell," I said.

Langston gave me a strange look, like how would I know the lead homicide investigator for the Suffolk County Police Department. I'd first met Chief Pell, who everyone nicknamed the Incredible Hulk because of his massive WWE muscled body, after I found someone murdered inside the mansion at the East Hampton estate Seacliff.

"I was happy," Langston continued, "that he didn't sit down to complete my interview. He just nodded his head at the Southampton detectives, and they left the room. A few seconds later both officers came back inside. The older of the two told me I could leave, and by older I mean about nineteen. Later, in the hallway I overheard one of the officers tell his partner there was a new development. Have no idea if it has anything to do with Blake Nightingale's case, but whatever it was, it caused Mrs. Nightingale to cry. I saw her through an open doorway talking to the same giant in the blue uniform, your Chief Pell. It's surreal about Nightingale's death. The way he was killed was something from a horror movie."

I couldn't help but butt in. "Did anyone mention the old murder?" In my head, I heard my cop father's voice telling me to take it easy. Knowing Langston lied yesterday about not knowing anything about Nightingale Manor's past or the old murder made me wonder if before becoming a movie director he'd been an actor.

Instead of answering, he totally ignored my question and instead addressed Felicity. "I've got good news. I just talked to Jeremy and he found another location for us to film. At least for the first episode. I'm scheduled to go check it out in an hour. Even though my opinion won't carry much weight because I'm in the doghouse for picking Nightingale Manor in the first place.

"Like me, I'm sure the authorities have asked all of you to remain nearby until they have a suspect in custody. I always spend Christmas in the Hamptons, so it shouldn't be much of a hardship, although I do hope they catch this fiend. What about you, Felicity? I have room at my place if you want to stay until the production schedule is reexamined?"

I think we were all relieved at the mention of a new location and the idea the production wouldn't be moving out of the area. It would've been a tough call on my part if they'd decided to stay at

Nightingale Manor to film. Serenity was the order of the day. I had a cottage to decorate and maybe a poetry book club to join. I could tell by Felicity's tight-lipped smile and lack of dimples she was conflicted about Langston's invitation, knowing he was one of the main suspects in the murder, motive or not.

Elle stepped in. "Oh, Felicity's all set. She's staying with me in Sag Harbor."

Felicity relaxed her shoulders and smiled. "Where have they chosen for the new location?"

"A place called Windy Willows. It seems the owner of the place, just like Blake Nightingale, is in desperate need of cash. Jeremy likes his bargains. We have to lock it in before they change their mind."

"Windy Willows," I squeaked.

Langston turned and asked, "You know it?"

"Never been there." I hadn't, but I knew whose family owned it. Windy Willows was the family estate of my ex-fiancé Michael's ex and current wife, Paige Whitney. Paige's father, Matthew Whitney, not only owned Windy Willows in East Hampton but also Whitney Publications. Whitney Publications was the parent company of *American Home and Garden*, the magazine where at one time I was editor in chief. If *Mr. & Mrs. Winslow* filmed at Windy Willows, it was doubtful I'd run into Michael and Paige off-season. They were probably off somewhere in the West Indies at some swanky winter resort. Just the thought of running into Paige, though, brought the Barrett welts to the surface, heating my face and neck. I unwrapped my scarf, knitted by yours truly, and put my hand on Langston's arm. "Did I hear you calling Sabrina's name a few minutes ago?"

If he thought I was a nosy Nellie, he didn't let on. "Yes. She almost attacked me about keeping the production at her estate. I told her it was out of my hands. She was quite upset. I thought it over and wanted to tell her that perhaps we could rent some of the 1930s items from Nightingale Manor and use them in the new location. But now that I think about it, I better wait and touch base with Jeremy until after we see the interior of Windy Willows. If its contents don't fit our time line, then perhaps we'll want to bring in a couple truckloads of 1930s furniture, art, and knickknacks from the Nightingale estate. Jeremy likes to stick to his budget, so it might make everyone happy. Including Mrs. Nightingale. She also asked again for a walk-on part if everything falls through. What are your thoughts, Felicity?" he asked.

I was flabbergasted. Sabrina Nightingale was concerned about a walk-on role in the miniseries the day after her husband was murdered? Shouldn't she be more concerned about mourning her husband's death or catching his killer—or even slightly worried she could be the killer's next target? I know I wouldn't want to stay at the estate after what happened.

"It might work," Felicity answered. "I just don't know if I'm ready to go back there until they find whomever killed Dr. Blake. How do we know Sabrina didn't kill him? You sure you want her in the production?"

I agreed with her on that one. And by the frozen grimace on Elle's face, I knew she also agreed.

He laughed. "You know showbiz, Felicity. Don't worry, we can always cut her out when editing. I bet the same person who killed the doctor is the one who came in from that door leading outside. They're probably long gone."

"Hope you're right," Felicity said. "This isn't the best start to what I thought was a fantastic premise for a series."

"I agree," Langston said wistfully. "But as you know from working on other projects, things don't always go as planned."

"True," she answered, shaking her head. "But murder?"

"I tell you what. Why don't we all go to Windy Willows together and check it out. I'll wait in my car. I have a couple of phone calls to make." He pointed to a navy Ford Explorer. "Then I'll drop you back here. The estate's not that far away."

Elle spoke up for all of us. "Of course, we'd love to." It was the first smile on her face I'd seen since the murder. "We'll meet back here as soon as we're finished at the station."

I wasn't quite sure how *fabulous* going to Windy Willows was. I said, "Why don't you three go together. I'll meet you there. I know where it is. I have something I need to do."

Elle gave me a look and mouthed the word *chicken*. She knew all about who lived at Windy Willows. The good news about Langston's invitation was it meant Elle and I would still be included in the production of the miniseries despite the murder and change of location. Plus, if I did run into Michael's ex and current wife, the high-and-mighty Paige Whitney, she'd probably avoid me, not wanting me to know her family had fallen onto hard times and had to contract out the family manse. I had the advantage. For once.

Felicity also looked relieved. "Then we better get going to the police station. Langston, I'll text you after we're done."

It looked like I'd be taking a trip to Windy Willows.

But before going, I planned to take a little side trip to Beauty Bar Salon and Day Spa.

Chapter 16

When we'd walked inside the small, almost quaint, Southampton Police Station with its amiable officers and designer coffee machine, I'd felt immediately at ease. I'd been chosen as the first person to be interviewed. The questions and answers had been kept short and there was no mention of Arden Hunter's murder. Neither Chief Pell nor Detective Shoner had been in the room, just two young officers who seemed at a loss as to what questions to ask in a murder investigation. And rightly so. In the past couple of years there had only been one murder in East Hampton and two in Sag Harbor. It had been decades since the town of Southampton, which included Shelter Island, had to deal with a murder.

It was sobering when I realized I'd been involved in each one of those murders, not to mention some oldies but goodies. While one of the officers took notes, I was asked to give a detailed montage of what we'd done to keep busy in the elevator until we'd fallen asleep. I knew what they were up to. They planned on comparing our stories. Looking for holes in the narrative. They wouldn't find any.

As the interview was winding down I thought I was in the clear until one of the officers asked if there was any way to prove the three of us had been in the elevator for the entire time the power had been out. I said I didn't think I could prove it, however, the others in the house—*who didn't have alibis*, I wanted to say—could confirm they hadn't seen us until we ran into the room and reported Blake Nightingale's death.

There was an awkward lull, so I stood, ready to leave.

The younger of the two officers asked, "Is that it? Are you holding anything back?"

The pen! Oops. "I did pick up something on the morning we found the doctor's body." I reached in my pocket and took out the plastic bag holding the pen. I reached across the table and handed it off, happy to be rid of it.

He read the advertising on the side of the pen, "*Nightingale and Lewis Dermatology*. 104 Poplar Street, Southampton, New York." He put the bag on the table. "Tell me where you got this and why you didn't turn it in immediately."

"It was on the basement steps, fifth step from the bottom. I originally saw it right after Elle, Felicity, and I were fleeing the basement after the elevator opened to, uh, Dr. Blake's corpse. I left it there for forensics, but then later when Dr. Lewis insisted we go down together so he could examine the body, I decided to pick it up, in case whoever killed the doctor decided to do the same. Do you think those spots are dried blood?"

He ignored me while his partner continued taking notes. "We'll have to see. Dr. Lewis, you say, wanted to look at the body? What did he discover?"

"Not much. He turned the body on its side but didn't see anything besides, the, um, wound in the chest from the ice pick."

"Did you touch the pen?" the one taking notes asked.

"No, I used a tissue to pick it up, then when I got home, put it in a baggie. You won't find my prints."

They appeared slightly impressed.

Before leaving the interview room, I was politely told to stay in the Hamptons area and not to inform any outside sources about the manner in which Blake Nightingale was murdered. I'd informed them that wouldn't be a problem. I understood their thinking. There had to be a link between the old murder and the new. Then I was directed to the front lobby, where I waited for Elle and Felicity while sitting on a comfy sofa sipping a decaf coffee and watching the door for those entering and exiting the station. In the back of my mind I was on the lookout for the woman who was suing Dr. Blake for her bungled surgery. I was sure that Sabrina had voiced her theory on who killed her husband. I had no idea what the woman's real name was, but last night I'd rewatched the *Bungled* episode on my laptop where she'd been featured post-surgery. Maybe it had something to do with my hearing loss and having to focus on a person's lips when they spoke, but I don't forget a face. I was sure if I saw her I would recognize her.

A woman walked into the station swathed in winter clothing. As she unwrapped her scarf mummy style, I was disappointed in her gray, almost-white hair and advanced age. No way was she the woman from *Bungled*. I picked up an ancient *Parents* magazine from the table next to me and pretended to be reading, peeking occasionally at the door. I wasn't a parent, and at this point might never be, but I got hooked on an article titled "Stop Saying No and Still Get Good Behavior." I planned on following a few of their tips for the next time Jo brandished her claws and refused to vacate my *New York Times* reading chair.

I moved on to the next article about how to clean smelly sneakers and almost missed her.

Little about her face resembled what she'd looked like on the post-surgery episode I'd seen. Her skin was tight and unwrinkled but there were lumps and crevices in all the wrong places, especially under her cheekbones, which reminded me of the skeleton in Nightingale Manor's attic.

The woman hadn't been coming in to the police station, she was being led out while yelling expletives at a female officer who kept a stoic face even though she had pinpricks of sweat on her brow.

Lucky for me, or so I thought at the time, a piece of paper had slipped from the screaming woman's hand, landing inches away from me on the floor. I waited until the pair left the station, scooped up the paper, took a look at it, then ran out with it clutched in my hand. It was the perfect excuse to meet Dr. Blake's unhappy guinea pig without making up one of my lame excuses. I wasn't good at fibbing even though I'd been practicing my poker face for Elle's assistant Maurice's monthly poker game in Sag Harbor. Maurice told me my poker face resembled his cat before she regurgitated a furball.

"Excuse me," I said, out of breath, reaching her just as she was putting a key in the lock of her Infiniti. The sun was still out, and the snow had melted, leaving small rivers draining into the sewers next to the curb. I leaped over, holding the paper in my outstretched hand. The woman must have thought I was going to assault her because she turned to me with her leg extended, kickboxing style. She was tall and solid, someone you didn't want to mess with, especially after hearing the growl coming out of her strange-shaped lips. Apparently, another bungled thing from Dr. Blake's surgery.

Before she could kick me in the jaw, I said, "You dropped this inside the police station." I held out the paper and she ripped it out of my hand. She scanned it, then stuffed it in her jacket pocket. "They didn't even make a copy, said they would do their own investigating. The buffoons!"

"I couldn't help notice how upset you were leaving the station." I kept my eyes downcast. "Are you sure you should be driving in such a state? I can call someone."

She opened the car door, then sat sideways, facing me. Tears streamed at a rate almost as fast as the water streaming into the gutter. "I'm not used to people being kind since this," she said, pointing to her face, "happened."

I reached into my handbag, retrieved a few tissues and passed them to her.

"Mr. Margulies told me not to come alone. He's out of town and won't be back until tomorrow. I should have listened."

I'd met the high-powered Hamptons attorney Justin Margulies on more than one occasion. If this woman was innocent of Blake Nightingale's death, she was in good hands.

"It's the first time I've been out in public. I'm not used to the press following me. Don't know how they found out who I was. Everything was supposed to be kept confidential. But now with this murder, I'm afraid to wake up tomorrow and open the paper and see my ghoulish face on the front page, accused of murder."

I tried to look like I didn't know what she was talking about, and it must've worked because she continued, "I'm sorry. You were just being kind, returning this." She pulled the paper from her jacket pocket and held it up. "It's proof I was nowhere near the murder scene. I'm sure you read in the paper about the murder of the doctor who did this to me." She pointed to a sunken area on her left cheek. "Have you ever heard of the television show *Bungled*?"

"It sounds familiar," I said, not wanting to lie.

"You're a very pretty woman with your lovely blonde hair and blue eyes. Don't ever get surgery for cosmetic reasons. I did when I was eighteen. The doctor did a poor job and then I tried to correct it and look what happened."

I thought about when I was younger and refused to wear hearing aids in middle school because of what all the other kids would say. How trivial it all seemed now.

A tear coursed down the woman's swollen right cheek. "I better get back, my son will be worried about me. I apologize for the scene I caused in the station. I'm still in physical pain and had a hard time being questioned for something I plainly didn't do." She laughed.

"You don't know what I'm talking about, do you? Thanks again for giving this to me. It's a photocopy, at least I listened to Mr. Margulies on that point."

"Are you sure you're all right to drive?"

"I'm sure. I only have to get to Bridgehampton. And it looks like the roads are better." She extended her hand. "Thank you . . ."

"Meg," I said.

"Pauline," she replied.

After she got inside her car, I closed the door, then watched her pull away.

Even though I believed in her innocence, I took out my phone and typed in her license plate number. Then I walked the half block to the Beauty Bar Salon, where I'd seen Sabrina Nightingale run in.

As soon as I walked inside a young girl ambushed me. She handed me a bottle of top-shelf water and led me to a small room with cushy seats. I sat, and she nodded toward a split of champagne in an ice bucket and asked if I would like a glass. I looked at her name tag. "Thanks, Trina. I better not."

"Of course, Mrs. Starling. I'll be right back with a fruit and cheese board." I decided to play along and let her think I was whoever Mrs. Starling was. I looked around the room. Soft classical piano music played in the background and the gentle mist from an electric atomizer filled the air with the faint scent of lavender. So, this must be what it felt like to be pampered Hamptons-style. I'd visited my share of top-rated salons when I'd been editor at *American Home and Garden*. However, it had been years since I'd been inside something this exclusive. I picked up a brochure and scanned the prices and saw the least expensive package was five hundred dollars for a cut and highlights, wash and blow-dry extra. I let Barb, my friend from Sand and Sun Realty in Montauk, cut my hair at her kitchen table. Then afterward we'd share a glass of wine on the front porch of her home overlooking Lake Montauk. I figured the money I saved not visiting a Hamptons salon would be better spent at an estate sale or flea market.

Trina came back inside and sat next to me. In her eyes was worry. "I'm sooo sorry, Mrs. Starling," she stammered. "Anthony is running a half hour late. Please excuse me, it's only my second week working here." She pulled her upper body away from me, like she anticipated a slap.

"Okay," I answered, still not technically impersonating anyone.

Trina seemed surprised I didn't throw a hissy fit. "Anthony said I'm to give you whatever you need in the meantime."

"Well, Trina." I stuck my nose a little higher in the air. "There is something you could help me with. You see, I was supposed to meet my friend here, Sabrina Nightingale. I'd been so busy getting my twin toddlers, Harry and William, ready for school and the time got away from me. Those boys take after their father, that's for sure."

"Oh, dear. I'm new here but I do know who your friend is. I'm afraid there was quite a scene about a half hour ago. The police were here and everything was quite chaotic. It seems there was someone posing as a client who turned out to be a newspaper reporter."

"That's terrible," I said, almost choking on my water.

"He took pictures of your friend and Anthony had to call the police. Beauty Bar protects their clients. It's just awful about her husband's murder. Just goes to show you, one minute you have it all, then the next minute it's gone." She clicked her fingers in the air.

"Indeed," I said, nervously glancing at my watch, waiting for the real Mrs. Starling to walk in and call me out. I stood and said, "I really can't wait. I must be off . . . twin stuff to do." It sounded lame, but she didn't seem to notice, too upset I was leaving.

"Oh, you can't leave. Anthony will have a fit."

"Have no worries, my dear. If he asks, tell him there was an emergency at the boys' academy."

She looked relieved.

"One more thing," I said, heading to the door.

"Yes?"

"What did the police do about the reporter?"

"They just escorted him out and Mrs. Nightingale called a friend to pick her up. Between you and me, Mrs. Nightingale didn't seem herself when she walked in. I guess it's normal considering what she's been going through. She must be on some strong meds. Didn't remember her appointment was for next week."

"Did you happen to see who picked her up?"

She hesitated for a moment and I thought she was going to catch on to my masquerade as one of the Real Housewives of the Hamptons.

113

Instead, she leaned in conspiratorially and whispered, "I was out in the back, having a cigarette. Bad habit. It was that other doctor from the show her husband starred in. She seemed quite relieved, her eyes rolled back in her head and she fell into his arms in a near faint."

Dr. Lewis to the rescue, I thought. I thanked her and gave her a twenty-dollar tip. She tried to refuse it, but I insisted. Still playing my part, thinking I'd just purchased a very expensive bottle of water. However, the information about Dr. Lewis had been priceless. I left without anyone in the front room the wiser.

It seemed deceased Dr. Blake's partner, Dr. Lewis, was involved with both Willa and Sabrina. The plot wasn't just thickening—it was coagulating.

Chapter 17

After returning from Southampton, I rapped on the front door of Little Grey. Through the window I saw Claire padding toward me barefoot, her toes pointed ballerina style. She opened the door, her face young and dewy like she'd just spent time over a pot of boiling water. "Are you sweating?" I asked, stepping inside as she held the door open.

"I'm experimenting with a new type of yoga that touches upon all four natural elements, fire, water, earth, and wind. *Experimenting* being the key word, seeing I almost scalded my face with steaming sage-scented water.

The front room looked completely different from the first time I'd walked into Little Grey. Then, the word *dilapidated* hadn't even covered it. With Claire's son-in-law's permission, I'd hired my go-to construction guys to plaster the walls, repair the staircase and unearth a second fireplace in the dining room that had been hidden behind a piece of 1970s paneling. A new fireplace mantel had been created by the owner of Montauk Woodworks. Billy used reclaimed wood from old fishing trawlers and had done a wonderful job making the second mantel a perfect match to the one in the living room.

Owing to the knowledge that Claire leaned toward minimalist and eco-friendly design, I'd risen to the challenge of decorating Little Grey. In return for my decorating services, I'd been thrilled my payment wouldn't be in cash. Instead, her son-in-law had told me that all the items in the attic, some over a hundred years old, were mine for the taking. What didn't go in my cottage could be stored in Elle's carriage house and used in future Cottages by the Sea projects.

Before she'd moved in, Claire and I had communicated via email about every room in the house. She'd shipped things from her Northern California home that she wanted me to incorporate into Little Grey. Her esthetic, if I could coin it in a few words, would be Natural Coastal Décor—bringing elements from outside inside. She'd loved the storyboards I'd sent her, and when she'd walked in the front door for the first time, she told me it was like coming home. In my opinion, there was no better compliment than that.

The house dated from the end of the nineteenth century, around the same time as the famous Grey Gardens in East Hampton and had the same architect, Joseph Greenleaf Thorpe. The wall between the dining room and living room had been taken down and the wide-plank floorboards sanded. The open layout was simple but had a rustic elegance. Claire had also sent a sofa and love seat on the moving van from California. I'd commissioned new slipcovers in a natural off-white cotton-duck fabric that set off the gleaming wood end tables and coffee table Claire inherited from her parents. They were made by George Nakashima, the famous American woodworker who fashioned pieces of furniture from large slabs of wood. The tables had smooth, polished tops and natural uneven edges. On top of the coffee table Claire had placed a copy of Nakashima's memoir, *The Soul of a Tree*, which talked about the time he was in an internment camp for Japanese-Americans during World War Two, the same place he learned the craft of woodworking. I knew from Elle and her time at Sotheby's that a Nakashima table could sell in the ballpark of thirty to eighty thousand dollars. I also knew, even though Claire barely survived on her small income, she would never consider selling them. Just like I'd never sell anything that had belonged to my mother.

"Come into the kitchen," Claire said, interrupting my thoughts, "I have the kettle on, and a Christmas fruitcake sent from my sister in London for us to devour. I know as a rule most of your younger generation hate fruitcake. But hold your opinion until you taste Melanie's."

"I never met a fruitcake I didn't like. I've been told by my father that when it comes to eating, I'm an old soul. Pot roast, one-dish casseroles, even Welsh rarebit are some of my favorites. As long as I don't have to cook or bake it, I'll eat it. Brussels sprouts excluded."

Claire smiled, then led me through the dining area with its long wooden table and rustic chairs. One thing that hadn't been changed were the Tiffany fruit and grapevine windows near the ceiling. Afternoon light in shades of pale green, mauve, buttercream and violet streamed down on us.

"Sit," she said, "I want to hear everything. I guess there's a disadvantage to not owning a laptop, and I only get nine television channels and rarely watch anything but PBS. My pay-as-you-go phone is all I need, along with the local Montauk newspaper, where I've yet to see any bad news. Even the paper's police blotter is as mild as milquetoast."

That's because you weren't here when I found a skeleton in a bungalow at the Falks' estate, only a mile down the road, I thought. Let Claire keep the illusion that all in the Hamptons is just what it seems. Because for the most part, it was.

Claire had been stunned when I'd shared what had gone down on Shelter Island. "So, are you sure that you and Elle are in the clear?" she'd asked. I told her I was, in a very *un*convincing tone. Then I told her about the police station and meeting the woman from *Bungled* who'd filed a lawsuit against Dr. Blake.

Unlike Claire, I watched television. When I'd returned home from Windy Willows, I'd put on the local Hamptons television channel to find they'd been doing a retrospective on Dr. Blake Nightingale, including that the estate had once been a mental asylum. They'd also shown old black-and-white images of the actresses Arden Hunter and Marian Fortune, along with clips from *Bungled* featuring the woman, Pauline, I'd just met in Southampton. Soon the world would know about the two murders, decades apart. The only thing the news circuit hadn't mentioned was the way Dr. Blake was killed because it hadn't been released.

I sat on a cushioned banquet bench original to Little Grey. It followed the curve of the multipaned bay window with a view of the ocean. Claire brought over an earthenware coffee mug filled with hot water and a lemon slice. She didn't drink coffee or tea, attesting to hot water and lemon's cleansing properties. *Keep it simple* was her answer to most things. A motto I tried to adhere to after moving to Montauk from Manhattan. Besides a few murders here and there, it'd been working.

As I sipped my hot water, I looked around the kitchen. It was barely recognizable from the first time I walked in. Back then it had been a bad 1970s dream with black and silver-foil wallpaper and black appliances. The only thing that had given me hope when thinking of the kitchen's renovation was the large window over the double farm sink, affording Claire a panoramic view of the Atlantic while scouring her potatoes and carrots. Duke and Duke Jr. had installed new kitchen appliances and a butcher-block center island made from recycled wood. They'd also stripped the kitchen cupboards down to their natural grain and had taken off all the cupboard doors, creating open shelving where Claire stored her handmade pottery and dishware she'd been collecting for decades, crafted by Northern California artisans. The shiplap walls were painted a creamy off-white.

"Wow. Double wow," Claire said, handing me a plate with a slice of fruitcake. "I feel sorry for the *Bungled* woman—a testament to the evils of reality TV. What that doctor did to her wasn't right."

"I agree. Speaking of wow. *You're* right, this fruitcake is amazing. I'm sure my dad would love the recipe."

Claire had been invited to Thanksgiving dinner and she and my father had gotten along famously. Claire even got along with my father's wife, Sheila. I still had a few qualms about the woman my father had recently married. I knew she had a good heart, and my father was happy. What more could I ask for? She just wasn't my mother. I owed it to my father to keep my mouth shut if I had any misgivings. Just like he'd done when I'd been engaged to Michael, the cheat. Detective Jeff Barrett always let me make my own decisions, letting me learn from my mistakes. And boy, did I learn from Michael. At the thought of Michael and his wifey, I told Claire about the filming location of the miniseries most likely switching to Windy Willows in Southampton.

Claire didn't see it the same as I did, even though she knew who lived at Windy Willows. She sighed. "What a godsend. Now I don't have to worry about you being in that house of terrors. I doubt you'll see your ex-fiancé or his wife. After all, it is winter."

A few hours ago, when Langston, Elle, Felicity, and I had walked into the foyer of the *Gone with the Wind*–style plantation mansion belonging to the Whitney family, I'd wished I'd brought a sage smudge stick to light so I could clear out the bad mojo. Most of the floor-to-ceiling windows in the first-floor rooms were covered in heavy velvet drapery, making it feel like we'd entered a funeral home. My fingers had itched to yank them open to let in the sun. "It was obvious after going from room to room," I told Claire, "following the director and Windy Willows' housekeeper, that Felicity and her crew would have to bring a semitruck's worth of furniture and décor. There was barely a stick of furniture left in the whole place. The only useful things were the built-ins from the mansion's original floorplans. We didn't go to the third floor, because the housekeeper said that's where the family stayed when they were in the Hamptons."

Claire added more hot water to my cup. "Look on the bright side, you're still part of the crew."

"You're right. Again," I said, grinning.

"The rumors you heard must be true that Whitney Publications is in financial ruin."

"Seems so. The mansion itself has been in the Whitney family for generations, along with the formal gardens that in spring are on the Hamptons Garden Tour. The location will be perfect for filming the miniseries."

"Good, then you'll be away from Nightingale Manor and I won't have to worry or call your dad."

I blew her a kiss, feeling lucky that of all the people who could have moved next door, it had been Claire. I stood and my napkin fell to the floor. I bent to pick it up. When anything fell to the floor from my table, Jo would be there on the ready, acting more like a Fido than a feline. I spied a second napkin under my chair. I grabbed it and noticed it had writing on it. I smoothed it out on the table and read Claire's beautiful script.

Sullen Grace
Joyous Pain
Splintered Calm

"Been looking for this?" I asked, handing the napkin to Claire. "New poem you're working on?" Claire had a penchant for writing lines on whatever surface was nearby. I'd read Emily Dickinson did the same, especially when baking in her Amherst kitchen. She would jot lines down on flour sacks, chocolate wrappers—whatever was handy.

Claire laughed as she glanced down at the napkin. "I don't remember writing this. Must've been during one of my middle-of-the-night trips to the fridge. A little oxymoronic, don't you think?"

"Not at all. It makes me think. Like all the carefully chosen words you use in your poetry. 'Splintered Calm' really hits home after the past couple days." Claire's wrinkled napkin reminded me of the paper I'd picked up at the police station after poor bungled

Pauline had dropped it. I hadn't had time to take a photo of it. However, after she'd driven away, I did write down the few key pieces of information I'd seen on it: her address on Lily Pond Lane in East Hampton and the name and address on the paper, a boutique hotel in Chelsea, the Riverside Hotel and Spa. It proved she'd stayed there Wednesday and Thursday, giving her an alibi for Blake Nightingale's time of death.

I stored away my questions for when I could talk to my ex-cop father. Then I realized he'd already hit the tracks, as in Am*trak*, on a luxury holiday excursion from Chicago to Colorado Springs to see his wife's relatives. Since he was a retired homicide detective, I'd told him if there were any *Murder on the Orient Express*-type shenanigans on board I was sure he'd be able to take care of them. Based on my past since I'd moved to Montauk, he'd told me he was more concerned about what trouble I might get into while he was gone. If he only knew the half of it—really a quarter of it . . .

"I can tell you're thinking about the murder," Claire said, placing her hands on her thin dancer's hips. I have the perfect remedy." She went to the kitchen drawer to the left of the sink and opened it. Then she pulled out a skeleton key tied with a faded green satin ribbon and waved it in the air.

"You're right, Claire Post! Time to start filling my cottage with a few trinkets from the attic and unpack the boxes in the extra bedroom. And I need to send a text to Duke Senior." I took out my phone and texted:

Time to go to my storage space and bring in the furniture and carpets. I'm ready to make my nest. Let's try to do it before the next blizzard. Dinner at Pondfare for you and Jr. as an extra bonus. Text me in the morning. XO, Meg

"That's my girl," Claire said with a huge grin.

• • •

Two hours later, I placed the fourth box from Little Grey's attic in the center of my great room. I'd been very selective, although it had been extremely hard to leave the rest behind. I knew the first rule of interior design: Don't junk it up! Actually, it was more like what William Morris, the great twentieth-century leader of the Arts and

Crafts movement, once said, "Have nothing in your house that you do not know to be useful or believe to be beautiful." I'd been designing the interior of my bungalow for what seemed like forever and I had storyboards, magazine clippings and a large-vision journal to prove it. The ocean vista and my gardens outside needed to meld with the choices I made on the interior. Editing was going to be a problem.

After feeding Jo her dinner, I put on my jacket and faux-fur-lined boots and went out to the design office I'd set up in the glass summerhouse designed by Little Grey's architect. In his original renderings that Elle and I found in a closet in a bedroom at Little Grey, Thorpe had called my summerhouse a folly. When I'd looked up the definition of a folly I found it was a structure built only for garden ornamentation that didn't serve a practical purpose. Not the case for me. I not only used my folly as an interior design office but also as a great off-the-grid place to hide out.

Not needing a flashlight because of the full moon, I followed a path behind my walled garden through a dense thicket of trees. Looking ahead I saw the small lamp by my drafting table glowing behind frosted panes of glass. Relief set in. I hadn't lost power during Wednesday's blizzard, which meant the oil heater was also working. I extracted the key from under the Chinese cement cricket outside the double glass doors and entered.

Each time I walked in, I smiled.

Buried behind junglelike vegetation, I'd stumbled upon the summerhouse two Aprils ago when I'd first found out the Eberhardt property was for sale. Its broken panes of glass in the roof and walls hadn't dissuaded me from the vision of its future metamorphosis. In the warmer months, I'd even spent time living in the summerhouse before my cottage got zoning approval. I had a penchant for small, cozy spaces, which was one of the reasons I decided to decorate small cottages in the area, not mega estates.

I'd furnished the summerhouse's interior with items I'd found at local garage sales or on the side of the road. There was no better place to go trash pickin' than the land of the Hamptons rich and famous during spring clean-out. My drafting table had been rescued curbside; all I'd had to do was buy a heavy-duty bolt from Hank's Hardware to secure the tilted top and make it as good as old. The bar stool I used to sit at the desk came from my favorite Montauk eatery, Mickey's Chowder Shack. It had been tossed outside, collateral after a bar fight between a pair of feuding fishermen too drunk to know what they were arguing about. All it had needed was a little wood glue.

I went to the stack of storyboards stored inside a wooden wardrobe that Elle and I'd found at a flea market in Southampton and extracted one. I also grabbed the completed storyboard for my cottage and the nine-by-twelve artist's portfolio from a basket on the floor filled with pages torn from home and garden magazines — one of my addictions, and an expensive one at that — drawn-to-scale renderings of furniture for each of my cottage's seven rooms, plus photos printed off my laptop from numerous décor blogs and websites, along with photos taken at past Hamptons designer showcases. I was a bit obsessive when it came to home décor. I put everything in a wheeled collapsible grocery cart.

On my way out, I passed a makeshift table I'd constructed from a salvaged hardwood door that I'd placed on sawhorse legs. Topping the table were an assortment of herbs crowning from vintage coffee tins and teal-glass Ball jars. Three pendulum, hard-hat grow lights hung from the glass ceiling — a little green to brighten up the winter landscape. Even though I was a terrible cook, I loved gardening and used my herbs to elevate my frozen or boxed meals to a palatable level. Foodwise, the winters were the toughest for me because Montauk Melissa's gourmet food truck, which always parked at Montauk's surfing beach, Ditch Plains, had closed for the months of December and January. I'd upgraded my indoor garden from last year to include different lettuces, arugula being one of my favorites with its distinctive peppery taste. I wasn't a chip off the old block, like my father when it came to gourmet cooking. I had yet to redeem the birthday gift my father had talked my friend into giving me: cooking lessons from Pierre Patou, the chef at Montauk's Pondfare. Maybe if I stalled long enough, the certificate would expire. My idea for a good recipe was like the one I used to make my tinted furniture stains: mix water and acrylic paint at a two-to-one ratio, brush the mixture on a sanded-wood surface, pat the surface with a paper towel to let the grain show through, dry it completely, then seal with a paste finishing wax.

After I checked the timer for the heater and lamp, I locked up, remembering to put the key under the cricket. As I wheeled the cart, I sang, "I'm dreaming of a White Christmas," realizing it was time to pick out a tree. I could smell the scent of pine already. All thoughts of murder at an old asylum on a secluded island faded with the thought of my first Christmas in my very own cottage, on my very own land.

When I opened the cottage's door, Jo was waiting in front of the fire with a sly look on her face. I left the cart on the porch and transported everything inside, leaning the two storyboards against the chair. I closed the door and put my hands on my hips, surveying the room. Sure enough, next to my knitting basket was the armless rag doll. I didn't think she could look more forlorn than she had before. But I was wrong. Josephine the Great had gone after what little yarn hair was left on top of the doll's head, leaving gashes in the thin cotton fabric. "No! No! Bad girl!" I said in a loud tone, then remembered the magazine article I'd read in the police station on disciplining your wayward children without using the word *no*. I had a feeling Jo was a lost cause as I watched her stretch and yawn. She always ended her yawns with a little squeak that I only heard when wearing my hearing aids. Then she curled in a ball on the rug in front of the hearth, her tail snapping a warning for me to back off.

"Fine, be that way. Stay there. I'm the boss and get the chair to myself tonight."

She didn't twitch an ear. I went to the kitchen, got a stack of four-by-six index cards, a marker and some cat treats from the cupboard. When I turned, Jo was sitting on my chair, sphinx-style. I anticipated her stealth move. "Vamoose!" I tossed the treats onto the carpet. Jo *cat*apulted off the chair, fur floating in her wake.

I quickly took a seat, brought the blank storyboard and a folding chair and leaned the board against the chair. Then I wrote down all the suspects for Blake Nightingale's murder on the blank index cards. I put Dr. Blake's name on the card in the center. If I'd been decorating an interior room for one of my cottages, the name of the room would go in the middle. I added Sabrina, Willa, Langston and Dr. Blake's partner, Dr. Lewis. Now that I'd met her, also Pauline. Then I jotted down what I knew about each and tacked the matching card under my suspect's name.

Sabrina Nightingale: Dr. Blake's wife. Having affair with Dr. Blake's partner? Assume because no children she inherits, and claims not to have signed a prenuptial agreement. Try to ask Detective Shoner.

Willa Sullivan: housekeeper/nurse, not happy with Dr. Blake before his death or Sabrina, his wife. Her son lived at Nightingale Manor until recently. Saw her and Dr. Blake's partner in a passionate embrace.

Langston Reed: director of Mr. & Mrs. Winslow, *lied about knowing about the old murder and the fact the estate was a sanitorium, had verbal altercation with deceased before murder.*

Dr. Greg Lewis: Dr. Blake's partner, upset malpractice insurance wasn't paid. Having affair with both Willa and Sabrina?

Pauline (find out her last name): Received botched cosmetic surgery performed by Dr. Blake on television show Bungled. *Is suing the practice. Seems to have alibi. Was staying at a hotel in Manhattan at the time of murder.*

The Invisible Man or Woman: Revenge on the doctor for something he did, and also knew about Nightingale Manor's past murder from the fifties. Left through the door leading out of the basement. NOT LIKELY.

Something to do with blackmail, like Dr. Blake mouthed to his wife on the ferry?

Before heading up to bed, I glanced at the names on the board, wondering if I shouldn't have added Marian Fortune's ghost on a card. "Jo, I think I'm losing it. Let's go up, I don't even want dinner."

At the word *dinner*, I got her attention. She'd already eaten but was always ready for seconds. When I'd first rescued her, she had a routine of sitting at the dinner table for her evening meal. All that changed when we moved into the new cottage. I hadn't minded her company at the evening meal, but my father's wife hadn't been too keen on having a cat at the Thanksgiving table, good manners or not.

I went to the cupboard and got out some peanut butter and put three spoonfuls in a small bowl then added some Sanders fudge on top. I figured the peanut butter's protein would keep my stomach from growling and the fudge, sent by my father in my quarterly Detroit care package, which also included Vernors ginger ale and Win Schuler's horseradish cheese spread and garlic bar chips, would just make it yummy. Then the two of us trudged up to the bedroom. It had been a long day.

I placed the bowl of peanut butter on the crate that I used as a nightstand, waited until Jo plopped down on her side of the bed, gave her a few treats, ate my peanut butter fudge mixture, then went to the small bathroom, where I washed up and brushed my teeth. After changing into an oversized NYU T-shirt, I climbed in next to her, closed my eyes, did my nightly gratitude list and dropped off to sleep.

I woke at two in the morning. Jo didn't budge when I left the warm bed. I grabbed my thick fleece robe and slipped it on. Then I crept barefoot downstairs, my toes popsicles on the cold wood steps.

Something had been bothering me and I knew the only way to calm my nerves was to go down to the beach and take solace in the ebb and flow of the serene waves. I needed to clear my head with a blast of icy salt air. I stepped into my boots, grabbed a flashlight, then went out the French doors to the deck. Pausing at the landing at the top of the steps, it hit me. Arden Hunter's and Blake Nightingale's deaths must somehow be related because of the empty suitcase in the attic with Arden Hunter's luggage tag. It hadn't been opened before Dr. Blake's murder because I'd looked inside the closet before taking the cursed elevator. Whoever took the contents had to have done it in the time between when we'd gotten trapped in the elevator and when I'd gone back to retrieve Elle's phone. None of the other suitcases were emptied.

The only problem was, who had it been? And why?

Chapter 18

Saturday, late morning snow twirled down on us in light fluffy flakes.

"Arthur, this is the one," Elle said excitedly. "Cut it down. Cut it down," she chanted.

Detective Arthur Shoner wore a Burberry overcoat, cashmere scarf and kid leather gloves. Rubber Totes covered what I'd guessed were either his black or cordovan Gucci loafers.

"Elle, are you sure?" His forced Grinch smile might fool Elle, but I could tell by the way he gripped the handsaw he wasn't in the holiday spirit. I knew he would rather be sipping a scotch and soda, his feet warmed by the fire at Southampton's farm-to-table restaurant, Home and Hearth. As would I. Instead of scotch and soda, though, I'd prefer hot chocolate. If Elle didn't choose a tree soon, the lunch hour would be over by the time we got there.

"Of course I'm sure, Arthur Theodore Shoner," Elle said indignantly.

I raised an eyebrow. "Theodore?"

He didn't answer, just gave me one of his penetrating gazes. His large dark brown eyes under lush brows had a way of seeing through you, making him a good detective, but not always an ally. Even if his fiancée was my best friend. Admittedly, there were mitigating circumstances in our relationship, owing to his skewed perspective. In his mind, I was always butting in to his murder investigations. I saw it as helping find a few killers here and there before another murder transpired — namely, mine. It was a double-edged sword that he had no authority in Blake Nightingale's death because the murder fell under Southampton's jurisdiction, not East Hampton's. It still wouldn't stop me from "butting in" to whatever he was privy to.

"Elle, this is the fifth one you've chosen then changed your mind on," he said, obviously at the end of his patience level. "Speak now, or forever hold your peace."

"It's perfect, Arthur!" Elle cooed. "I'm sure. This one is it."

He rolled his eyes, winked at me, then crouched in front of the seven-foot Douglas fir. I had ulterior motives for hurrying our tree odyssey along. I looked forward to picking his brain over lunch. If he wouldn't share anything, I'd enlist Elle to find out what she could on her side.

The temperature was in the mid-forties. I unzipped my down jacket, removed my scarf and put it in my pocket. "Can we get on with it? I'm cold and hungry," I whined. "I'm not fun to be with when I'm cold and hungry." I wasn't really cold, but I was hungry and wanted to tug at Elle's nurturing heartstrings.

So far, Elle's tree had passed the smell test, the full-branch test, and the perfect-height test. I'd found my perfectly *imperfect* tree three minutes after the tractor pulling our wagon dropped us at the edge of the tree farm. I had a penchant for choosing trees no one else wanted. My father coined them my "Charlie Brown" trees. Last year, Jo had destroyed my Charlie Brown tree, knocking it down every time I set it up. That was until I had the brilliant idea of getting Jo her own tree. I'd found a fake one, unopened, still in its box, at a recent estate sale for only five bucks. I planned putting Jo's tree on my screened porch, hanging assorted catnip-stuffed toys from the branches and spraying it with pine air freshener. Then I would release the beast and let her go to town. Hopefully, she'd leave my tree alone.

"Okay, Elle. Here we go," he said.

Finally.

"Stop-p-p-p!" Elle screeched. "I see a nest."

Sure enough, near the top of the tree was a birds' nest.

"I'm sure those birds have long since flown the coop," he grumbled. "Ms. Barrett found her tree as soon as we stepped off the wagon. Once you put all your junk on it, you won't even notice a tree underneath."

"Junk?" she asked, visibly miffed.

Oh, boy.

Elle's cheeks flushed pink, along with the tip of her ears where they were sticking out behind vintage faux-fur earmuffs. "I'll have you know my collection of German glass ornaments was featured more than once in top home and garden magazines." She stuck out her bottom lip.

He left the saw on the ground and came to her, then pulled her into his arms. While they cuddled, I went to the tree and gently lowered the branch with the nest, peeking inside. "No eggs."

"Even so, I can't take this tree. They'll be back in the spring, their home destroyed, and I'll be to blame," Elle said, stepping next to me.

I tapped her on the shoulder. "Look behind you." An overloaded wagonful of tree shoppers dressed in Santa hats and garish holiday sweaters were coming toward us caroling, "Oh Christmas Tree." It felt like we were on the set of *It's a Wonderful Life*.

Thinking of movie sets, I nudged Elle. "Heard anything more from Felicity?" Elle had called last night about the decision to go ahead with filming *Mr. & Mrs. Winslow* at Windy Willows. She'd also told me there was a good chance they'd be using items from Nightingale Manor for the interior.

"All I know is, I don't plan on going back to Nightingale Manor anytime soon," Elle said, a stubborn set to her jaw.

"I wouldn't mind going back, but after they arrest Dr. Blake Nightingale's killer. I'm still banking on it being one of the four not in the elevator with us."

Elle's head snapped in my direction. "I assumed Felicity would go alone, make her choices, then send them on to Southampton. Our job would be to inventory as we unpacked the boxes. I would like to eliminate Langston Reed as a suspect. You do realize we'll be working with him at Windy Willows and he's one of your four." Her brow furrowed, and she looked up at the nest.

Detective Shoner advanced toward us. He said, "Sooo, Elle, what's it gonna be? This tree?"

"Yes, Elle. My stomach is growling," I said. "Remember, for every tree you cut down they plant another. Look over there." I pointed to a section of land where baby trees grew in neat rows." The tractor pulling the wagon stopped three trees down from us. I picked up the saw and handed it to Detective Shoner. "Elle, you better make a decision on this tree before someone else snaps it from under your pert little freckled nose."

Elle scurried up to her fiancé. "Hurry, someone might steal my tree. Cut it down, Arthur! Cut it down!"

• • •

Thirty minutes later we arrived at Home and Hearth. It was one of those rare restaurants where when you walked inside you felt transported to another age. On either side of the dining room were two fireplaces. The smell from the burning white birch logs brought back memories of Michigan in the winter. Each Christmas my parents and I would travel four hours Up North to my grandfather's house in Traverse City. There'd be snowmobiling and ice skating, then, following a meal of Great-aunt Helga's schnitzel and noodles, we'd gather around the long wood table in the formal dining room for a game of Michigan Rummy, a combination of poker and rummy played on a colorful game board the size and thickness of a plastic tablecloth. Grandpa called the room the formal dining room but there was nothing formal about it, especially when all my aunts, uncles, and cousins gathered around. Under the table, my grandpa's schnauzer Heidi would bite our ankles whenever we moved. We never thought of putting Heidi in another room. She ruled the underworld and we'd better keep our stomping feet in check. I smiled inwardly at the memory.

Home and Hearth co-owner Molly Stevenson came toward us, menus in hand. She greeted us with a bright, cheery smile. Her gray hair was in a long braid down her back, her pale gray eyes sparkling in recognition when they met mine. Even though she was in her late sixties or early seventies Molly's skin glowed with youth. Last fall, when we'd manned the silent auction table at a benefit for Harvest for the Hungry, she'd shared the history of her family-run restaurant. Home and Hearth had been farm-to-table way before it came into vogue. Like many of the early Hamptons settlers, the Stevensons had once been potato farmers. When half of their land was sold to developers they bought the restaurant in Southampton and continued to grow their own food. From a fruit, vegetable, dairy and egg standpoint they were completely self-sustainable.

"Meg, so good to see you. I have a perfect table for you between the hearth and the tree. Come this way." The rich wide-plank wood floors gleamed in the firelight. Even though it was early afternoon, the sky outside was dark and light snow was falling at a steady pace, making me feel cocooned and warm, happy to be inside. Sprigs of pine tied with raffia hung from exposed wood pillars. The restaurant's walls were adorned with handloomed rugs and shelves of pottery made by artisans from the nearby Shinnecock Native American Reservation. The Shinnecock tribe had been in

Southampton for generations and were very active in the Southampton community.

We embraced, and I introduced her to Elle and Detective Shoner, then she led us through the crowded dining room. Keeping to the organic theme of the restaurant, I saw that their Christmas trees were alive, resting in huge clay pots, ready for replanting in the spring. They were simply decorated with hanging pinecones, stringed cranberries and popcorn. After we sat, she handed out menus with the day's specials. The menu changed from day to day. Creamy corn and butternut squash chowder in a bread bowl was the first special listed. I needed to look no further.

After we ordered I tried to think of the best possible way to bring up the Nightingale investigation to Detective Shoner without sounding nosy. I opened my mouth to speak, but Elle beat me to it. "Arthur has something he wants to tell you. I can't." Her eyes watered, and she looked away. So, this was the thing making her so melancholy. I reached over and grabbed her hand, then looked at Detective Shoner.

He cleared his throat and said, "I've been offered a promotion."

"Well, that's great." I looked at Elle. "Isn't it?"

She sniffled. "Tell her where, Arthur."

"Okay, I give. Where?"

"Manhattan," he answered.

"And that's bad? Why?"

Elle snatched her hand away from mine. "Because when we get married, we'd have to move."

"I could think of worse places."

"I can't leave Mabel and Elle's. I can't leave Sag Harbor. I can't leave Maurice. And I most certainly can't leave you, Megan Elizabeth Barrett."

"I'm so relieved."

Elle gave me a questioning look.

"I'm relieved. From the way you've been acting, I thought you or your detective fiancé had a terminal disease or something."

"Might as well have," Detective Shoner said, shaking his head.

"Now, hold on a minute. I'm not making you choose me or Manhattan," Elle said, putting her napkin to the corner of her leaking eye. "I support your promotion, it's just . . ."

"I told her I can come here on the weekends. My job is as a liaison between the press and the DA's office. Monday through Friday."

I felt like I was the mediator in a divorce hearing; one looked at the other, then back at me, waiting for me to proffer my solution. "I'm sure you'll work it out. Manhattan's only a hop skip and a jump away."

"Yeah, off-season," Elle said, her cheeks flushing under her freckles, making them stand out even more on her makeup-less face. "In the summer it'll take him six hours to get to Sag Harbor."

"It's not set in stone. Ms. Barrett is right. We'll work it out," he said.

That was the first time he'd ever said I was right. Even though I had been numerous times in the past. Much to the dismay of his male ego.

Molly came toward us carrying a tray. Saved by the food.

She placed my chowder in front of me and I took my open palms and fanned the aromatic steam wafting off the bread bowl closer to my nose and inhaled. "Thanks, Moll. Smells heavenly." I took my spoon and dipped just the tip of it in, then brought it to my mouth and blew. Then I swallowed.

Molly looked on, holding her breath.

"Curry," I said. "Delish. That was a nice surprise. Love the sweet and savory components."

"Bingo! It is curry. You sound like your father. I guess you wouldn't be surprised whose suggestion the curry was?"

"Hmmm."

"Your father. He was in last fall and told me he loved the recipe and suggested a touch of curry. He was right. It really elevates it to another level."

My foodie snob father, I thought. I stuck my spoon in the thick chowder again and took a large spoonful. "Amazing. I hope he didn't insult you with his suggestion?"

Molly laughed. "Are you kidding? Every time it goes on the menu it's our best seller." She glanced at Elle and Detective Shoner, who'd also ordered the soup.

Molly put her hands on her hips and smiled. "Will your father be here for Christmas?"

"No, he's going to Colorado to visit Sheila's family."

"Well, if you talk to him, ask if he made the last recipe I emailed him. We've become foodie pen pals."

"Promise."

A server came up to Molly and whispered something in her ear. "Small emergency," she said to us. "Seems we have at least three a day." She gave me a quick peck on the cheek and said, "Enjoy, everyone."

"Oh, we will," Elle said, dabbing the corner of her mouth with a colorful handwoven napkin also made by the Shinnecock tribe. Detective Shoner gave Molly a thumbs-up, his mouth full of chowder. Then Molly followed the harried server toward the kitchen.

After we finished our soup, Molly sent over a plate of eggnog fudge. Two minutes later, not a morsel remained.

"I can't believe I've never been here before. I'll sure be back soon, Ms. Barrett," Detective Shoner said.

I figured it was now or never to take advantage of everyone's lifted spirits. "So-o-o, Detective Shoner, how's the Nightingale investigation going? Have they arrested anyone yet?"

"That's it!" Elle said, clanking her spoon against her apple-green earthenware mug filled with cocoa. The next table looked over. She lowered her voice, but her brown eyes blazed. "I insist from here on out, you call Arthur, Arthur. And you," she said, turning her head, "call Meg Meg. Not Ms. Barrett."

"Okay. Okay," we said at the same time.

I threw up my hands in surrender. "It'll be tough, but I'll really try. If we're on a first-name basis, Arthur, does that mean I'm privy to what you know about the murder? After all, if we do have to go back to Nightingale Manor we should know who's in the PD's crosshairs."

His neck turned red, then the rosy hue traveled up to his cheeks.

I guessed I hadn't handled that too well. "Okay, before you get angry, here are a few points about what makes this case different than the others Elle and I have been involved in. We have no connection to Nightingale Manor or Dr. Blake. With the exception of Langston Reed, I'd never met any of our suspects before going to Shelter Island." Before he could respond, I hurried on. "I brought with me a list of things that need to be looked into. I have a copy for you, Det . . . Arthur." I handed one over and Elle leaned in to read over his shoulder.

I looked down at my copy. I hadn't written it as a ploy to overstep the competent job of the police, I actually sat for an hour in front of my laptop, wanting to get all my questions on paper so I could relinquish them and let them go to the powers that be. I knew if I didn't share all my what-ifs, I'd lie awake night after night worrying someone else might die and I could have done something to prevent it. Plus, I felt in my bones that the old murder was somehow related to the new.

1. Is Sabrina Dr. Blake's sole heir in the will? They had no children. When a newspaper reporter trapped her inside Southampton's Beauty Bar, Dr. Greg Lewis came to her rescue and she supposedly swooned into his outstretched arms.

2. Why did Langston Reed lie about knowing about the old murder of Arden Hunter? What was he looking for in Blake's office's filing cabinets when Dr. Blake confronted him?

3. What did Willa have against Dr. Blake? He let her son live with them until Sabrina made him leave. Dr. Blake blamed her for not paying the malpractice insurance. She and Sabrina had fought. Sabrina accused Willa of having an affair with Dr. Blake that Willa didn't dispute.

4. Dr. Greg Lewis was overheard threatening Dr. Blake on Wednesday after Dr. Blake threatened him. He was found embracing the Nightingale's housekeeper, Willa. He also came to the rescue of Dr. Blake's wife, Sabrina. What happens to the practice following Dr. Blake's death?

5. Pauline, no last name, the person suing Dr. Blake for her botched cosmetic surgery, seems to have an alibi for Dr. Blake's death. She also has Justin Margulies as her attorney, so she must've had a good case against him. Was she suing the practice, the show, or Dr. Blake himself?

Random questions: Does Arden Hunter's murder have anything to do with Blake Nightingale's death? What about the tickets in the rag doll and the suitcases that were opened in the attic during the time of Blake's murder, plus the letter between the floorboards — any bearing on the modern-day murder? And the cause of death? The ice pick, or was he drugged first? Why would he lay on the hospital bed if not incapacitated — did the wound cause his death? And why were the lights on in one of the rooms at the gatehouse when I went to the attic to retrieve Elle's phone after the power returned?

Was time of death around 2 a.m., when we heard the howling in the elevator?

When Arthur looked up from the page he said, "Was your dad giving you inside info on the case? And what's all this business about a note and suitcases? Elle told me about the tickets in the doll. I still don't see how it would have anything to do with the murder of Dr. Blake Nightingale.

I told him no, my father hadn't given me any info. Then I explained about the tickets, the suitcases, and the argument between Langston and Dr. Blake. Too late, I realized by Elle's wide-eyed stare, I should have taken the detective aside to have him read my musings.

After taking it all in, he folded the paper and put it in his jacket pocket. Then he threw down his credit card and said, "Lunch is on me, ladies."

"That's it? That's all you have to say? I think it would be nice if you could clear up anything you know, or any suspect we can eliminate."

"We, Meg Barrett?" Elle scolded. "Let Arthur and the Southampton PD, along with Suffolk County, handle things. It has nothing to do with us. You did a good job with your list and turning in the pen to the Southampton PD. Let it rest and we'll get on with doing things we love. Like furnishing your cottage tomorrow so you can decorate for Christmas."

Elle was right. Tomorrow morning, Duke and Duke Jr. were

scheduled to bring everything from my storage locker to the cottage. I would let go of everything and everyone on the list with one exception. Langston Reed. I didn't cotton to working with a killer no matter what the perks. Instead of one day at a time, I thought, eliminate one suspect at a time. Once he was in the clear, I would breathe easier about working at Windy Willows.

"But Elle, you just told me this morning that there's a chance we might have to go back to Nightingale Manor. I'd feel more comfortable going back if I knew what the cops are thinking."

Elle turned to her fiancé. "She does have a point."

Concern clouded his eyes. "I'll be candid with the two of you. They have no top suspect, it's too early. Southampton PD is following an angle of a homeless person who for the past couple of years has been sneaking inside boarded-up homes on Shelter Island during the winter. The handyman from Sylvester Manor saw him in the woods the day Mr. Nightingale was murdered. I don't think he's our man, though. Last year he left a note to the homeowners thanking them for letting him stay. The guy always includes a couple hundred-dollar bills along with the note. Other than that, everything's in the preliminary stages. And I can tell you the coroner confirms time of death around two in the morning." He looked at me.

I thought back to when Langston told us that when he was at the Southampton station he'd overheard there was a new lead. The wealthy vagrant must have been that lead.

Our waitperson came over and presented the check. Arthur grabbed it. He said, "I appreciate your intel, Meg. I promise to take it very seriously and follow up on every detail. Even the old murder. If the two of you do go back to the estate, I'll send an officer with you. Elle's safety is my utmost concern."

"What about the coroner's report? Anything unusual?" I asked, trying to keep the open lines of communication flowing.

"Nothing, except the wound to the chest."

"How about the doctor's will? Is Sabrina his heir?"

He wouldn't make eye contact.

"Raise your eyebrow if I'm right?"

He did.

"And how about Willa's son? How old is he?"

He turned to Elle and said, "We should get *eighteen* of those chowders to go."

I liked playing this game. Willa's son was eighteen. I didn't want to push my luck with any more questions after he gave me one of his old "stay out of police business" looks. I wanted to say, how would a homeless person know enough about the old murder to strap Dr. Blake to a bed and kill him with an ice pick to the heart? I opened my mouth then closed it.

Don't push it, Meg Barrett. Don't push it!

Chapter 19

I left my Woody, with my rescued tree tied to the roof, parked in front of Home and Hearth, and strolled over to Main Street. Snow was falling but it was the kind of snow I welcomed: fluffy and light, the flakes so large I could almost make out their individual patterns. Elle and *Arthur* had left for Sag Harbor to put Elle's tree in water, and I decided to do some peace-of-mind sleuthing.

Yesterday on my way to Beauty Bar, I'd passed Southampton Aesthetics, the former practice of Dr. Blake Nightingale and the current practice of Dr. Greg Lewis. I was curious about Dr. Lewis's part in the practice. Wondering why he always seemed to be in the background on *Bungled*. Was he playing both Willa and Sabrina? And if so, why? I hadn't been privy to Dr. Blake's will, and probably wouldn't be. Even with the malpractice lawsuit and loss of revenue from *Bungled,* I'd venture a guess the fifteen-plus acres that made up the Nightingale estate would sell in the double-digit millions. But where would that leave Dr. Lewis? If Sabrina was the only heir, that might give Dr. Lewis a reason to comfort her in her time of need. Willa, on the other hand, might just be an old friend. That was doubtful seeing the way I'd found them locked in each other's arms. More like friends with benefits? And there was always the possibility Dr. Lewis was just a really great guy, like everyone kept telling me.

I approached the office. Over the door, a tasteful white wood sign, etched with gold script, read *Southampton Aesthetics.* The white clapboard shop on Main Street looked like the others surrounding it, as if it had been part of Southampton since it was established in 1640, when a Shinnecock Native American guide led a group of colonists to the perfect spot for a settlement. Southampton was the oldest and largest Hampton but didn't become a summer destination for wealthy New Yorkers until the 1860s, when a doctor from Manhattan turned his wealthy friends onto the beauty and restorative nature of the unspoiled terrain.

I neared the door just as it was flung open from the inside. One step closer and I would've been knocked to the sidewalk and needed my own plastic surgery. Willa! I turned my head so she wouldn't see me, but not before noticing her red face and clenched fists as she strode away, her short legs moving quickly toward an old Volvo station wagon. I waited until she was inside the car. Not once did she look my way. I hurried inside and entered a posh, elegantly decorated waiting room. An empty waiting room. With the murder all over the headlines, I wasn't surprised. Near the end of the room was a small window. I expected a receptionist to be sitting on the other side, but no one was there. I walked over to the ledge in front of the window. It was filled with beauty brochures promising the fountain of youth. It was amazing how many options there were. I swiped one of the pamphlets just as a young five-foot-eleven amazon with perfect cheekbones and rich ebony skin came into view.

She slid open half of the window and said in a posh English accent, "My apologies, love. Have you been waiting long?"

"No," I answered, realizing I wasn't really dressed like one of Southampton Aesthetics' usual patrons. I zipped my jacket to my neck to hide my favorite flannel shirt, washed about a billion times and about a billion years old.

The young woman didn't seem to notice. Her eyes hadn't met mine and her left hand was fidgeting with a letter opener, turning it over and over until I wanted to reach inside and wrench it out of her hands. The potential weapon in her hand reminded me of why I'd stepped inside; I wanted to talk or at least learn a little more about Dr. Lewis.

Almost a minute passed until she looked up. Her eyes were filled with tears and her lower, perfect lip was trembling. "I'm so sorry, I just got some really bad news."

I grabbed a few tissues from a box on the ledge and handed them to her.

She took them and blew her perfect nose, which had a tiny diamond stud on the left side. "He can't do that. Can he?" Somehow, she'd lost her English accent.

"Do what?" I asked gently, handing her another tissue.

"Shut down the office until he finds another partner. Dr. Blake promised me new cheekbone implants." Her voice took on a whiny tone. "Now I'll never make it to Milan."

"Isn't there another doctor here who could do it?"

She sniffled. "That old goat." She looked over her shoulder. "That's why he's closing the office until he can find another partner. His hands shake so much he can't even do a Botox inject—" She caught herself and finally looked me in the eyes and sat up straighter. "Did you want to make an appointment for a consultation? Just so you know, there's a fee for the consultation and the doctor doesn't take insurance."

"You just said they were closing the office."

"I didn't say that. It's temporary. I'm supposed to start booking for April."

Was I in a parallel universe? "Um, sure. Is there any way he could give me a quick consult? If I feel confident in his suggestions, I'll wait until spring for my procedure." I held up the brochure. "I want to do this." I had no idea what *this* was because I'd picked it up randomly.

She looked at it and said in a snotty tone, "Just come back in the spring."

All compassion I felt after her recent crying jag vanished. I didn't appreciate her condescending attitude. It felt like I was in the Beverly Hills boutique Julia Roberts's character walks into in the movie *Pretty Woman*. But I kept it together. "Can't you just ask if I could have just a few minutes with the doctor? Don't you think he would appreciate you trying to get business scheduled for when you come back to work. He'll think you're indispensable."

"He's with someone. Now, be on your way. I have to call my agent. I'm not waiting around 'til April, especially after the murder and the fact I haven't been paid for the entire month of November or this month, either."

"Oh, so you don't need references? Okay, fine. I'll leave."

She looked torn. She put down her phone. "Don't move, I'll see if he's free."

I waited, looking at the art on the walls, all impressionistic in soothing beach colors. There was one spot where a large picture was missing. I would probably find it for sale in one of the art galleries in Bridgehampton.

She came back to her chair, sat, then glowered at me. Instead of filling me in, she picked up her phone and made a call.

I remained seated until she hung up, then I went to the window. "Well?"

"Well, what?"

"Can he see me?"

"No, I told you, he's with someone."

"Okay, I'll leave." I shifted from one foot to the other. "But do you mind if I use the, uh-h, potty?"

Potty? What was I, three?

She looked at me like she wanted me to prove I needed the bathroom. "Third door on your right," she said grudgingly, then picked up her phone again. The door buzzed. It seemed strange to be buzzed into a doctor's office like it was a high-security prison.

There were voices coming from the end of the hallway. The receptionist told me the third door on the right was the bathroom, and that left two other doors I could peek into. It was becoming a pattern, me faking the need to use the bathroom. It hadn't worked the first time at Nightingale Manor, I hoped it would this time.

The first door I passed was open. It looked to be an upscale version of a doctor's examination room. The second door was closed. I quickly turned the knob and slid inside, making sure to close the door silently. Dim light came through a small window near the ceiling. I went to a large glass desk and turned on a small lamp. *Pay dirt!* I was in the deceased doctor's office. Five framed photos of Sabrina were arranged on his desk. That was my first clue. Another clue was a line of photos on a shelf behind the desk. They showed Dr. Blake arm in arm with famous celebrities and politicians. I had no idea what I was looking for. A threatening letter exposing a blackmailer? A datebook? I riffled through the drawers, knowing datebooks were an archaic tool because most people used their phones to store appointments. Plus, I still saw black fingerprint dust on the front of the drawers and top of the desk, meaning if there had been anything, the police would have found it. There was a photo of Sabrina and Dr. Blake on the steps leading up to Nightingale Manor. I took it down. The grounds surrounding them were amassed with hydrangeas, azaleas and lilac bushes bursting with vibrant spring color. Something was different about Sabrina. I realized what it was: she looked ten years older than she did now. Maybe I should consider getting some work done. After all, age thirty-four was approaching. Sabrina's hand was grasping her husband's forearm and she had a grimace on her face. Maybe that's why she looked older? I followed her gaze and spotted a teenage boy in the woods where one of the dogs had found the rag doll. I quickly swiped the photo from the frame and stuck it in my back pocket. I had a theory the boy was Willa's son.

As I went to stick the frame back on the shelf, I heard voices coming through the radiator on the south wall of the office. I crept closer, reached in my bag and put my hearing aids up to full volume. One quiet, unassuming voice definitely belonged to Dr. Lewis. The other voice sounded familiar, but I couldn't figure out who was talking.

"I don't see how the lawsuit has anything to do with my partner's death?" Dr. Lewis said.

"We've ruled out the patient suing the practice as having killed Dr. Nightingale, however we learned something interesting from her," the other baritone voice said.

I leaned in closer, scorching the tip of my right ear on the radiator. Covering my mouth, I stifled my whimper.

The other voice continued, "It seems that it was you, Dr. Lewis, who she remembers seeing wearing a surgical mask when she came out of surgery. We also know from the woman's lawyer that you've recently been diagnosed with a condition that precludes you from performing surgery. Did you kill your partner because he planned on telling the world about the surgery? A source told us your malpractice insurance wasn't paid up. You would be ruined either way. I would say that's a pretty strong motive for murder."

Dr. Lewis didn't answer. After a few seconds of waiting, I got up from my crouched position. Still holding the pictureless frame, I went back to the shelf and shoved it behind a photo of Dr. Blake and former First Lady Hilary Clinton. The frame tipped sideways, starting a domino effect. Two of the pictures flew off the shelf, hit the corner of the filing cabinet and crashed to the floor. The sound of shattering glass was amplified by my hearing aids. Or so I thought.

I held my breath, waited a few seconds, then set them back in the order I remembered. Then I kicked the broken glass under the bottom of the shelf.

The door flew open, and who should walk in? The Incredible Hulk, Chief Pell from the Suffolk County PD.

"Ms. Barrett. Fancy meeting you in a dead man's office."

He and Dr. Lewis stepped inside.

"What's she doing here?" Even though he was visibly upset, Dr. Lewis kept his voice at an even keel.

"I'll be asking her that myself. Would you like to accompany me to my car, Ms. Barrett? Unless, Doctor, you want to charge her with breaking and entering?"

I took the brochure from my back pocket and flashed it in front of Chief Pell's crimson, angry face. "I'm here for a consultation for this." I was happy to have the brochure as an alibi. Weak as it might be.

Chief Pell took it from me and read the cover. "Implants for your derriere, Ms. Barrett. How amusing and frivolous at the same time. I would have never guessed you went in for this kind of stuff." He winked, then put his hand on my elbow to guide me out. "Well, Doctor? What will it be?"

Dr. Lewis looked at me with his kind eyes. "I'm sorry. We're closing the office for a little while. I'm sure you understand. Leave your info at the front desk and I'll let you know when we reopen."

"I take that as a no? You're not pressing charges?" Chief Pell said, a definite edge to his voice.

"Of course not," Dr. Lewis answered, shocked. The deep eggplant-colored circles under his eyes told of many sleepless nights.

"Let's go, Ms. Barrett," Chief Pell said in a thundering baritone that made both Dr. Lewis and me startle.

I shook his hand off my elbow and left the office ahead of him, walking calmly down the hall and into the waiting room. I'd always admired the chief. He was a straight shooter and had been awarded many commendations. But just because I admired him didn't mean he could put his hands on me. I felt him behind me, then he passed me and held open the door leading outside. I walked out, chin held high, brushing off the malicious grin the pretty receptionist had given me as I'd passed. Maybe she should be on the authorities' suspect list.

Once outside, I said, "What can I do you for, Chief?"

"It's not unusual, Ms. Barrett, to find you snooping around a crime scene. That's more than par for the course, but you might want to be a little more circumspect."

"I didn't see any crime scene tape. I was just curious."

"I'm sure you were, Ms. Barrett. And clumsy."

"Call me Meg." I grinned, showing him my pearly whites.

"Okay, Meg. Detective Shoner assured me that you, the set designer and his fiancée have an iron-clad alibi for Dr. Nightingale's murder. If that's the case, what are you doing snooping around my investigation? This one doesn't concern you."

"Don't get mad at Arth . . . Detective Shoner. I went rogue." I bent my head and looked down at his large feet. He must have to get his shoes special ordered online. "There's a chance Elle and I will continue to work on the miniseries. We'll feel better when someone is arrested. And seeing we have an insider's connection, you can be sure I'll share everything with the police."

He raised an eyebrow, looked down, raised his hand, then quickly lowered it, as if he wanted to pat me on the head like I was an errant puppy, then reconsidered.

"Did the pen have Dr. Blake's blood on it?" I asked, batting a few eyelashes and looking up at him.

"Stay out of it, Ms. Barrett. We've got it covered."

"Meg. Will do," I chirped.

As he walked away, I thought, *Nobody puts Baby in the corner.*

Chapter 20

Montauk's small downtown area was quiet, a shell of itself compared to when the invasion of the summer people descended on Memorial Day. The volunteer fire department had decorated the small downtown area with colorful lights, the streetlamps were wreathed in holiday greens with large red bows. Snow had started to accumulate on the sidewalks and rooftops and was still falling as I got out of the car and headed toward Old Man and the Sea Books.

I felt lighter now that Detective Shoner knew everything about the murders, old and new. I'd stopped in East Hampton on my way back from Southampton to see if there were any steals at the Pink Ribbon Thrift Shop, not that I needed anything with all my fixer-uppers waiting in Elle's carriage house, not to mention the truckload of furniture arriving on my doorstep tomorrow morning and boxes packed in my guest bedroom. I'd just needed the distraction after getting caught in Dr. Blake's office, which had been followed by a phone call from Cole when he told me Christmas didn't look good. He promised to come for New Year's Eve. Seeing he was always willing to travel to me, instead of me going to him, I couldn't get upset. After I'd booked the job at Nightingale Manor, all of Cole's and my plans for the holidays had to be rearranged. Now I wasn't sure what my future held when it came to *Mr. & Mrs. Winslow*. Or Cole.

The steady wind chafed my cheeks and I wrapped my scarf higher on my face, wishing I'd chosen the heavy wool scarf my father had given me last Christmas instead of one of my handknitted holey ones. Glancing toward the end of the street, I saw a sliver of the steel-gray Atlantic. The seas were rough and the whitecaps on the waves foretold of the winter storm inching its way toward us. After listening to the weather report this morning, I'd felt relief knowing I wouldn't be on Shelter Island when the storm hit sometime tomorrow night or early Monday morning.

Half of the shops in Montauk were closed during the winter months, including A Little Bit of Everything, the first stop for vacationing summer tourists needing to stock up on sand pails, shovels, kites, wave boards and sparklers for the Fourth of July.

Lucky for me, Fudge 'n Scoops, on the corner of Edgemere and Elmwood, was open year-round. They didn't just sell fudge and old-time candy, but also homemade ice cream. When I'd first moved to town I would ask for one scoop of fudge brownie, one scoop of banana, and a half scoop of peanut butter, then mix them together while Katie, the owner, looked on in amusement. After I gave her a spoonful, she'd added it to the menu—Barrett's Banana Brownie Bombshell.

I opened the gate on the white picket fence in front of Old Man and the Sea. The fence was draped with live pine garlands and small twinkling aqua lights. The bookstore had once been a run-down three-room fisherman's cottage until Georgia turned it into her bookshop. I was relieved to see a lamp glowing through the frosted storefront window. The bookshop's posted winter hours were from eleven to three, but sometimes Georgia stayed later. Lucky for me, this was one of those times. The temperature had dropped twenty degrees since our early afternoon at the tree farm and I knew there would be a fire in the hearth, the teakettle plugged in, and Mr. Whiskers ready to greet then ignore me. I wanted to pick Georgia's competent born-and-bred Hamptons resident's brain about film director Langston Reed.

A bell jingled when I walked in. Georgia wasn't alone. It was easy to figure out who was sitting in one of the wingback chairs in front of the hearth. Barb Moss's signature beehive updo, reminiscent of Marge Simpson's, crowned from the back of the wing chair. Barb and I became friends shortly after I'd moved to Montauk. She owned Sand and Sun Realty and had rented me my small oceanfront cottage. She'd also brokered the sale for the land my current cottage sat on.

Barb jumped up, her hair not moving a smidge. "Meg! So happy to see you." Her luminous green eyes always looked gleeful, like someone had just told her a funny joke. "How'd you know we were talking about you? You just missed Claire. She filled us in about what you've been going through. I'm so sorry, honey. Wish I could stay but the grandkids have descended for the weekend." She came toward me and gave me a kiss on the cheek. "My daughter and son-in-law are off for a ski weekend. Based on the last text from my better half, their vacation seems well deserved. Jack and I might need one when they come back to retrieve the little darlings."

Georgia, the proprietor of the bookstore who occupied the other wing chair, stood and went immediately behind the counter to fill my mug, adorned *I heart NY*, with hot water. Barb threw on her jacket, and as she passed by whispered, "Call me later. I want to hear everything." Then I kissed her plump cheek and she whizzed out the door. Frigid air snaked its way inside as the door jingled shut.

Wordlessly, Georgia extended my cup of hot water and presented me with a basket of tea choices. I chose an orange-spice herbal, which she opened then plunked in my cup. It was my job to go to the counter and add my desired amount of honey. "Put a bottle on my tab," I called over my shoulder. Then I poured a generous amount of locally produced Lighthouse Honey into my cup, swiped a bottle off the shelf, and stowed it in my handbag.

"What tab? Merry Christmas. Have a seat," Georgia said, sitting back down in her chair and extending her stockinged feet toward the fire.

Barb's vacated chair was still warm and smelled like Chanel No. 5. I placed my cup on the table between us, slipped off my jacket, then kicked off my boots. Mr. Whiskers came from the back room, where Georgia kept used books. He sniffed my feet, then went to his cat cave on the shelf behind the sales counter.

"Should I be insulted?" I asked Georgia. "I'm wearing clean socks?"

"Mr. Whiskers isn't a snob. Very pedestrian, in fact. You should see what he brought home from the garbage behind Chips and Fish last night. He only wants to know if Jo's still in your life. He's been quite enamored with her ever since you babysat him when Doc and I went on our triathlon weekend."

Weather permitting, Georgia was a consummate athlete. She liked to bike to the lighthouse and back on most mornings. When she wasn't biking, she was yoga-ing, tai-chi-ing, or Zumba-ing. Her brain was just as fit as her body. Sexagenarian Doc and septuagenarian Georgia had been dating for months and I wouldn't be surprised if Georgia caught the bouquet at Elle's wedding.

"Too bad Josephine didn't feel the same way about Mr. Whiskers. Had to keep her locked in my bedroom after the fur went flying," I said, picking up my cup and blowing on the rising steam that scented the air. "Poor Mr. Whiskers still has a scarred ear to prove it."

Georgia laughed and took off a knitted hat in a snowflake design that covered her short gray hair. "Do I have hat head?" she asked. "I was just gonna close up, but I want to hear about your latest shenanigans. I'll let Doc know to pick me up in a half hour." She put on a pair of reading glasses and took out her phone, then typed a message.

"I don't want you to change your plans for me."

She looked up. "Why the panic in your voice? You haven't filled Doc in on what's been going on, have you? Or, I assume, your father either. Am I right?"

"Well . . . Hmmm, right as rain. Where did that expression come from, anyway?"

"Don't try to deflect. It most likely came from the English, where it rains so much it's just a normal fact of everyday life—a truism." Georgia took off her reading glasses and put her phone away. "I understand. Doc can be a little overprotective when it comes to his surrogate niece. I'm surprised you wouldn't want to pick his retired coroner's brain like you've done in the past."

"Actually, I want to pick your brain about Langston Reed."

Her eyes opened wide and I saw she was up to the task.

"From what Claire told us, I can't imagine a reason Langston Reed would want to kill Dr. Blake. I don't see a connection."

"So, you know both men?"

"Never met the doctor, but Langston's grandmother was a good friend of my mother's. I haven't seen him since he was a child, but I've followed his career. His family has been in the Hamptons for ages. Dr. Blake I only know from television."

"I knew if anyone knew about Langston, it would be you. Was his family wealthy, or is he a self-made man?"

"I think his mother's side of the family had some money. His grandmother, Bunny Fortune, was very involved in the arts. That's how my mother met his grandmother, they were on the same Bridgehampton art committee."

"Say what!" My mouth dropped open. "His grandmother's last name was Fortune? As in Marian Fortune?"

Georgia leaned forward in her chair and looked at me. "Wow!"

"Wow!" I said back. "Was Fortune her married name?"

"I don't think so, it was her maiden name that she took back after one of her divorces. You know the Hamptons High Society."

This was better than she thought. They might be getting closer to the connection between the old and new murders. "So, you know the story of the old murder committed by Marian Fortune?"

"Of course. It's been all over the news. But I surely didn't know about it when it happened. Even though I grew up here, I would have been about a year old when the murder took place. I'll admit after Claire came in, I did a little online research about the old murder. I do know Langston's grandmother's first name wasn't Marian, it was Bonnie, but everyone called her Bunny. If you go into the Southampton Art Museum there's a wing dedicated to her. Still don't see how what happened in 1950 could be related to the doctor's murder. Unless we're talking about a ghost story?"

Remembering that I promised not to disclose how Blake Nightingale had been murdered, I decided instead to tell her about the rag doll and my finds in the Nightingale Manor attic. I knew Georgia would keep quiet about the ice pick, I just didn't want her to slip and tell Doc, my protector, who would most likely spill the beans to my father, ruining his holiday in Colorado. I did tell her about the argument between Dr. Blake and Langston. "I don't know why Langston lied to us later when he said he didn't know about Arden Hunter's murder."

We chatted for a few minutes about things not related to the murder. I reveled in the normalcy of it all. Thirty minutes later, I stood. "I better run. Fat cat will be waiting impatiently for her dinner." I finished my tea, loving the orange-honey flavor that had settled at the bottom of the cup.

"Just leave your mug on the counter. I'll rinse it out later with mine."

"Thanks, Georgia."

She turned her wise eyes on me. "Okay, scoot," she said. "But before you go, I have something for you." She got up and went to the section of books labeled *Poetry* and extracted a white hardcover and handed it to me. It was titled *Robert Frost*. Pictured on the cover was the proverbial forked road from his famous poem. Underneath the picture it read *Including Discussion Questions*.

"Claire told me about you meeting Patrick Seaton. She also said if you come in to take this."

"Ahh, how conniving." I paused at the thought of a poetry group that included Patrick Seaton. For a millisecond I forgot about Langston's possible relation to murderess Marian Fortune. Then I remembered Patrick was the screenwriter for *Mr. & Mrs. Winslow*. "Thanks, Georgia. What do I owe you?"

"A gift from me. Claire wants me to join their little group, too. But I have so much going on, I don't know if I have the time. But you should do it. I know a little tidbit you might enjoy hearing. The last time Patrick and his publicist—"

"Beautiful publicist," I added.

"Not half as gorgeous as you. Anyway, they didn't seem to be getting along. So the door's open." Then she hesitated. "If you want it open?"

"I'm pretty busy too."

"Claire certainly is a great addition to our circle, isn't she?"

"The best," I answered.

"Maybe you could bring Cole along to the poetry club?" She winked.

"You devil. Maybe I will."

"And if you do decide to join, might I suggest you redeem the gift certificate Barb gave you for your birthday for cooking lessons with Chef Patou? You don't want to poison anyone, do you?"

"Poison . . . Hmmm, maybe I should speak to Doc. Or you could. Just see if they found anything in Blake Nightingale's system besides champagne."

"All roads lead to mystery and murder with you," she said, laughing. "I'll see if he can find anything out, nonchalantly. What about Elle's fiancé? Can't he get the info?"

"It's under Southampton's jurisdiction. He probably could, but I don't want to push it."

"Doc and I have been discussing the case. Did Doc know you were working at Nightingale Manor?"

"No. When we met on Monday at Paddy's I told him about *Mr. & Mrs. Winslow* but not the location. And so far there hasn't been any mention in the news of the miniseries being filmed at Nightingale Manor. I have to say, Doc does look pretty fit. Is that any of your doing? He even ordered oatmeal instead of eggs benedict."

She smiled. "You'll be happy to know he's lowered his cholesterol and is off his meds. And his heart is a happy ticker."

"That is good news."

Georgia bagged the book and handed it to me. I donned my coat, slipped on my boots and headed for the door. Mr. Whiskers followed.

I looked down. "Masochist. Sorry, buddy. Don't want to be responsible for what my wayward feline does to you next."

Georgia laughed and scooped him up. "Keep in touch. I expect updates from you for my peace of mind."

I saluted. "Yes, ma'am." Then I opened the door and stepped into the bracing wind.

• • •

After returning home and feeding the beast her dinner, I took my laptop to the card table and started my search. I typed in *Bunny Bonnie Fortune* and *Bridgehampton*. Bingo. A dozen pictures popped up on the screen of Bunny from when she was in her early twenties, always in a society photo at some art installment. There was also a photo attached to her obituary. Even in her later years, Bunny was a handsome woman. I scanned the text in a *New York Times* obit and found Langston Reed listed as one of Bunny's three grandsons, as was a nephew named Grayson. The same name in the letter from Arden Hunter that mentioned Grayson as Marian's son. It was just as Georgia said. Langston Reed was Marian Fortune's great-nephew. If Bunny was still alive she would have been of a similar age to Marian Fortune. Perhaps a little bit older. I continued searching the web until my eyes started closing and Jo told me it was time for bed by plopping all of her twenty-three pounds on my laptop's keyboard. The same thing she liked to do during a board or card game. "You cheeky thing," I scolded. "I saw your boytoy, Mr. Whiskers, and his ear is healing up nicely. No thanks to you."

Jo's eye looked away, and she had that cat-ate-the-canary smirk on her mouth.

"Shoo, shoo. I need to sign off. You win."

For once she listened, but not before swishing her huge Maine coon tail near my mouth. A layer of fur stuck to my lip gloss. "Ugh! What am I going to do with you!" I, for one, was never a cat lover. Dogs had always held a special place in my heart. Especially after meeting Cole's three-legged dog, Tripod. When Detective Shoner, aka Arthur, and Elle talked me into adopting Jo, I'd only acquiesced when promised inside information on a murder case I was involved in.

Now, I couldn't imagine not having her in my life.

After wiping my mouth with a tissue and the keyboard with a duster, I went to turn off the laptop. Raising my finger above the Off button, I paused. There it was, second line from the bottom of the page. A Long Island *Newsday* article with the headline "Bunny Fortune Defends Sister in Murder of Famed Actress."

Chapter 21

Sleep had been fleeting and my mind was still fogged from the knowledge that Langston Reed's great-aunt murdered Arden Hunter, but I still managed to get up Sunday morning from my warm, toasty bed and dress in anticipation of the arrival of Duke and Duke Jr., along with the truck of furniture from my storage unit.

I was in the kitchen on my second cup of coffee when the light near the kitchen door flashed. My heart hiccupped. I galloped to the door and opened it.

"Elle! What are you doing here?"

"Is that any kind of greeting? You think I would miss helping you arrange your cottage to those floor plans we've been going over for months? Plus, I brought you a present in the back of my truck."

I glanced behind her and saw something humongous covered in a heavy moving blanket and secured with bungie cords. I also saw about a foot of snow. Thankfully, I had a snowplow company on retainer and they'd already been and gone. "What is it?" I asked her, clapping my hands in excitement.

"You gonna let me in? It's cold out here. You can't see it until after the truck arrives."

I ushered her inside. After giving her a bone-crushing hug, I closed the door. "I can't believe you drove here in all this snow. It's not like you at all, you rogue."

"Like the mail carriers, *Through rain, sleet, or snow* — I'm here to deliver your early Christmas present. Plus, Arthur told me the roads were all salted and cleared. It pays to have a cop as a fiancé. Smells heavenly." She passed me then beelined to the coffeepot on the counter, took a mug from the cupboard and poured herself some dark roast. Something had changed. I had a feeling it had to do with her fiancé and a decision about his new job. I let it go. She would share when she wanted to.

After adding milk and sugar to her coffee, Elle turned. She scanned my face with her large chestnut eyes and said, "You look awful. Are those dark circles from yesterday's mascara?"

"Thanks. No. They're from a bad night's sleep."

"Too excited to unload the truck?"

"Not exactly." I told her about what I'd learned about Langston Reed and Dr. Lewis.

"Oh, boy. But what does it all mean? I see Dr. Lewis's motive. But why would Langston kill Dr. Blake?"

"I don't have an answer to that. I looked at some old streaming episodes of *Bungled*, and it's true they don't show one clip of Dr. Blake doing the actual surgery."

"You have to admit, Dr. Blake was tons more handsome and personable as a television personality compared to his partner. But I would love to ask . . ." Elle's phone rang. She pulled it from the pocket of her down vest and answered. "Hi, Felicity . . . Are you sure? . . . I'll ask her . . . I'll have to tell Arthur, so he can have an officer meet you. Of course. I'll call you as soon as I talk to him. Can you hold on for a sec?" She tapped the screen and turned to me. "It's Felicity. Should I tell her about Langston? She's heading to Nightingale Manor. Langston is meeting her there with a moving van and they're picking out the furniture to go to Windy Willows. She wants us to come and pack up some boxes of smalls. She shouldn't be alone. Especially after what you told me."

"I wouldn't tell her about Langston until you ask Arthur. I doubt her life is in danger."

"Famous last words." Elle took the call off hold and said into the phone, "Okay, Felicity, I'm going to call Arthur right now. Meg's coming too. See you soon."

Elle placed another call and walked out onto the screened porch. I took a seat at the card table. I had to catch my breath. Things were happening too fast and I was the type that needed to analyze and put things in their proper place, like when working on one of my decorating boards for a client's cottage.

When Elle came in from the porch, she gave me a thumbs-up. "Arthur's going to meet us at the ferry. He called ahead for someone from the Southampton PD to go to the Nightingale estate. They should get there the same time Felicity does."

Elle went to the kitchen, grabbed her coffee from the counter, topped it off and went to the window. "Truck's here!"

I hurried to the kitchen door, opened it and propped open the vintage aqua screen door that I'd found at a Brooklyn salvage company. The door had reminded me of one you might find in one of my favorite movies, *To Kill a Mockingbird*.

I called over my shoulder to Elle, "Do you mind collapsing the card table and chairs?" I'd already moved the boxes I'd packed from Little Grey and stacked them with the others in the guest bedroom. "I'm gonna run upstairs and put in my hearing aids and make sure Jo is locked in the bathroom. Not that she'd escape into the snow, but she might purposely trip Duke or Duke Junior."

"Sure," she answered, laughing. "I told Felicity we would be on the eleven o'clock ferry. And we'll be going home on the four o'clock. I'm not taking a chance the storm comes twelve hours early. And we aren't taking that elevator."

"Agreed. Did you tell Arthur about Langston's tie to the old murder?"

"Yes."

"Great," I said, making my way to the staircase.

"He also told me to tell you that the woman who was suing Dr. Blake for malpractice is in the clear. They have her on video surveillance at a hotel in Manhattan during the time of death."

I had already learned that yesterday when I'd been eavesdropping. In the past Arthur and Chief Pell never got along. The chief always thought the detective was too concerned about his fancy attire and the A-list functions he attended to be a real cop. Time and time again Chief Pell was proven wrong. Maybe he had something to do with Arthur's new job in Manhattan. I had a vision of us catching Dr. Blake's killer and Arthur getting an accommodation and promotion. "I never really thought she was guilty, but at least we can take her off the list." I recalled the piece of paper she'd dropped at the Southampton police station and how torn up she was. I was hopeful the press wouldn't find out her last name.

When I came back downstairs, the area rug in the main room was down and Duke and his son were coming through the doorway carrying my sofa. I didn't realize how much I missed it and almost jumped on top and let them carry me Cleopatra-style to the designated spot Elle was directing them to. "Come back a little . . . to the left, no, a little to the right . . ."

That was my girl.

My home would soon be *my* home.

Chapter 22

Arthur met us at the ferry. When we'd pulled up he was outside his car chatting with Captain Chris. I saw him hold his phone up to the ferry captain's face and the captain nodded in the affirmative. Elle parked the pickup next to Arthur's Lexus. Then she motioned to him to hurry and come over. Arthur raised the heel of his right hand to say we should stay put. That wasn't a problem seeing the outside temperature was somewhere in the low twenties, not counting the windchill. The skies were partly cloudy with peeks of sun, but the choppy seas and whitecaps on the bay forecasted another storm was on the way. It was scheduled to hit hard around midnight but leave quickly thereafter. As I'd learned many times since moving to the east end of Long Island, when you're surrounded by water, Mother Nature could be very fickle. At the thought of being stranded again, I realized Elle was right, we needed to get in and out of that house of horrors as quickly as possible.

"Hope your fiancé's getting some good intel about the case," I said, checking my phone. I'd contacted Doc to see if any of his PD fishing buddies could find out the details on Dr. Blake's autopsy, falsely reassuring him I wouldn't go near Nightingale Manor, because at the time I hadn't planned to. I was hopeful if there'd been anything worthwhile relating to who killed Dr. Blake, Arthur would have told me. Or at least his fiancée, for her safety alone. I recalled Langston telling us that on the night Dr. Blake was murdered, he'd consumed a lot of champagne. I wondered if there was anything more in that champagne.

I'd reread the newspaper reports on the internet and realized something—Dr. Tobias Nightingale had been the only witness to Arden Hunter's stabbing with the ice pick. It wasn't a case of he said/she said, it was more a case of the doctor said, the insane accused would have no say. What if Marian had read the note from Arden telling her about the tickets in the rag doll and had been the one who had torn the doll's arms off to search for the train tickets? When Arden didn't show up, she went to search her out?

Too many questions, but hopefully after confronting Langston about his great-aunt, Marian Fortune, they might get some answers.

Elle was biting her cuticles, no doubt nervous about getting to Nightingale Manor before something else happened. Trying to distract her, I said, "Have you and Arthur chosen a date, or at least a month for your nuptials?"

"We had a long talk last night."

"And?"

"We're going to try to do the long-distance thing. He gets out early on Fridays, so if he hits the road, it shouldn't be that bad. He might even have the use of a helicopter."

"Who knows," I said, "maybe you'll see more of him than you do now. His position on the East Hampton Town PD keeps him busy and stressed. The new job sounds pretty cushy."

"We planned on getting married in the spring, nothing fancy . . ."

"In my walled garden," I added.

"Yes, but we might have to make it September. See how the job goes."

"Still a beautiful time out here."

Our conversation was shortened by Arthur opening the driver's side door. "Okay, sorry about that, but I've just learned something very interesting."

"About the Nightingale murder?"

"Yes, Ms. . . . Meg. Hop out. We'll take my car on the ferry."

"Do you have an emergency roadside kit in your trunk?" Elle asked as we got out.

"A what?" he asked.

"A foldable shovel, flares, a special blanket to go under the wheels if you get stuck in the mud or snow. Need I go on?"

"No. I don't have any of that. I do have a jack and spare tire. I usually depend on my police radio if I need help."

"Well, buster, you're getting one for Christmas. Especially if you'll be making the commute from the city on the treacherous Long Island Expressway. You can grab mine from the truck's bed."

"Aye, aye, Captain Gorgeous," he said, laughing. "I like the role reversal, it's usually me giving you the concerned-father speech."

Elle smiled.

He got the emergency kit from the bed of the pickup and put it in the trunk of the Lexus, then we hurried to his car.

"A few minutes in this weather, you might freeze to death fixing a flat tire," I said, opening the backseat door, happy the car was still running and was warm and toasty inside.

"No, Meg. Get in the front seat," Elle ordered from behind.

"Thanks, pal." I held the door as she got in the backseat, then closed it. I opened the front passenger's side door and sat, then pulled the door shut just as a wicked gust of air caused all the papers on Arthur's dash to scatter everywhere. *Oops.*

Arthur opened his door and got inside, then turned his head toward the backseat and gave Elle a questioning look as to why I was sitting next to him.

"Meg needs to be able to read your lips on the ferry," she said. "The background noises are too loud for her to hear about what you've just learned from the captain. This way she can listen and read your lips at the same time."

"How considerate, buddy," I said, looking back at her and throwing her an air kiss.

"Plus," Elle added, "now I can lie down, not look out the window at the rough seas, and while I'm closing my eyes, I'll repeat a few mantras and prayers there won't be another dead body at Nightingale Manor when we arrive."

I wanted to laugh her off, but I'd had the same thoughts.

Arthur put the car in Drive and we went up the ramp to the ferry. He turned to me, making sure I could read his lips and whispered, "Why are you holding my papers, Ms. Barrett?" The fact he used my last name wasn't lost on me.

"When I opened the door, the wind blew them off the dash and I nicely collected them for you." I grabbed the disorderly pile from my lap and offered them to him. "I wasn't snooping, it was the wind. I swear."

He arched a thick black eyebrow but didn't question me further. Now I was dying to see what information was on them.

We parked next to a pair of utility trucks from the electric company, and as if reading my thoughts, Arthur grabbed the papers from my lap and stuffed them in the arm console. After we were settled in, I couldn't hold it any longer. "So, what were you talking to Captain Chris about, Arthur?"

"I haven't even called it in to Southampton PD yet, but in a nutshell, the vagabond who frequents closed homes on the island during the winter months was rescued by Captain Chris and taken to a men's shelter in Sag Harbor."

"When was that?" I asked.

"Wednesday around noon."

"How do you know he's the same man the handyman from Sylvester Manor spotted?"

"I have a videotape of him. There were security monitors at the last house he left. I showed the ferry captain the video and he confirmed he's the same guy. One less suspect to worry about."

"And then there were four," I said. "Sabrina Nightingale, Langston Reed, Willa Sullivan, and Dr. Greg Lewis. Am I right?"

He didn't answer. Even though this case wasn't under his jurisdiction, he was playing things close to the vest. As in bulletproof vest.

After the ferry docked and we were directed down the ramp, Elle said from the backseat, "No more murder talk. Focus on the road. Look for black ice."

"Yes, Mother," Arthur said, pulling onto the narrow two-lane highway that followed the east side of Shelter Island.

"Meg, tell me more about your Patrick Seaton? Any romantic meetings?" Elle asked, not too coyly. "Any discussion about *Mr. & Mrs. Winslow*?"

Arthur grinned at me. "*Your* Patrick Seaton?"

"I told you," Elle said. "The screenwriter for the miniseries is Meg's mysterious neighbor who used to leave her sad classical poetry verses on the beach."

"It does sound familiar."

I hadn't told Elle about the poetry book club both Claire and Georgia were pushing me to join. When it came to pushy, especially relating to my love life, Elle wore the golden crown. "I thought the script was marvelous. Patrick really captured the feel of the pre-World War Two time period, even mentioning the rise of Adolf Hitler and unrest in Europe and Japan. But the best part was how he's developing Lara Winslow's character. Not the norm for the 1930s. Patrick made Lara Winslow the true detective in the series. In this case the *Mrs.* is the brains and the *Mr.* more the eye candy.

And what eye candy that Dillon King is!" Elle moaned from behind them. "I'm glad Mr. Seaton still has Lara dressing in the glamorous styles of the day."

"Brains and beauty," I added.

"Hey, watch it! What am I, chopped liver?" Arthur asked, sticking out his lower lip.

"You know you're the love of my life . . . I wouldn't say eye candy, you're more like a caramel machiatto—a taste of dark espresso topped with whip cream."

"Get a room," I said.

Arthur swerved, avoiding a branch in the middle of the road, and we all went sliding.

"What was that!" Elle screeched. "A dead animal, a body?"

"Just a branch, my love."

"No more chitchat. Concentrate, Arthur."

"Yes, ma'am, your wish is my command."

The island seemed stark and cold with its leafless trees and snow-covered terrain. Even though the temperature in the Lexus was near eighty, a chill set into my bones. Twisting my body around to face the backseat, I said, "I really think the series is going to do well. I just hope it gets produced. After reading the script we have a better idea of the setting and it will be easier to see what props we need. I'm glad we already went through the Christmas decorations. I assume the murder weapon will be supplied by Felicity's prop department. I don't know where we would find one of those at Nightingale Manor."

"Meg!" Elle scolded. "I'm sure we won't have to find *that* prop at Nightingale Manor."

Finally, up ahead, I saw the low stone wall designating the boundaries of the Nightingale estate. We passed between the stone pillars and I glanced at the gatehouse. There was movement in the gabled window on the second floor. "Stop! Someone's inside the gatehouse!"

"And why is that of importance?" Arthur asked, coasting to a stop.

"I thought it was unused. Who would be inside? The day we found the body, after we were freed from the elevator, I went to get Elle's phone. When I looked out the window there was a light on at the gatehouse. It was that same window." I pointed.

Elle tapped me on the shoulder and I turned to read her lips. "Didn't Felicity tell us that the Nightingales were moving to the gatehouse when the crew came to stay in the main house?"

"Yes," I answered. "But the production company, actors and crew aren't scheduled to come until the end of January."

"I think we should worry more about Felicity being alone with Langston than who is in the gatehouse," Elle said.

"You're right. Sorry, Arthur, we better get to the house."

He gave me a weird look, then pulled away and we snaked up the long drive. I knew I'd seen a curtain flutter in the above-mentioned window but kept it to myself.

"I wonder if it's status quo for a big-time director to help stage the set. It would seem Felicity could handle it. Especially with our help," I said.

Arthur parked in the front circle behind a Southampton Police cruiser, Langston's Explorer and Felicity's rental car. As soon as he turned off the engine we hopped out of the car and bounded up the cement steps like a trio of superheroes.

Only, once we got inside there was no one to save.

Yet.

Chapter 23

We found Felicity and a female officer, introduced as Officer Hall, from the Southampton PD in the kitchen being catered to by Willa. It brought back memories from the first time I'd walked into Nightingale Manor's kitchen and felt only cozy vibes and the promise of wonderful baked goods. Today felt very different.

Willa turned when we entered. She looked like she'd aged ten years since the last time I'd seen her. Her rosy cheeks looked ashen and her eyes dull. I could tell it was a chore for her to smile, but she did when she saw us.

"Girls," she said. She raised an eyebrow when she glanced at Arthur. Elle introduced him as her fiancé and a detective on the East Hampton Town PD.

Willa's mouth formed a small *O*. "It's a sad state of affairs. I was just telling Felicity that last night when I gave my notice, Mrs. Nightingale insisted I stay on at Nightingale Manor and I agreed. I'm very worried about her. I don't think she's slept since her husband's death and she's on so many antidepressants and sedatives. They just don't seem to be working."

"Is she here?" I asked, because no one else did.

"No, she must have left early in the morning. I myself have been sleeping late. The coffee's on a timer, and I know she had a cup before I came down to the kitchen. Detective, I hope they're close to finding who did this to Blake. I know it would bring us all peace. This is a big place to be rambling around for just the two of us."

Before he could answer, I said, "Felicity, is Langston here?"

"I haven't seen him," she answered.

Elle and I had pointed out Langston's Explorer to Arthur when we'd parked.

Trying not to let Willa, who was still a murder suspect, notice the Barrett blotches sending pinpricks of heat to my neck and cheeks, I said, "Felicity, we better get crackin'." I put my arm around Elle's shoulders. "This little lady wants to leave before any precipitation begins."

Elle laughed a fake laugh, then said, "The calm before the storm. Ha, ha."

As soon as Felicity stood, Elle grabbed her arm and pulled her out of the kitchen and into the hallway. I followed.

Arthur remained inside with Willa. He didn't have an excuse to leave like we did. We were, however, followed out by Officer Hall. I told the officer a brief synopsis of what was going on and asked if she wouldn't mind going to look for Mr. Reed, who was possibly at the gatehouse. She hesitated at my directive but must have figured that since I came in with Detective Shoner, I had some position of authority. Even if I didn't.

When the officer left, Elle said, "Let's move into the drawing room. We can talk and work at the same time."

Felicity looked from my face to Elle's. "I've only known the two of you for a little while, but something squirrelly is going on. I can tell."

Elle giggled, but it came out more like she was choking on a chicken bone. I walloped her back with the palm of my hand as we moved into the foyer and then the drawing room.

"Something's different here than before," I said. Empty cartons were scattered in the corners of the mammoth room, labeled with the words *Drawing Room*.

Elle walked to the center of the Aubusson rug. "I know what it is. The mansion isn't freezing."

There were about ten pieces of furniture with yellow sticky notes attached to them designating they would be going on the truck. Felicity or Langston had chosen the exact items I would have after reading the script and knowing the time period. I had to wonder where Sabrina was. It seemed she'd want to be here with Langston. Unless he already promised her a walk-on part.

"Thanks to Willa, we have heat," Felicity said. "Her son is scheduled to come here tomorrow. She told me she doesn't want him to catch pneumonia. Per Willa, it seems Sabrina doesn't care about the heating bill or much of anything lately."

While Elle explained about Langston's ties to Arden Hunter's death through his great-aunt, I beelined it to the window and watched the officer walking toward the gatehouse. She reached the steps to the main entrance, and when she put her foot on the first step, Langston Reed exited. He held something in his hand that I saw him shove in his jacket pocket.

I moved away from the window and looked around the room. There were about a dozen Deco pieces in the room, the rest were from the Victorian and Edwardian time period with a sprinkling of Art Nouveau. Exactly the furnishings and accessories Jack Winslow's elderly great-uncle would have had in the 1930s. The detective couple's walk-up on the lower East Side of Manhattan would be more Art Deco or traditional pre–World War Two.

I picked up a magnificent glass vase. Elle looked over and said, "Oh, my. We must bring that one to Windy Willows. It's a signed Emile Galle cameo-glass hydrangea vase." I brought it over to her and whispered, "I think Langston is on his way. It was him in the gatehouse." Glancing at Felicity, I gave her a weak smile, which she returned. I could tell she didn't know what to make of Langston being related to Marian Fortune. After all, they'd worked together on other projects and for all outward appearances he'd seemed most genial, especially compared to the show's producer.

"We should definitely take that," Felicity said. "I've put paper and bubble wrap in those boxes. There should also be a marker and a pad of paper inside to write down what goes inside. The boxes are already numbered and coordinated with the pad of paper."

I took the vase to a box near the foyer, wanting to catch Langston when he came in. I had no idea where Arthur was. He needed to have a chat with Langston Reed. Keeping my mind busy, I slowly wrapped the vase like it was a living thing, afraid of breaking it after Elle had also added that the vase was worth somewhere in the forty-five-thousand-dollar range. I wondered if Sabrina knew the worth of the contents inside the mansion. What Willa said about Sabrina being overly upset about her husband's death didn't fit the Sabrina I'd witnessed in the past couple days. She seemed less concerned about her husband or even the value of a cameo vase and more concerned about getting a cameo role on the show.

I heard the front door open, then close. Things like doors closing had a vibration to them that I felt. It was true that when one of your senses was lacking, you made up for it with the others.

Langston appeared through the archway between the drawing room and foyer, stomping the snow from his boots and pant legs. When he peered in, I noticed his face was flushed and his eye's bright, almost like he'd had some kind of awakening. He confirmed my thoughts by kicking off his boots and calling to Felicity, "I'm going to run up to the attic and see what decorations you've picked out for the holiday scene. No need to come. Stay here, I can handle things up there."

Then he was gone.

Felicity looked flustered. Arthur came into view and she said, "Detective, Langston was just here and he—"

"I know," he said, looking at Elle, "I was privy to his entrance."

"Oh, Arthur." Elle ran to him. "I thought you'd abandoned us."

"I was in communication with the officer who saw him coming out of the gatehouse."

I put the vase in the box and came over to them.

Arthur continued, "I've also been in contact with Chief Pell from Suffolk County. I told him everything about Mr. Reed's familial connection to the old murder. He told me to take it easy when doing any kind of interrogation, apparently they've been friends for years."

"But . . ."

"No buts, Ms. Barrett."

Elle gave her fiancé a chastising look, I assumed because he called me by my last name.

Arthur walked over to where Elle sat and said, "Just stay put in the meantime. There's no physical evidence that Mr. Reed killed Blake Nightingale. This is out of my jurisdiction . . ."

"But . . ." I said again.

He didn't say anything, just put his hand up and continued, "We passed on the information about his ties to the old murder and we have to leave it at that. I've been promised Mr. Reed will be questioned, it just won't be by me. We have to let it go."

"I'm glad Chief Pell is vouching for him. Can't have a better endorsement than that," Elle said.

"What a relief," Felicity added.

I would let them stay in their little bubbles, but I wasn't about to let down my guard. I've learned too many times, you never knew what went on in someone else's mind.

Arthur sat in the corner of the room while we packed away things to take to Windy Willows. After we'd finished, I said, "Arthur, do you have any objection to me going over to the gatehouse and checking it out?" Something was bothering me, and I knew what it was: the light in the gatehouse that I'd seen from the attic after the murder.

"It was searched already. Knock yourself out."

"Do you mind if I go, Felicity?"

"No, but Elle and I need to go up to the attic and see what holiday things Langston has chosen, then box them up. The truck for the furniture is coming soon."

"I assume Detective Shoner will accompany you?" I asked.

Arthur looked up from his phone. "Of course."

Elle came over to me and whispered, "Don't be long."

"I won't," I said, grabbing my coat off the chair. On my way out of the room I asked, "Felicity, is it normal for the director to take such an interest in the staging process?"

"It's not unusual. Woody Allen had a say in all his movie interiors. I don't think Langston is that hands-on as a rule. But I think he feels pressure to make things right with Jeremy and the other investors."

I padded in my stocking feet to the mat by the front door and slipped on my boots. I glanced out the small window next to the double front doors; thankfully there was no precipitation, however sooty dark clouds had blanketed the sun. I checked my watch. We had an hour and a half until the time Elle wanted to leave for the ferry. Even though Arthur was our escort, him and his Glock, I didn't want to dawdle.

But I did want to check out the gatehouse before we left the island.

Chapter 24

I ignored the charming décor and furnishings of the cozy gatehouse, something very unusual for me, and sprinted up the spiral staircase to the second floor. It took a few minutes until I got my bearings and found the room that I'd spotted from the attic on Thursday. It was the same room where I'd seen movement in the window when we'd pulled onto the grounds. It wasn't a guest room, more like a storage room filled with items that looked like they might have belonged in someone's mid-twentieth-century office.

There was a black Underwood typewriter missing its *S* key sitting on top of a metal desk in front of the room's only window. Wood filing cabinets covered one wall. The other wall had built-in bookshelves filled with old newspapers, Rolodexes, staplers and other office odds and ends. Also on the bookshelves was a stack of framed diplomas. I pulled one out and saw Tobias Nightingale's name written in old-fashioned pen-and-ink script on yellowed paper. It listed him as an intern at Kings Park State Psychiatric Hospital in 1939. In my research into Nightingale Manor Sanitorium, I'd found references to Kings Park as being one of the first state hospitals to use prefrontal lobotomies on Long Island. It seemed that was where Dr. Blake's grandfather had learned the tools of his trade—the tool being, of course, an ice pick. Next to the stack of framed medical certificates was a large metal box with an antique iron padlock, corroded with age. There wasn't a key. Underneath the lock was a fine dusting of reddish powder, as if someone had attempted to yank on it and rust from the padlock had fallen to the shelf below.

"I didn't know Mrs. Nightingale sanctioned the guesthouse contents to be used in our production?" a familiar male voice said from behind. I looked for a weapon but all I spied was an old single holepunch. I grabbed it. The only good it could do was to pierce someone's earlobes with the hope it had been over ten years since their last tetanus shot. Gripping it in my hand, I slowly turned around.

It was no surprise that Langston Reed stood in the open doorway.

What was surprising was the hammer he held in one hand and the sharp-edged chisel in the other.

I took a step backward toward the window, hoping someone in the main house's attic, preferably someone with a gun, happened to be gazing out and saw me.

I took another step back.

Langston took a step forward.

Back.

Forward.

My tailbone hit the metal desk.

It seemed the jig was up. "I, uh, was sent here by Willa," I stammered. "She said last night she'd noticed a light was on and wanted me to turn it off." It sounded lame, and he must have thought the same, because once more he advanced toward me.

Unless I climbed up on the desk, there was nowhere else for me to go.

Chapter 25

Instead of pounding me on the head with the hammer or sending the chisel into my chest, Langston went to the metal box with the padlock. He put the chisel against the lock then brought down the hammer. "Damn!" he muttered. Then he tried again. This time the lock snapped open, and red dust made a small cloud in the stale air. He sneezed.

I said, "Bless you." Even if he killed me, like he'd done to Dr. Blake, I planned to go out like the lady my mother would've been proud of.

"Thank you," he answered.

I couldn't help but edge closer to him as he lifted the lid to the box. Inside were three black leather journals. The top one had the year 1949 etched in gold on the cover. Langston took it out, put it to the side, then picked up the one below. It read 1950.

The year Arden Hunter had been murdered.

"I know all about your great-aunt," I whispered from behind. "And so do the police. In fact, Detective Shoner is here, waiting to talk to you." Not exactly the truth. But close enough.

"Fine," he said, as calm as could be. He opened the journal and flipped through it. When he found something that caught his interest, he went to an old swivel desk chair in the corner of the room and sunk into it. It groaned under his weight, the seat tilting to one side. His eyes never left the page of the open journal.

If I wanted to, I could run out the door and make it out of the gatehouse with no problem. But the curious gene, handed down from my cop father, kept me frozen in time. I really wanted to know what was in that journal.

After a few minutes, which ticked by like hours, Langston looked up. He blinked as if noticing me for the first time. "It's here. Just as she said."

"What's there?" I asked, trying to keep my voice low, not wanting to break him out of his reverie.

"He admits it was his fault. Not outright, but here it is. After Arden Hunter's death it looks like he had his own mental collapse. No wonder he wasn't heard from again. I have a feeling he spent the rest of his days here. In the gatehouse. The coward."

"Whose fault?"

"Dr. Tobias Nightingale's. The person who accused my great-aunt of murder and caused her to be imprisoned in a mental hospital for years. My grandmother and mother believed her, but the hospital never did."

"Is that why you murdered his grandson, sins of the father, and all that?" The words came out before I could stop them.

A voice from the hallway said, "Yes, Mr. Reed, please enlighten us." Arthur stepped inside the room and stood in front of Langston. He was followed by the officer from Southampton. Her gun wasn't drawn, but her hand was on her holster.

Saved in the nick of time.

Or so I thought.

Chapter 26

"I've already written most of the documentary in my mind. It will be a tell-all on what really happened the day Arden Hunter underwent her lobotomy. Dr. Tobias Nightingale must have screwed up the operation and accidently killed her," Langston said, his eyes bright like he had a fever. "My great-aunt's diary tells of how it really went down. She and Arden were meant to run away and take a train to Manhattan the night before Arden's scheduled lobotomy. However, Dr. Nightingale moved the procedure up a day. A kind nurse named Mary told my great-aunt about the change of schedule and my great-aunt went to the basement to stop it. But it was too late. When she arrived, Arden was already dead on the operating table. My great-aunt got agitated, and rightly so. The doctor forced her to breathe in ether, put the ice pick in her hand, then gripped her wrist and shoved it into Arden's heart. Afterward he gave her more medication. When the police finally arrived, she was in restraints and drugged senseless. The sanitorium was closed immediately. Soon after Dr. Nightingale all but disappeared. My grandmother even tried to get Arden's body exhumed. Back then, because Shelter Island was so small, Dr. Tobias Nightingale was also the island's sole medical examiner and he'd done the postmortem himself. There was even an underground holding area in the hospital's basement for the bodies."

I shivered at that last statement.

"All my grandmother's efforts failed," Langston said, "but now we have proof."

We were in the drawing room. Langston sat next to Arthur on one of the love seats that flanked the fireplace. I sat in the chair next to Langston. Elle and Felicity sat on the other love seat. Everything Langston said rang true and matched the rag doll with the train tickets inside, the letter in the attic and the kind nurse Arden had mentioned in her letter. Langston handed the journal from the gatehouse to Arthur, who handed it to Officer Hall.

"You can see how deranged Tobias Nightingale was," Langston said. "Look at the macabre drawings in the margins. And his handwriting."

The officer opened the journal but her face didn't show any emotion. From where I was sitting I couldn't see a thing.

Langston kept talking. "My grandmother told my mother that right after her sister was sent to a state mental hospital, Nightingale Manor Sanitorium closed. Shortly after, my grandmother took a trip to Shelter Island to confront Dr. Nightingale, but the house was boarded up, and a groundskeeper who lived in the gatehouse shooed her away with a rifle and a threat of charging her with trespassing. She never heard about Dr. Tobias Nightingale again. After she read his obituary a few years later, my grandmother finally gave up."

"But how did you end up choosing Nightingale Manor for *Mr. & Mrs. Winslow?*" I asked.

"Months ago, when we were in the beginning stages of scoping out the area for the miniseries, I saw an ad in the *East Hampton Star.* I felt it was a sign from the universe. I've always been curious about the story. After we signed the contract for Nightingale Manor, I went to visit my great-aunt. She's still distraught over the death of her infant, along with what went down with Arden Hunter, plus she's had dementia for quite a few years. Even though she's ninety-five she seemed quite lucid when she told me the story of her 'dear friend Arden.' Then she handed me a box filled with notebooks where she'd written her own story, all claiming her innocence. The ramblings of the unwell, the doctors had told my grandmother year after year when she tried to get her sister Marian cleared of all charges."

Everyone was silent for a few minutes, digesting what we'd just heard.

Finally, Langston asked Arthur, "Do I need a lawyer?"

"I'm not in charge of the investigation," he answered. "But I'm pretty certain you will need to answer some questions either from Suffolk County or Southampton. Only someone who knew ahead of time about how this actress Arden Hunter died would be able to stage a copycat murder."

"Well, I might have known, but so did Sabrina, Dr. Lewis and even Willa. It was everywhere in the papers when it happened, not impossible to research. Willa is the one who confided to me that Dr. Blake had told her the gatehouse was where his grandfather, Dr.

Tobias Nightingale, spent the remainder of his years. And of course, Sabrina was privy to the story. After I let Blake know I knew about the old murder of Arden Hunter, he told Sabrina. On the night Blake was murdered, Sabrina begged me to keep the production at Nightingale Manor, worried that between the *Bungled* lawsuit and the lapsed malpractice insurance her husband's family skeletons might come prancing out of the closet. Sabrina gave me the key to the gatehouse and I was there all night until the power came back on. I returned at daylight. I promised Sabrina a walk-on part, but it was well worth it to find that journal."

"Why didn't you say all this in your statement to the police?" Officer Hall asked. It was the first time she'd spoken since we'd come back from the gatehouse. She wasn't one for small talk. An admirable quality.

Langston drew in a long breath, then exhaled, seeming to center himself. "I wasn't done searching the gatehouse. When the power went out I hadn't even a flashlight, just the one on my phone, which soon died. I needed to come back. Today was the first time I was able. But I didn't kill Dr. Blake in revenge. He had nothing to do with his grandfather's actions. I'm not a murderer."

"I believe you," I said, trying to lift the heavy cloud of malaise with my upbeat voice. I wanted to tell him that I had proof back at my cottage that what his great-aunt said was true. I held back, knowing things were still uncertain on who did kill Dr. Blake.

Felicity added her own vote of confidence. "So do I."

There was still doubt in Arthur's eyes, along with Officer Hall's.

A phone buzzed. Officer Hall took hers from her pocket and looked down. "It's a message from Chief Pell. He wants me to ask Mr. Reed if he wouldn't mind meeting him at the Southampton station." She nodded toward Langston. "We can leave now for the ferry."

Langston stood tall, putting both his arms in front of him, like he was waiting to be cuffed. Officer Hall also stood. She was a lot shorter than Langston, but the way she held herself made her appear an equal match.

"I just planned on doing a movie that would vindicate my great-aunt," Langston said. "That was all."

"No need for cuffs, Mr. Reed," Officer Hall said in a steady voice with a slight New York accent. "Chief Pell was very clear about that."

After they left the room, Elle said, "We need to catch the ferry too. I don't like the look of that gloomy sky. Plus, if Langston isn't the killer, that leaves Willa, Dr. Lewis, and Sabrina. Dr. Lewis and Willa are here, right now. Maybe they killed Dr. Blake together. Remember, Meg, what you told me about finding them together?"

Arthur raised his furry eyebrows and pursed his lips, as if holding back from calling me Ms. Barrett, and reading me the Detective Shoner Act for not telling him about the Willa and Dr. Lewis connection. Then I recalled that I had put their liaison on the paper I handed Arthur at Home and Hearth yesterday. He mustn't have given it a second glance.

"Dr. Lewis is here?" I asked incredulously.

Elle brushed back a lock of hair that had fallen over her right eye. "Yes. He came to the door looking for Sabrina when you were in the gatehouse. She was supposed to show up this morning at nine in Southampton to meet with him and a solicitor about Blake's will and the future of the practice, Southampton Aesthetics. She never showed up."

I recalled Willa saying Sabrina had been out bright and early.

Felicity stood, and Elle and I followed suit. "Now that Langston has left," Felicity said, "I need to cancel the truck. I hope it's not too late. Something keeps stopping us. This whole project seems doomed to failure."

Elle looked nervously at her fiancé. "Maybe this place is haunted and has a mind of its own."

Arthur stood. "Stuff and nonsense. Let's stick to our plan for the four o'clock ferry to Sag Harbor. First, I want to have a word with Ms. Sullivan and the doctor. I'll meet you in five minutes." He turned to go, then turned back. "Felicity, I want you to leave with us. You can follow us to the ferry. We still don't know who killed the doctor."

Elle blew him an air kiss. He winked then left the room.

"So," I said, rubbing my hands together. "It seems things are progressing along. At least Langston's ties with Arden Hunter and Marian Fortune are out in the open. For once, I agree with Detective . . . Arthur. Until they find out who killed Dr. Blake, we stay away from this place. Do you agree, Felicity?"

"Wholeheartedly," she answered, glancing wistfully around at the cartons in the room. "Any chance we could load some of these in your pickup, Elle?"

"We took Arthur's Lexus. There isn't much room, but between our car and your rental we should be able to bring a few cartons back to the mainland. We can store them in the carriage house for the time being."

"Great, let's get going," I said.

"Before it's too late," Elle added.

Her statement hung in the air and I felt a chill even though I was standing in front of a roaring fire.

Chapter 27

The caravan left Nightingale Manor. Arthur hadn't been too happy that the backseat next to Elle was filled with boxes, making it hard to see out the back window. Not to mention his full trunk. He'd better get used to it. Because once they married, Elle, like me, was prone to rescue things curbside, or stop at an estate or garage sale, or two or three, without warning. Felicity's rental car was also packed. She followed closely behind. We passed the gatehouse and I breathed a sigh of relief. At least everything having to do with the old murder was out in the open. I turned to Arthur and reminded him that when Sabrina showed up they needed to confirm Langston's story that he'd spent the night at the gatehouse. I believed Langston's version of the events. Making a movie made more sense as a way of vindicating his great-aunt. My gut said he wasn't a killer. Which left us with Willa, Dr. Lewis and Sabrina.

Light snow started falling, swirling in the blustery air and making me feel like I was inside a snow globe that someone had just shaken. The water beyond the estate's stone wall was softened by the haze of snow, and glancing to my left at the thicket of pine trees, I saw, again, how beautiful the grounds were. I took a mental snapshot to replace the one of Dr. Blake strapped to the bed in the basement. I forced my thoughts back to earlier in the day when Duke and Duke Jr. brought in the nineteenth-century apothecary cabinet Elle had brought for me as a housewarming gift. Elle had known about my obsession with apothecary cabinets. I looked to my left, daydreaming on what I could put on the cabinet's shelves and in the clear glass drawers.

Something out the window caught my eye after we passed through the stone pillars. "Stop!" I yelled loud enough to cause feedback in my hearing aids. Arthur put his foot on the brake and we skidded to a stop.

"What the heck, Meg!" Elle shouted. I looked back and saw two boxes had tumbled onto her lap, hiding her upper torso.

"Look over there!" I said, pointing. Felicity must have seen what I'd seen because she'd gotten out of her car and was running toward a large bush. On the other side of the bush, a car had plowed nose-first into the low stone wall that followed the perimeter of the Nightingale estate.

"Oh, my," I heard Elle say as both Arthur and I bounded from the car and followed Felicity.

When we were a short distance from a silver Mercedes, we saw the front driver's side door was open.

When we reached the car, we bent and looked inside.

"It's Sabrina," Felicity said. "She's unconscious but alive. I don't know how long she's been out here, but she's really pale. She might have hyperthermia. And she's really wedged in there."

Arthur said, "Felicity, get in the passenger's seat and try to pull her torso toward you so I can free her legs."

I stepped out of the way. Sabrina didn't look good; her forehead was leaning against the steering wheel. Her skin was the same color as the snow at the top of the fence. The front of the Mercedes had impacted the stone wall with such a wallop that most of the stones had broken apart and lay crushed under the car's wheels. The airbag hadn't deployed, so maybe the impact hadn't been as bad as it looked.

Elle came trotting toward us. "Is there someone inside?"

"Drive the car over here!" I shouted back. "It's Sabrina. She's alive." *Not for long in this cold,* I thought. The Mercedes had been hidden behind an azalea bush, nose to the wall. I'd caught the glint of its silver bumper after we'd passed through the stone pillars. It was a miracle I'd looked to my left, the opposite direction we would have been traveling to get to the ferry.

Felicity tried to help free Sabrina's long giraffe legs from under the steering column. Only after Felicity managed to remove Sabrina's high-heeled boots was Arthur able to pull her out. I hurried to help him carry her to the Lexus. Sabrina's body was as limp as a rag doll's, reminding me of Marian Fortune's armless doll. I noticed the tips of her fingers were starting to turn blue. Why hadn't she worn gloves? The outside temperature was in the teens, even colder when she'd left the house in the early morning. And how had she ended up going north? Southampton, where she was going to meet Dr. Lewis, was in the opposite direction.

Elle ran over and told us that she had the heat blasting. Felicity opened the door to the backseat and removed the boxes, placing them on top of the stone wall. When we laid Sabrina on the backseat, she stirred for just a second. Just enough to let us know she was still alive.

"We should take off our coats and place them on top of her," Elle suggested.

"Good idea." Felicity took off her coat.

After Elle draped her jacket over Sabrina's still form, Arthur and I followed suit.

"Arthur, there's a thermal blanket in the emergency kit you put in the trunk. Get it." I had a feeling Elle would never let him forget it was her idea to transfer the emergency kit from the pickup to his car. Then Elle turned to me. "You'll have to get in with Felicity."

I gave her a thumbs-up and hurried to Felicity's rental and moved the boxes in the front passenger's seat into the back. As I leaned in to get inside, Arthur called out, "Should we try to make the four o'clock ferry?"

I looked at my watch, then looked at the sky. The snow was steady but still manageable. "Willa's a nurse, and Dr. Lewis might still be at the manor," I shouted over the blustery wind. "I don't think we should take the chance of missing the ferry."

He hesitated for only a second, then shouted back, "Okay."

I got in the car and we waited until the Lexus passed through the stone pillars. As we followed them up the long winding drive, I murmured under my breath, "Hope we made the right decision."

Turned out we hadn't.

Chapter 28

Not only was Willa at Nightingale Manor but so was Dr. Lewis. We'd brought Sabrina up to her room, which was more like a luxury suite—something you might see in an episode of TV's *Victoria*. All that was missing was a scepter, crown, and throne. Her room-sized closet/dressing room was about the size of my kitchen and great-room combined. Even Elle, who had her own room full of vintage clothing and jewelry, was jealous.

Willa and Dr. Lewis shooed us out of the room. Before closing the door, I glanced at Sabrina's pale face. There were no cuts or bruising from hitting the steering wheel. Her seat belt had been on. It must have saved her.

Arthur hadn't called EMS because Dr. Lewis had reassured us that he knew how to handle hyperthermia; there was nothing they could do that he couldn't. Plus, we had another problem, we'd missed the four o'clock ferry back to Sag Harbor. At the rate the snow was falling we wouldn't make it onto the next one and might end up skidding into a wall like Sabrina had done.

A few minutes later, we were sitting in the kitchen around the fire. We'd already raided the cookie jar and polished off two of the four loaves of orange-cranberry bread warming on the counter. If Willa didn't turn out to be Dr. Blake's killer, Felicity said she'd see if she couldn't get her to come over to Windy Willows and be the crew's housemother and chef. Arthur had found a bottle of scotch in the pantry, but he held off drinking any until he was sure there was no way to leave the island. The flicker of lights told him it was time for that drink.

Tabitha came and sat on my lap. Even though I owned a cat, I wasn't a touchy-feely cat person. I was like a parent who thought my kid was cute and adorable no matter what heinous crimes they committed, but from an outsider's view my kid was just an obnoxious brat. Jo was a brat, but she was my brat. Tabitha had stinky fish breath, but I'd bet Willa loved her as much as I loved Jo.

"So, it looks like we might not leave the island," Arthur said. "I've made sure my office knows where I am. It seems the pantry is stocked with food and spirits, so would anyone like to join me in a drink?"

"Count me in," Felicity said. "I have a crazy proposition on how we could spend our time. What if we took turns reading the script for the pilot of *Mr. & Mrs. Winslow*? It might help us make sure there aren't any late-1930s items we might have forgotten to pack up. The furniture's already been tagged for when the truck comes."

"Great idea," I said. "It would be fun to play out all the parts. But are you sure with the recent developments with Langston, the miniseries will move forward?"

Arthur handed Felicity a glass and poured three fingers of scotch.

"Thanks," she said. "Of course, *Mr. & Mrs. Winslow* will continue. I don't know if the series will take place in the Hamptons, but I'm sure if Langston gets arrested, Jeremy won't have a problem finding another director." She took a sip, then another. "That warms your bones. And takes the edge off. Especially knowing we might have to spend another night here. Regardless if it's with or without a killer on the loose." Her words hung in the air for a few seconds before she said, "I'll get a pen and paper and we can assign roles from the script."

Felicity went rooting through kitchen drawers looking for a pen and paper. I remembered seeing a desk in the pantry that Willa must use and told Felicity to check there. When she came out, pen and paper in hand, she sat at the table and we fought over roles. The script was fifty pages long. As Felicity wrote down each person's part, she told us that usually one page of a screenplay equaled about one minute of the episode or movie.

"I only have one copy of the script, so we'll have to pass it around," Felicity said with a slight slur to her voice. "I want you to know I feel comforted by everyone's presence—especially yours, Detective."

"I don't think we have anything to worry about. It stands to reason if Ms. Sullivan or Dr. Lewis murdered Blake Nightingale, they wouldn't have any need to kill one of us. This might be one of those cases where the perpetrator goes unpunished."

I bristled at his statement. I knew from my father's point of view, catching a killer not only made the public feel safer, but also gave closure to the victim's family. Sabrina was the only family Dr. Blake had and she was upstairs unconscious fighting for her own life. Unless she was the one who killed her husband, then perhaps

179

Karma had come calling. I kept my thoughts to myself and brought my empty plate to the sink and rinsed it. As I was putting the plate in the dishwasher, Dr. Lewis entered the kitchen.

Everyone looked expectantly at him.

"I think she's going to be fine," he said as he went to the urn, grabbed a mug from the tray and poured himself a cup of coffee. He turned and said, "Willa is going to stay with her. She's in and out of consciousness and probably won't remember what happened. As I've told Willa, it's par for the course when dealing with hyperthermia. The tip of her pinky toe on her left foot might be permanently damaged from frostbite, but other than that, she's one lucky woman."

It was like one of those flashes you get when you keep trying to find a solution to a problem and the answer hits you on top of the head with a proverbial brick. I went to the coffee urn, my hand shaking, and grabbed a mug and filled it. I brought it to the table and announced, "I'm going to bring this to Willa, I'm sure she needs some respite and caffeine."

Felicity put the pen down and looked up at me.

I had to use my right hand to steady the arm holding the mug.

"Are you okay?" Felicity asked.

"Yes. Just a chill. I'll be right back."

I hurried out of the kitchen, down the hall, and ignored the elevator and took the staircase in the foyer to the second floor. Spilling coffee on the Persian runner as I went. Coffee stains were the least of my, or anyone else's, worries.

When I reached the top of the stairs and took a few steps, I heard the front door close with a bang. My hearing wasn't good enough to hear a door open, but it sure was good enough to hear the door slam and the resounding vibration that followed in its wake.

I kept walking until I got to Sabrina's sitting room. Looking down at the cup of coffee, I realized I'd lost half of its contents on the way up. I tiptoed inside, moved to the open door of the bedroom, and peered in.

Willa held a pillow in her hand. I watched, in what seemed like slow motion, as she brought the pillow to just above Sabrina's face. She paused for only a second, then pressed down, covering Sabrina's nose and mouth. Sabrina twitched like a beached flounder. I had a second to react. I heaved the mug at Willa. But missed. From behind, I heard a male voice, "Mother! What are you doing!"

I turned and saw a younger version of Dr. Blake Nightingale. He had the same amber wolf eyes.

Willa looked over, then crumpled to the floor, taking the pillow with her.

Chapter 29

"How did you know it was Willa?" Felicity asked me an hour after Arthur had handcuffed Willa and set her in the chair in the kitchen by the fire. Poor Tabitha nuzzled her as tears fell like water dripping from a sun-struck icicle. Willa's son, Donnie, had sat mute in the other chair.

Elle, Felicity, Dr. Lewis, and I were in the drawing room, huddled around the fire even though the room was warm. Arthur had stayed in the kitchen, keeping an eye on Dr. Blake's killer, and Willa's and Dr. Blake's son. He'd never drawn his gun. There'd been no need. Willa was as docile as the deer I'd spotted from the window of the attic the day I went to retrieve Elle's phone. Willa had admitted to killing Blake after he refused to sign a check for Donnie's tuition at Princeton. Apparently, Sabrina had forbidden him to spend one more penny on her husband's illegitimate son. In a fit of rage, Willa stabbed an inebriated Blake with a pen to the heart. Being a nurse, there'd been no mistaking her target. Bull's-eye! She transferred him onto a gurney, then flipped him onto the old hospital bed and finished him off with the ice pick. As for Sabrina, Willa admitted giving Sabrina some kind of sleeping pill in her coffee, upped her benzodiazepines, carted her to the Mercedes in a wheelchair, put her in the passenger seat, drove the car into the wall, then transferred Sabrina to the driver's seat.

I took a sip of scotch. "In answer to your question, Felicity, when Dr. Lewis said Sabrina's pinky toe had frostbite, it set off warning bells. I thought back from when we first arrived at Nightingale Manor. Willa had done an about-face on her feelings for Sabrina, saying she felt sorry for her. It just didn't ring true. I also remembered the position we'd found Sabrina in in the car. Sabrina is at least five feet ten, yet the seat on the driver's side was pushed close to the steering wheel; the passenger's side seat was all the way back. Detective Shoner went to the controls on the electric seat, but the battery had died so we had to pry her out. I also noticed Sabrina had no head wound but her head was resting on the steering wheel when we found her. Sabrina would have been traveling in the opposite direction for her appointment. The car had been hidden behind the only bush in front of the stone wall, leaving enough time for her to freeze to death before someone found her. But it wasn't just that. What really caught my attention was when I saw the pen you'd taken from Willa's desk in the pantry. I noticed it was the same as the one I'd found on the steps after the murder, only without the blood."

"Didn't it have an advertisement on it for the doctors' practice?" Elle asked, leaning in. "I don't think it would be a stretch for Willa to have it in her desk drawer."

"True, but the pens were old. They were from before the practice changed its name to Southampton Aesthetics and the address printed on it was different than modern day. It's a guess, but I remembered Willa had worked at the practice years ago, before they changed their name. Am I correct, Doctor?"

Dr. Lewis rubbed the area between his brows. "I haven't seen one of those pens since the mid-nineties."

"Dr. Lewis, did you know that Donnie was Dr. Blake's and Willa's son?" Elle asked.

"We all did, even Sabrina," he answered.

Elle's chocolate eyes opened wide. "I assume after Sabrina's death, he would be heir to the Nightingale estate?"

"Yes," he answered, shaking his head.

"After a DNA test," I added.

He stood.

"One more thing," I said. "Dr. Blake was holding something over your head, can you tell us what it was?"

He hesitated. "I better go check on Sabrina."

"Please, Doctor. Answer my question."

"Blake threatened to tell everyone that I performed the operation on the patient that is suing us after I'd recently been diagnosed with a neurological disease. The charismatic Dr. Blake Nightingale had been a showman, not a surgeon. He went to med school somewhere in the jungles of South America, but never learned how to perform real cosmetic surgery. He was basically a dermatologist who could only do injectables. He even froze at the sight of blood. I performed all the operations on *Bungled*, with the exception of the last. It was the only time I'd had to give up because my hands started to palsy. It wasn't until afterward that I got the diagnosis. Blake took over on the last operation and we all know the results. I tried to fix what he'd done to her, but it was too late."

"Why didn't you tell someone?" Felicity asked.

"Blake threatened to lie and say that I'd done the operation. The patient only remembered my face before the anesthesia hit her. It was also my face she saw when she woke up because Blake had to do some promo shots for the series. I had no recourse but to bow to his demands. Although, now I see, I was just as culpable as he." He looked down at his trembling long-fingered hands. "They seemed to have a mind of their own, my brain couldn't control them. I've promised our bungled patient to make everything right, monetarily and physically. I've been in negotiations with Mr. Margulies, her attorney. Blake wasn't too keen that I went behind his back—or should I say his façade. He was still trying to solve things through saying she'd signed a nondisclosure and waiver promising not to sue. We all know if negligence is involved those waivers are null and void." Dr. Lewis met my eyes. "Don't ever let fame and fortune turn you from your true calling. A guilt-free mind and a passion for what you do is more important than any television contract or an invitation to celebrity events."

"One last thing . . ." I said.

"Will this really be your last question?" he asked calmly.

The doctor was hard to ruffle. "When I saw Willa leaving your office yesterday, why did she look so angry?"

"She wanted me to help her contest Blake's will so his son would inherit instead of Sabrina. Tired of all the subterfuge, I said no."

He left the room and the three of us looked at each other.

"I feel sorry for him," Elle said, "but because he kept quiet on who really performed the surgery, it caused a lot of suffering for that poor woman. Even made her a suspect in Dr. Blake's murder."

"Agreed," I said. And Felicity nodded.

• • •

A couple hours later, Arthur came into the drawing room. He explained that he'd locked Willa into one of the sitting rooms on the second floor. "It has one of those couch thingies that women used in the old-fashioned days to faint on."

"A chaise?" I offered.

He shrugged his shoulders and held up a skeleton key. "She won't be going anywhere until morning."

Elle walked over to him and gave him a hug. "My hero."

He blushed, then said, "She's confessed to everything. She did it for her son. And this is an awful thing to say, but I think the kid was disappointed her plan didn't work. That's the reason I locked him in with his mother. How do we know he didn't have a hand in the whole thing?"

"Good thinking, Detective," I said. "Hope you checked to make sure they can't escape through a window and you had them empty their pockets."

"Yes, Ms. Barrett, there are no windows and I checked the only drawer in the room. No tools or keys for escape. Has anyone looked outside? There's no way any of us are getting out of here tonight."

"Well, I'm hungry," Elle said. "Meg, let's go see what we can scrounge up."

I was happy she wasn't upset about the weather. It seemed having your fiancé by your side made all the difference. Plus, I didn't think any of us worried about Willa coming after us. Then again, I would have never pegged her as a cold-blooded killer. Which she was. I knew as events unfolded we would find out if the murder was premeditated or second degree. I got up and followed Elle into the foyer. "You know I can't cook."

"Let me come with you," Felicity called after us, laughing. "I think I saw some leftovers in the fridge."

"Oh," I said. "In that case, I'm a pro at leftovers. I think I saw some herbs on the windowsill. Maybe I can teach you gals a thing or two about leftovers."

Elle gave me "the look," and I grinned.

When we entered the kitchen, Tabitha was sitting in Willa's chair, meowing. I scooped her up, and Elle followed with a bowl of water and food. I brought her to the drawing room and handed her to Arthur.

Elle reached into his pocket and extracted the key, saying, "I think we should bring her up to Willa. Soon enough, Tabitha will need a home." She looked over Arthur's head to me.

Oh, no, you don't, I thought. They'd bamboozled me into adopting Jo, and look where that had gotten me. Then I smiled.

"For now, she belongs with her owner," Elle directed, then elbowed her fiancé. "Let's go, warden."

"Instead of a last meal, you're giving her a last pet," I said.

I didn't believe we were going too easy on Willa. She would soon pay the price for what she'd done. And on top of that, she'd lost her only son.

Chapter 30

Lights on a trellised archway twinkled outside the doors to Pondfare. The outdoor fireplace had a fire burning and there was just the right amount of snow for a perfect Christmas Day. We filed inside the restaurant and Bella, Pondfare's co-owner, came up to me. "Meg, we have your table for seven ready."

"It's only going to be six," I said.

Bella gave me a knowing look and glanced at the rest of our group: Doc, Georgia, Claire, Arthur, and Elle. No Cole. Felicity had flown home to her husband but promised to be back for Claire's New Year's Eve party. *Mr. & Mrs. Winslow* would start filming at the end of January with Langston Reed as its director. We'd already staged the main room at Windy Willows. Almost everything they were using on set came from Nightingale Manor. Sabrina had wanted Langston and Jeremy to reconsider filming on Shelter Island, but with the stigma of the estate's murderous past, they'd stuck to Windy Willows. Luckily for me, I hadn't run into my ex-fiancé, Michael, or his wife, Paige, at Windy Willows. And I made sure to hide whenever Paige's father and my former employer and owner of *American Home and Garden* magazine, Matthew Whitney, showed up. I could only imagine what lies Paige had told him about me. Serenity was once again my mantra. With that thought, I suddenly realized I hadn't run into Cole's ex-girlfriend and my archnemesis, Tara Gayle, in months. And that was a good thing. Except for Cole being grounded because of bad weather in North Carolina, I was determined to enjoy Christmas dinner, hoping Cole, my father and his wife would make it for New Year's Eve at Little Grey.

"Right this way," Bella said, grabbing some menus and leading us to a table overlooking Montauk's Fort Pond. As usual, the restaurant was packed. Chef Patou had been at the helm since I'd moved to Montauk. He was a colorful character and a runner-up on TV's *Top Chef Challenge*. Many times, his loud voice could be heard coming from the kitchen, demanding something or another from one of his underlings. Bella had told me his bark was worse than his bite. She should know because she'd just married him.

I put my napkin in my lap and said, "Elle, you should have your rehearsal dinner here."

"Wow. Great idea," she said. "Whaddya think, Arthur?"

He looked up from his phone, a pained look on his face.

"Oh, no. Don't tell me, you have to leave?" she asked.

A waitperson put down a platter of crostini topped with goat cheese, cranberries, and rosemary then filled our glasses with sparkling water.

"And then there were five," I said, grabbing a crostino from the center of the table and stuffing the entire thing in my mouth. Olive oil dribbled down my chin and I caught it with my napkin. Ready for another, I looked to the center of the table. The large platter was empty. "Elle, I think once Arthur starts his job in Manhattan, you'll probably see more of him."

"You might be right. He never gets weekends off here. And part of his hiring package is access to a helicopter."

"Hey," he said, "I'm right here. You're talking about me as if I'm already gone. However, I do have to go." He leaned over and gave Elle a smooch. "You know what I like, order me something to go. Promise to make it up to you."

He stood, and I said, "Nothing to do with the Nightingale case, I hope?"

Doc gave me a fatherly look. "Come on. It's Christmas, missy."

"Not a thing to do with the Nightingales," Arthur said, looking festive in his red-and-white Nordic-style sweater, not his usual designer suit and tie. I liked the look and knew Elle had a lot to do with it. "Nice sweater," I said.

"Good thing I brought a dress shirt and jacket in the car." He glanced at Elle. "Will you be able to get a ride home if this turns into an all-night deal?"

"I can take her home," I said.

"Thanks, Meg."

• • •

After we finished our appetizers and main course, we moved on to dessert. I'd chosen Pei mussels swimming in garlic, shallots, and parsley for my appetizer, followed by a pork tenderloin with apricot apple chutney and watercress pine nut salad with Spanish prosciutto.

Doc said, "Arthur sure missed out on a fantastic meal."

Elle pushed her plate forward, not a morsel remained. "I ordered him the lamb ribs, they were fantastic."

Georgia put her napkin to the side of her plate. "So, now that everything is tied up relating to Nightingale Manor, I'm happy you'll be able to concentrate on the set of the miniseries."

"And stay out of trouble," Doc added, wiping his white beard and directing his gaze at me.

I ignored him. "Yes, the case is closed. Forensics came back that Willa's prints had been on the pen advertising the old practice, along with Blake Nightingale's blood. Not a surprise. Especially after her confession. Sabrina is completely recovered, Willa is in prison, and the practice lost the lawsuit and Pauline was offered a million-dollar settlement that Dr. Lewis isn't contesting."

Elle took a sip of her cabernet then said, "Felicity told me as a way to get a walk-on part, Sabrina is cooperating with Langston Reed on the documentary he's planning to make after filming *Mr. & Mrs. Winslow*."

"Wonder what part she'll get?" I asked.

"I already know. She's going to be a gangster's moll."

"Well, it seems Sabrina got her wish," Elle added. "There was even a happy ending for Tabitha, Willa's cat."

"Ugh," I said.

Elle laughed. "Just be happy Willa didn't have a dog. At least Tabitha and Jo ignore each other."

"I guess I'm lucky Tabitha doesn't put up with Jo's shtick. You'd never guess she's fifteen, except she sleeps a lot."

Georgia grinned. "What cat doesn't?"

"Uh, Jo. She's always up for some high-jinx or another." My perfect scenario with Jo loving the fake Christmas tree on the porch with the hanging catnip ornaments didn't pan out as I'd planned.

"I've got the best supplement to put in Tabitha's food," Georgia said. "I put it in Mr. Whiskers' and I swear he's acting like a teenager again."

"Do you put the same thing in Doc's food," I said, smiling. Ever since he met Georgia, he'd been carrying on like a teen. I almost missed his constant interference in my life.

"No, but last week he did eat a veggie burger for the first time."

Doc grinned. "Georgia, tell her what was on top."

"Sautéed onions, shitake mushrooms, blue cheese and veggie bacon."

"Veggie bacon!" he exclaimed. "Why'd you have to ruin it by bursting my bacon bubble."

The waitperson brought everyone's dessert. Georgia, Elle, and Claire had ordered white chocolate soufflé with crumbled peppermint bark shavings on top. Doc and I got the traditional pumpkin pie and crème fraîche and clinked our coffee cups in memory of all the Christmases in the past we'd shared with my father in Detroit.

Even without my father and Cole, I realized I was still surrounded by family. All was well, and as I glanced out the window at the softly falling snow hitting the frozen pond, I felt warm and snuggled in a blanket of gratitude for all the people in my life.

And as cliché as it sounded, Tiny Tim's words came to mind . . . *God bless us, every one!*

Chapter 31

"Only thirty minutes 'til midnight," Elle said, reaching up and strapping a pointy gold-foiled cardboard hat to my head.

"Ouch! You snapped me with the elastic."

"Serves you right. You need to bend down more."

"I'm not really in the New Year's Eve mood."

I went to take the hat off and Elle slapped my hand. "Leave it! No pity parties. Arthur's not here, either. Blame Mother Nature for making you and Cole star-crossed lovers, once again."

"I don't think I remember what he looks like."

"Don't you video chat?"

"Rarely. He's always on the open seas delivering one of his sailboats, no cell service."

"Well, let me take a few pictures of you. You look lovely."

"I can't compare to you," I said, laughing. Unless the invitation said black tie, I dressed like most thirtysomething women in the Hamptons: jeans, T-shirts, boots in the winter, sandals or sneakers — or tennis shoes, as we'd called them in Michigan—in the summer. The only way you could tell me from a visiting celeb was my jeans and footwear didn't cost in the five-hundred-dollar range. For upscale parties like tonight, I'd added a blazer, my mother's pearls and diamond stud earrings, and borrowed a pair of Elle's vintage designer shoes and a handbag.

"Nice dress," I said.

Elle never bowed to peer pressure when it came to what to wear. "It's from the 1939 movie *Bachelor Mother* starring Vivian Leigh and David Niven. I'm no Vivian Leigh and the waistline is a little tight, thanks mostly to your father and his meals, but I love the color and it matches my Schiaparelli jewelry."

"I can relate about the waistline. I can barely fit in my jeans." Ever since my father had arrived, I'd been scarfing down gourmet meals at a rate of three times a day, twenty-four-seven. He'd made most of the hors d'oeuvres for the party, and under his tutelage I'd even contributed a few of my own simple no-bake appetizers. I couldn't decide which one was my favorite, so I'd kept circling the dining room table, sampling them all until I came up with my favorite—panko-crusted crab cake bites with roasted pepper and chive aioli. A close second were the mini beef Wellingtons.

It was a small gathering: Claire; Elle; Barb and her husband; Georgia and Doc; my father and Sheila; Felicity, who had to leave her husband back in California because of his job; Morgana, Barb's sister, who was a dispatcher for the East Hampton Town outpost in Montauk; two members of the Poetry Book Club; Karen, who owned the needle arts shop in town; and Maurice, Elle's shop assistant, who'd left his partner at home with a cold.

"Oh, my," Elle said, bringing her hand up to her mouth. I followed the direction of her gaze and saw Patrick Seaton enter Little Grey. For a minute it felt like all the oxygen had been sucked out of the room and was replaced with a fresh ocean breeze.

I was caught off guard. He sure cleaned up nicely. His coat was open, and I saw he'd also dressed in jeans and a blazer, only instead of a T-shirt he wore a white dress shirt. I took a step toward him.

Our eyes met, and he said, "Meg . . ."

I took another step, and just as I was a foot away, a woman stepped through the open doorway and stood next to him, grabbing his arm. Her cheeks were flushed from the cold.

"Meg," he repeated, "I'd like you to meet my publicist, Ashley Drake. She's thinking of buying a summer place out here."

I was saved by Claire, who welcomed them and took their coats.

They'd come late to the party. I realized ever since I heard Cole wasn't coming, I'd been constantly checking the door for Patrick. Last Tuesday, succumbing to Claire's peer pressure, I'd attended my first Poetry Book Club meeting. Since then I'd been trying to deal with my feelings toward Patrick, secretly hoping that once I'd gotten to know him, he wouldn't be as attractive. But I'd been intrigued even more. Over moussaka, we'd finally discussed the murder at Nightingale Manor and found we not only shared a love of classic nineteenth-century poetry but also Louise Penny's books featuring Inspector Gamache and the cozy town of Three Pines.

Now, here he was smiling at me. The only problem was, Ashley, his book publicist, was looking at him the same way I was.

I extended my hand. "Nice to meet you, Ashley."

Instead of shaking my hand she gave me a double-cheeked air kiss.

I took a step back, not because I felt accosted, but the Yves St. Laurent shoes Elle had loaned me were a half size too small and the heels way higher than I was used to. I teetered. Patrick caught my elbow. He pulled me toward him and I smelled his clean intoxicating scent. Or maybe it was just that I was intoxicated. I'd already gone over my two-drink maximum figuring I could crawl next door if need be, peeved about Cole not ringing in the New Year with me.

"Thanks-s-s," I slurred. Tonight, his eyes appeared more teal than green.

Ashley grabbed my other elbow and whispered something in my ear. My hearing aids were set at their lowest volume because of the party's loud background chatter. I thought she'd said, "You have shrimp cocktail sauce on your shin." I looked down and saw nothing there. Then she pointed to her chin. I grabbed a napkin and dabbed the area. Patrick winked at me and the Barrett blotches surfaced.

"Get ready," Claire called out. "Ten minutes and counting. Grab your champagne flute and a couple sparklers."

"It's my fault we're so late," Ashley said. "We had a party in East Hampton I insisted Patrick attend. I think he's a little miffed with me. But we have to get him in the public eye, create some buzz about the upcoming miniseries." I waited for her to take a breath, but she kept going. "Patrick's told me all about you. I was hoping maybe you could keep your eyes out for a small cottage in Montauk on the water I could fix up. I know oceanfront is out of my means, but maybe something on Lake Montauk or even Fort Pond?"

I wasn't expecting to like her, but she had an open easy smile, not to mention she was stunning with her long, silky dark hair and large hazel eyes with thick lashes. She seemed to have tons of energy that I bet made her effervescent in a crowd. However, I couldn't picture her lounging by a fire reading a book of poetry. I commiserated with Patrick on wanting to spend a mellow New Year's Eve at Claire's, instead of some Hamptons high-brow party. "Ashley, have you been introduced to Barb Moss from Sand and Sun? She was my realtor who found Little Grey and the property my cottage sits on."

"No," Ashley said, "would love to meet her."

"Come."

"I'm gonna check out the food," Patrick said. "Quite the spread." He raised his eyebrows.

"Don't worry," I said. "My father made most of the food."

"Most?"

"Full disclosure, I made two dishes, the marinated mozzarella and the cheesecake bars."

"Under Daddy's supervision, I hope?"

"Ha, ha, funny. But yes."

I realized we'd totally left Ashley out of the conversation. When I turned to her, I saw a surprised look on her face. "Ready to meet Barb?" I asked.

"Sure."

As we moved across the room, she said, "I rarely see Patrick laughing about anything. I'm sure you know the story about him and the tragedy."

"Yes."

"You are a good influence on him, I think."

I felt embarrassed and confused at the same time. "You'll love Barb. She knows everything about Montauk. She won't lead you wrong. And when you find a place, I'd love to come see if Cottages by the Sea can be of service."

Barb was in the corner of the living room talking to Elle and Felicity, their gazes fixed on Ashley and me. After introducing Ashley, I went back to the dining room, where I saw Patrick talking to my father and Sheila. Before I could join them, Claire tapped her spoon against her champagne flute. "Okay, everyone, five minutes and counting. Let's go out to the deck and light our sparklers."

Everyone filed outside and crowded on the wood deck overlooking the Atlantic. Claire went from person to person, lighting sparklers. Someone started the countdown, "Ten, nine, eight . . ." I elbowed my way through until I was standing next to Patrick, and I joined in, "Seven . . ."

A huge dog the size of a St. Bernard bounded up the steps. He wore a black bow tie over his collar. "Tripod!" He crashed into me, stood on his hind legs and pressed his lone paw onto my collarbone. I went flailing back. Patrick broke my fall, but not until we were both on our backs looking up. Tripod jumped on top of me, lapping my cheek with his long, slobbery tongue.

"Four, three, two . . ."

"Surprise! Happy New Year," Cole said, looking down. "Seems I made it just in time." He wore one of his undecipherable grins.

"Happy New Year," I said.

"Happy New Year," Patrick said.

"Happy New Year," Tripod barked.

If not happy, it sure would be interesting, I thought.

Meg and Elle's Think-Outside-the-Box Guide to Repurposing Vintage Finds

Meg: Create a barista station on your kitchen counter. On a large antique ironstone platter or vintage tray place a coffee/teapot, vintage sugar bowl, napkins, a glass or cream pitcher filled with teaspoons—or anything else you can think of. It's a decorative way to keep things organized and makes cleaning the countertop a breeze. You could also lean a chalkboard behind the tray and write the day's coffee or tea blend, maybe adding a little saying like, *Start the day with a good cup of coffee (tea) and gratitude for another sunrise.* Large serving trays or compartmentalized wicker trays are also great for pop-up bars when entertaining.

Elle: For the sewing-challenged like me, make no-sew pillows using fabric glue. Change your pillows to match the season. You can even use vintage tablecloths or curtains to make your pillows.

Meg: You can also place vintage lace, linen, and patterned tablecloths on trunks, side tables, and coffee tables when entertaining. All-white linens brighten a room and let your guests know you are giving them the white glove treatment. If any wine spills, try dabbing the stain with a white cloth (never rub) then put the tablecloth taut over a bowl, centering the stain, sprinkle with salt and pour boiling water over the stain. Afterward, depending on the age of your linens, hand or machine wash.

Elle: I collect small vintage finger bowls in chintzware and transferware patterns and use them to sort my jewelry on my dresser.

Meg: Turn your windowsill into a year-round herb garden. Plant herbs in old green-glass Ball jars or vintage coffee or tea tins. Just make sure the room gets southern light and you mist the herbs with water, especially during the winter months.

Elle: Small vintage pottery vases can be used to store makeup brushes, lipstick, mascara and eye pencils.

Meg: Display a collection of similar items together to make a statement. Look for the unusual: groups of souvenir Empire State Buildings, Liberty statues, Eiffel Towers; vintage box cameras, binoculars, field and opera glasses; or stack three sets of different cups and saucers on top of each other in three rows. Don't overdo it. Make sure the area around your collection is clean and clutter-free so they come off as one statement.

Elle: Make one-of-a-kind magnets out of pieces of vintage costume jewelry. Buy button magnets at your local craft store and use permanent glue to connect the back of your chosen piece to the magnet.

Meg: I have a fixation with glass cloches, bell jars and domes. Things I put under my domes are small antique books, an ironstone creamer with dried flowers, seashells, photos, vintage postcards, and so on. The ideas are endless. During the holidays, add a bottle-brush tree, vintage valentine, a bunny or lamb figurine, mini pumpkins or pinecones. Place the cloche on top of a stack of books, bread plate, or small basket.

And remember a modern home can meld perfectly with that little touch of antique or vintage. **Wishing you great finds!**

YEAR-ROUND PARTY PLEASERS

Jeff Barrett's Roquefort/Fig Flatbread

1 pound fresh (or thawed) Italian bread or pizza dough
Olive oil or corn meal
Four tablespoons Dalmatia fig spread, warmed
1/3 pound Roquefort/blue/gorgonzola cheese, crumbled
Four thin slices prosciutto

Pre-heat oven to 425.

Stretch and roll out the dough to a rectangle approximately 10 x 12 inches and place on a pizza peel dusted with corn meal (if you have one, and you also will be using a pizza stone on which to bake the bread), or place on an oiled baking sheet. Cover the dough with plastic wrap and allow to rest and rise for 45 minutes.

When the dough has gotten puffy and the oven hot, spread the fig lightly across the face of the dough. (Note: the fig spread will be much easier to work with if it has been microwaved for 15 seconds to warm and soften.) Next, sprinkle the cheese in small bunches (rather than evenly). Then place the prosciutto slices on top, covering the majority of the flatbread.

Bake the flatbread for 15 to 20 minutes until golden brown on the edges. Cut the flatbread after cooling slightly into small squares and serve.

Meg's Marinated Mozzarella Balls, Artichokes and Olives

1/2 cup olive oil
1/4 cup red or white wine vinegar
1 garlic clove, finely grated
1 teaspoon dried Italian seasoning
Fresh herbs, any of the following: thyme, rosemary, oregano, basil, parsley
Zest of 1 small Lemon
Salt/pepper to taste
1 12-ounce jar marinated artichokes, drained
8-ounce mini fresh mozzarella balls in water, drained
1-1/2 cups pitted and stuffed green olives (you can also mix in pitted kalamata olives), drained
chopped pistachios (optional)

Mix olive oil, vinegar, garlic, Italian seasoning, herbs, lemon zest, salt and pepper.

Toss artichokes, mozzarella and olives into oil mixture until evenly coated. Marinate 30 minutes before serving.

Sprinkle with chopped pistachios (optional)

Meg's Easy Cheesecake Bars

2 packages refrigerated crescent rolls
2 packages (8 ounces each) cream cheese, room temperature
1 cup white sugar
1 tablespoon vanilla extract
1 stick (1/2 cup) butter, melted
3/4 cup cinnamon sugar

Preheat oven to 350 degrees. Grease a 13 x 9 baking pan with cooking spray.

Lay one roll of crescent rolls in a single layer on the bottom of the pan. Pinch together any seams, stretch to fit bottom of the pan.

In a bowl, use an electric mixer to beat the cream cheese, white sugar and vanilla until combined. Spread over first crescent layer.

Unroll the other crescent roll on a cutting board. Pinch seams and stretch so it is same size as pan. Carefully lay it over the top of the cheesecake filling. Pour the melted butter over the top, and evenly sprinkle cinnamon sugar on top.

Bake for 30 minutes. Let cool completely before chilling in the refrigerator. Cut bars and store covered in the refrigerator.

Claire's Cranberry Pineapple Punch

4 cups pineapple juice
4 cups cranberry juice
2 liters ginger ale
Juice of 1 to 2 limes
(You can also add 2 cups of rum)

Garnish:
2 limes sliced
1 cup of fresh cranberries (frozen to keep the punch cold)

About the Author

Kathleen Bridge is the national bestselling author of the Hamptons Home & Garden Mystery series and the By the Sea Mystery series. She started her writing career working at *The Michigan State University News* in East Lansing, Michigan. A member of Sisters in Crime and Mystery Writers of America, she is also the author and photographer of an antiques reference guide, *Lithographed Paper Toys, Books, and Games*. She teaches creative writing in addition to working as an antiques and vintage dealer. Kathleen blissfully lives on a barrier island in Florida. Readers can visit her on the web at www.kathleenbridge.com.

Printed in Poland
by Amazon Fulfillment
Poland Sp. z o.o., Wrocław